IS THIS THE VILE NECROMANCY OF
THE PRIESTS OF SET?

When he saw the priests drag Roganthus's body through the Gate of the Dead, Conan lost all reason. Charging across the bloody sand of the arena, he reached the wooden door just as it was closing in his face. The door banged shut behind him, and he was instantly blind. He heard shouts and the scuffling of feet nearby, and felt the impact of robed bodies. He raised his sword and, even as his blade and knuckles slammed into the low ceiling, felt the hilt wrested out of his grip. An urn broke over his head, flooding his eyes with blood, and he blacked out.

Conan awoke, tried to stand; almost immediately he reeled. As he pitched forward, his eyes met a horrific sight. There on a raised stone slab—supine, and laid open with hooks, brass clamps, and wooden splints—was the slashed-open body of Sistus, the young gladiator late of Dath's company.

**The Adventures of Conan,
published by Tor Books**

CONAN
THE
GLADIATOR

—BY—
LEONARD
CARPENTER

A TOM DOHERTY ASSOCIATES BOOK
NEW YORK

This is a work of fiction. All the characters and events portrayed in this book are fictitious, and any resemblance to real people or events is purely coincidental.

CONAN THE GLADIATOR

Cover art by Ken Kelly
Maps by Chazaud

PB
339-9216

A Tor Book
Published by Tom Doherty Associates, Inc.
175 Fifth Avenue
New York, N.Y. 10010

Tor® is a registered trademark of Tom Doherty Associates, Inc.

ISBN: 0-812-52492-6

First edition: January 1995

Printed in the United States of America

0 9 8 7 6 5 4 3 2 1

To Catherine and L. Sprague de Camp

Contents

Contents

CHAPTER 1
Night-Cats

The public-house at Thujara was no gilded palace. Its walls of sun-baked mud were thick enough to stand before the harsh winds of the Shemitish plain, turn aside leopards, and blunt the spears and arrows of roving bandits. It had a tile roof tight enough to keep out winter sleet and summer dust-storms. Its doors and shutters were secure against sneak thieves—those, at least, who had not been locked inside for the night.

The inn's kitchen had sheep stew, coarse bread, and raw wines and ciders that were no more sickly or sour than the pressings of other rural districts. The place was, in all, very little different from a hundred other inns Conan had squatted in during his travels. It was cozy enough, and he thanked

Crom he had coppers enough to afford its shelter for a few more nights.

Hulking over the long plank table that served as a counter, he took careful stock of the local women. A hardy lot, these Shemitish maids—thick and supple in the haunch and breast, sharp-eyed and sharper-tongued, with ill-kempt hair that hung down in charcoal or reddish curls.

Ellilia, now, the kitchen-keeper, made a healthy armful . . . as did Sudith, the innkeep's pouting daughter, a wild crocus blooming along a barnyard fence. Alas, most of these country wenches were discouragingly homey and settled. And unimaginative, far too ready to fend off an innocent question with the swipe of a roasting-fork or a splash of scalding soup.

The two current exceptions sat on the bench at either side of Conan, flirting gaily with the handsome Cimmerian. One of them, Tarla, was no real contender: a thin slip of a girl, barely approaching the estate of womanhood. She enjoyed playing at feminine wiles without fully knowing what they meant; to her, the outlander's thick-muscled bare chest, his square black mane, and his foreign-looking blue eyes signified only status and prestige, a handsome trophy in the flirting game. Yet Conan tolerated her brash experimentation; he bantered with her as half a child and half a maiden, without making demands on her.

The other female was Gruthelda, the stablemaid. She had all too clear an idea of the relationship between the sexes, likely gained from watching the antics of the horses and asses under her care. To her credit, she had the braying laugh and the good strong teeth of a well-fed mule; less fortunately, there was something in the roll of her eye and the stumble of her speech that made Conan believe she must have been kicked by one. Sitting with Gruthelda was lively exercise; the lass would make some stockhand a sportive mate.

He had just been letting the girls share his trencher of spiced oat gruel when there came a stirring from outside the inn—a chorus of voices and the skirling of some high-pitched instrument. It was not yet dusk, and the oaken door was not bolted; instead it swung open to admit a string of newcomers—mountebanks of some kind, three in number. They marched in and issued a grand proclamation, singing in turn as they made a prancing circuit of the tavern.

"For your delight and idle delectation," one said.

"Be you of noble rank or common station," the next proclaimed, to a riotous fluting.

"We hail you to our sumptuous display,
A Circus offered here on market day!
Rare feats of prowess, strength, and wizardry,
Strange fearsome beasts, and maidens fair to see,
All will disport at Festival tomorrow.
Come be amazed, nor shirk us at your sorrow!"

The first in the line was a broad muscular man, almost Conan's height and more than his girth. Bare-chested, he wore a brightly sequined kilt, rope sandals, and a wide leather belt with the brightly polished clasp of a contest champion. His face, framed by jet-black curls, bore full, sensuous features and a coarse lip that curled in an arrogant expression. As his march brought him toward the central table and toward Conan, his glance took in the Cimmerian's smoldering gaze and massive physique. Hackles rose almost visibly; then he strode on, scarcely acknowledging the implied challenge.

Conan, seeing the strongman and feeling natural skepticism and irritation at his overblown bearing, was nonetheless instantly distracted by the second marcher. This was a female, dressed in a tight sheer costume that both concealed and advertised the firm athletic flesh prisoned underneath. From neat slippers to bare shoulders, she was clad in fine silk, a sheer green fabric that seemed almost to have been sewn taut against her skin; only a narrow fringe of skirt hung about her hips as a flimsy pretense at modesty. The shiny cloth fitted with extra tightness over her breasts; these were ample but pressed flat, probably to prevent sway during violent acrobatic movements. Her brown hair, of unknown length, was tied back in a neat braid at her nape. Her hands and arms were hard and graceful, bare of any rings or bracelets that might interfere with her craft.

The sight of this female athlete, so different from the farm and village women of Thujara, gave rise to a new set of cravings in Conan's soul. He had known girl-warriors before; crack sailors, too, and dancers in the great cities. This was in truth his favorite type of woman, he realized ... or at least, a welcome change. Suddenly forgetful of the two farm maids who fawned against him, he half rose from his bench and reached out a hand. He sought to detain the prancing performer and perhaps offer her refreshment or lively conversation.

"Paws off, you oversized lumpkin! Let the parade pass unmolested."

Drawing back his hand from a sharp rap on the knuckles, Conan turned to stare at the third member of the band, a squat, square-faced midget dressed in a gray baggy-sleeved cape and pointed black cap. Lashing out with a small man's quickness, he had struck Conan's hand with the end of a silver flute—which, until then, had tweeted in skillful crescendoes between alternate verses of the marching song. Moving briskly past, the musician regarded Conan with bright, alert eyes from a face that was square-featured and not unhandsome.

"Wait, fellow, that was most ill-mannered," Conan protested, standing up and endeavoring to pull free of his girlfriends. "I only meant to invite the lass to stop awhile and talk, or mayhap share a puncheon of ripe cider. I would compliment you all on your fair costumes and fine talents. Especially the lady, there—"

"Enough, woodsman!" A gruff baritone voice overrode his as the bemuscled leader stopped and turned. "We have business to attend to."

"True indeed," the lovely acrobat said, her kohl-dark eyes looking at Conan with unamused interest. "There is our march through this village to complete, and a whole great circus to be made ready in time for the market fair tomorrow—"

"Plenty indeed to occupy us," the muscleman

finished for her, "instead of crowding in here to soak up warm, weak horse-trickle with an ill-mannered country lout." Wrinkling his nose at the aroma of the beaker in Conan's hand, he moved up opposite him and expanded his chest. Conan saw that, in part, he was only acting the character of the arrogant champion; but there was something heart-felt in it, too, something scornful and personal in his manner.

"And what if I bundle your thick carcass out of the way?" the Cimmerian challenged. "Will there be enough room then for the lady to sit down and share drink with her admirers?" He blinked past the oiled shoulder of the titan to the skeptical-looking woman. "For, if I can yet receive civil treatment from you and your friends here, I might then be inclined to follow along and help you with your night's chores back at your tenting-ground—"

"Enough of your impudent drivel!" the strong-man barked. Barging forward, he gave the Cimmerian a flat-handed shove on the chest, causing him to lurch backward and slosh part of his drink onto Gruthelda's bosom. "Now, sit on that bench and be quiet, Outlander, before I knot your arms and legs around it to keep you there."

"So it comes to grapples, then." Handing his cup to Gruthelda while keeping his eyes on the big man, Conan drew several deep breaths and arched his body into a wrestler's crouch. Arms spread wide, he balanced on tiptoe, holding his weight high.

"What, a tavern skirmish?" his adversary crowed. "I, Roganthus the Strong, accept your challenge!" The performer began to spread himself in an identical crouch to Conan's, but raised a flat palm in warning. "First rid yourself of that pig-bleeder there, lest you find yourself skewered by it in a fall." He pointed to the small dagger sheathed at Conan's belt—a mere paring-knife really, its blade scarcely exceeding a hand's-breadth.

"This? If you wish it."

Unlacing the sheathed weapon from his belt, Conan turned to his giggling, giddy seconds. He handed it to Tarla, whom he judged less likely than Gruthelda to use it in an excess of girlish excitement.

As he turned back to confront the strongman, he felt an iron hand clamp the side of his neck and bear down hard. His turning body fell into a blind, lurching half-step; he flailed his arm to clutch at his attacker and instantly felt it grasped and twisted in a wrestler's skillful hold. Propelled roughly across the floor, driven off balance into the side of the long inn table, he plunged over it and tumbled onto the hard dirt floor.

"A throw! Your kind attention, gentlefolk!" Dizzy, Conan heard the midget's gruff voice shouting. "The first fall out of three—unless, of course, there's a pin. Your bets, everyone! I, Bardolph, will guarantee them." The small man was now making the circuit of the place, collecting money and scribbling tallies on a wax tablet. "Remember, good friends, Roganthus is so far undefeated!"

Conan sprang to his feet and stalked angrily toward the strutting, posturing performer. "That was no honest grapple, you rogue!" he thundered. "This time you'll not catch me off guard!"

His complaint was echoed by yells, both derisive and supportive, from inn patrons who'd risen from their seats to form a ring of spectators. Newcomers jostled in through the door as well—summoned hither by the noisy circus parade, no doubt, and by the yells. A fight was a rare treat in Thujara, a town that lacked diversions, and Conan was a foreigner whom few cared to stand up for; so the crowd, in general, howled for his blood.

"Have at me, Northerner," Roganthus crowed, "unless you want to back down! Only two more tumbles will acquit your honor. Fear not, I promise to be gentle with you!"

Even as Roganthus sneered and taunted, Conan was upon him, lunging with blinding speed to throw a hammerlock across the mountebank's brawny neck and shoulders. The strongman's flesh was oiled, however, and the Cimmerian's fingertips raked across the firm skin without catching hold. His adversary ducked and delivered a block, a low, powerful shoulder-butt to Conan's midsection. It drove him only a few shuffling steps backward— until something bulky rammed into the hollows behind his knees and toppled him over, once again onto his back.

Blinking away stars from his fall, Conan belatedly realized it must have been Bardolph, already scuttling across the room to collect more bets, who had tripped him up. The midget's presence underfoot was no accident, the Cimmerian felt sure as he rolled to his feet.

"Another fall, Northerner, and so soon?" Roganthus blustered for the benefit of the crowd. "Poor fellow, you must learn not to stumble over innocent bystanders!" He turned in his crablike stance to face his attacker—but this time Conan did not bother to raise himself upright. Darting on all fours with pantherine speed, he locked an arm around the showman's thick knee, lifted, and twisted.

As the giant reeled and doubled over, Conan took the full weight of the man's torso onto his shoulders and hoisted him bodily into the air. Turning in place to confuse his opponent, he raised the writhing man high overhead and flung him down flat on his back to the tavern floor. The thudding impact brought a grunt from Roganthus and a respectful silence from the crowd.

"Well-done, Conan!" the loyal Gruthelda cried. "You threw him good, now pin him down! Step on his neck!"

But as Conan knelt to apply his weight more judiciously, the supine man arched up from the floor and grabbed hold of the Cimmerian's throat and trunk, exerting sudden leverage to try and flip him onto his back. Conan responded by prying his attacker's knee out from under him and driving him forcefully into a bench of the central table, toppling it.

Roganthus recovered and lashed back like a wounded python; the two proceeded to roll and grapple across the tavern floor, scattering furniture and spectators alike. Thrashing on their knees in the dirt and the muck, each groped and flailed for

an advantage. At length Conan managed to clamp
an arm around his adversary's neck and lever him
over onto his back. But as he bore in to subdue
Roganthus with a stranglehold, the giant gave off a
low, involuntary groan.

Suspecting a trick, Conan clenched the man's
throat only lightly while peering down into his
face. The strongman did not lash out or try to topple him, but rolled his eyes and muttered pitiably,
"Ow, by Set, you should not have doubled me
backward across that bench! That was a foul move
indeed! I think you must have cracked my
shoulder-bone."

"The match is over, then?" Conan asked, loudly
enough for the others to hear. "You yield to me as
the better fighter?"

"Why, no," Bardolph the flute-player interrupted
at once. "Of course he does not!" Striding forward,
the diminutive man was able to glare down indignantly at Conan where he crouched on the floor.
"The contest is halted due to a foul, naturally! All
bets are impounded—though in truth, you should
lose by forfeit."

"Why, that's nonsense," Conan objected, rising
up to his knees. "I bested him fairly enough—"

"How can you argue over such a thing while a
man lies here in pain?" The beautiful acrobat knelt
beside Roganthus. Smoothing his rumpled, muddy
hair, she kissed his clammy brow. "Poor fellow,
can you get up?"

"I think so." Roganthus let the muscular female
haul him to a sitting position, with Conan gingerly
propping him up from the other side. "Aii! By the

feel of it, my knee is sore wrenched!" Trying to stand upright, he faltered and leaned heavily on the woman. "I may need your help getting back to camp."

"Let me aid you," Conan volunteered. He looked the woman performer straight in the face. "I bear him no grudges after an honest brawl."

"Very well," she said, returning his gaze. "If you want to try and set things aright—"

"No, never!" Roganthus protested angrily, turning on Conan. "I would not trust this oaf to carry a sack of stale cow-flops!"

"Now see here, you great ill-tempered hulk, I can hardly carry you," Bardolph the midget pointed out. "Helping you is the least this farm-ruffian can do, after maiming you unfairly." As he spoke, the small musician was already shoving aside furniture and gawkers, clearing a path to the door.

Conan kissed his tavern-girls goodnight, then he put his back forcibly under the arm of the hobbling man, who resisted him at first and tried to shove him away, in spite of his game knee. Meanwhile, the female acrobat braced Roganthus more closely, careful of his sagging, injured shoulder. The party then started for the inn door—not as grandly as they had entered, but with no less comment and attention from the villagers.

Outside, twilight gathered over the grainfields and pastures of the Shemitish plain. The four of them, with Conan half dragging his resentful burden, headed out between the trees and buildings of town, west toward the pinkish-gold sunset.

Along the way, Conan learned that Bardolph and Roganthus were both Kothians by birth. The shapely acrobat, whose sultry face bore a catlike Stygian cast, was Sathilda, a native Shemite. Their troupe consisted of a dozen or so itinerants from diverse lands, most of whom were currently occupied setting up circus stalls and tending the animals.

The encampment soon came into view, nestled off the road beside a tree-lined stream. Bonfires flared, illuminating two brightly painted wagons, low tents, and dark shapes that hulked bright-eyed in the shadows. Fit-looking nomads, the males were, dressed in shabby finery. The women, clothed likewise in silks, busied themselves cooking and laying out bedrolls.

"Ooh, my shoulder!" With his loud groans, Roganthus announced their arrival. "Handle me more gently, you rawboned lummox, lest you compound the damage you have done already! Bring me drink, and plenty of it, to ease this distemper!" While he scolded, Conan and Sathilda lowered him onto cushions before the fire. Others came to see what had happened and, on hearing the strongman's moans and complaints, resentfully eyed the Cimmerian. He found himself wondering whether he might be mobbed or stoned; yet he stood his ground and returned their looks defiantly.

"Well, since you have crippled our star performer, you may as well do the chores assigned to him." The speaker was a lean, gray-bearded elder with the excess height and craggy facial features of a Bossonian: Master Luddhew, as the others respectfully addressed him. After looking Conan skeptically up and down, he waved a rawboned old hand at an open tool-crate containing metal stakes and a heavy iron mallet. "Sathilda will show you what needs to be done."

Taking up a flaming brand from the fire and striding proudly before him, the female acrobat led him up to a level open meadow where long timbers and thick ropes were laid out on the grass. "These supports need to be staked out firmly," she explained to him. "One loose rope could ruin my act, and lay me up worse than Roganthus."

Working under her supervision, Conan drove metal spikes deep into hard earth, knotted lines around them, and hoisted gaily painted beams vertical. Between the uprights, the two stretched a sturdy tightrope along with various rope ladders and trapezes. Sathilda tested every fastening, occasionally tightening a knot or admonishing Conan to drive a stake deeper. When the work was finished, she handed him the torch, swung herself barefoot up onto the rope, and poised there gracefully for a moment. She then performed a dazzling series of loops and flips around the trapezes, landing neatly on the ground. "That will do for now," she informed Conan with a smile. "You may share our supper if you wish."

A few venturesome townspeople had followed Conan and the others out to the camp, arriving in twos and threes as sunset faded. Already the circus folk worked the crowd for silver; blankets had been laid out before the biggest fire, with various nomads showing off their talents. On one, a female seer called Iocasta knelt in a peasant dress and turban, dealing out pasteboard cards and telling fortunes to squatting farmers.

On another blanket a gambling game was in progress, punctuated by the clink of coins and the rattle of dice in a bone cup. And farther on, inside a circle of attentive males, a plump, buxom dancer gyrated and dipped in a sequined halter, girdle, and a mist of veils, moving to the strains of Bardolph's flute and a thumping tymbal. Keeping the time with bangles shaking across her belly, the woman doubled over backward most charmingly, picking up thrown coins with her teeth.

Conan paused but a moment to stare over the men's shoulders; then he turned and followed Sathilda to the smaller fire that lay beyond the wagons. There, inside a scattering of idle nomads, she bent over a cauldron and dished steaming viands into wooden trenchers for herself and Conan.

Amid the stares of the others—and most particularly Roganthus, where he lolled now in a drunken half-doze—the Cimmerian hunched down beside the woman and ate. He exchanged few words with his hostess, sensing that, for now at least, most everything about her circus life was openly revealed to him. After scorching his mouth on the piping stew, he waited quietly while she dispensed wooden cups of spirit drawn from a small, spigoted cask.

It was fiery stuff that went straight to his head; he almost staggered when, moments later, he climbed to his feet at her silent summons. She led him away toward the back of the camp, into the deeper shadow of the circus wagons. There a sparse bedroll lay outspread on the grass; he saw her kneel beside it, smoothing and straightening it.

As he picked his way through the shadows, a rank, familiar scent drifted to his nostrils, making his neck-hairs prickle. There was a lazy clattering near at hand . . . then the shifting of heavy chain links and the feathery rumble of a low, bestial growl.

Whatever it was, it was black. Solid black. He could easily have stumbled over it in the darkness. From the dull mass of its shape and the broad space between the glinting yellow eyes, it was no mere panther. It must be a night-tiger, fully grown.

Sathilda made him flinch by placing her cool hand on the back of his neck. "The animals come in handy," she murmured in his ear. "They scare off the wild beasts and the prying farmers."

Entwining him in her arms, she drew him down onto her pallet. Her embraces proved to be vigorous and athletic. Fiercely taxing the muscles he had already strained while fighting and toiling that evening, the woman made him pant with exertion.

While resting after their first prolonged, sweaty bout, he found himself wondering whether this, too, was one of the strongman Roganthus's evening tasks. Yet he kept silent on the matter . . . being too sober to ask such a dangerous question and too sublimely intoxicated to care.

CHAPTER 2
Spawn of Titans

The market fair at Sendaj transformed the squalid riverside hamlet into a bustling assemblage of tents, stalls, and festive crowds. From earliest dawn the peasants began arriving with their donkeys and oxcarts, hauling in produce from outlying farms. Soon the village street filled up with Shemitish farmers and herders in their best fleece vests and embroidered kaftans. At the far end of the bazaar, the fringed pavilions and guyed towers of the traveling circus drew in the simple folk by the dozens.

"Come," Master Luddhew proclaimed from atop a keg by the roadside, "bear witness to wonders from the far corners of the world. See beautiful Sathilda and her famed troupe of Imperial Acrobats of Kordava, the capital of fair Zingara in the

West! Marvel at Bardolph and Iocasta, magicians and seers most extraordinary, who bring us sorcerous wisdom from the crypts and temples of remote Turan, Land of the Sunrise! Gape at strange beasts out of the haunted jungles of the South! And, right here before you, here stands Conan the Mighty, far famed as the Strongest Man in Nemedia, touring here to show off the skills and physical feats of his lusty race of northern giants! Observe the great Conan now, and obtain a rare glimpse of supernatural strength and prowess!"

Luddhew, balancing expertly atop his cask, turned and signaled with a flourish of his velvet cape. Conan stepped forward across the open wagon-bed that anchored one end of the curtained circus enclosure. He wore the same costume of kilt and sandals that Roganthus had worn in Thujara on the evening of the parade, right down to the broad, polished belt-clasp at his midsection. His square black mane was trimmed, combed, and adorned with a polished metal circlet that gleamed gold from his brow—which, between performances, had to be wiped free of green stains from the base metal. Raising his arms above his head wrestler-style, he flexed his muscles to show off his massive physique.

"There he is, half-human, half-titan!" Luddhew bellowed to the crowd. "Look there, at the power in those mighty thews—what a fine, splendid brute of a man! To see him use his godly strength, and learn if any pair of challengers from our audience can defeat him at wrestling throws, just give your coppers to the gatekeeper, right up there at the front of the wagon. Conan the Mighty's demonstration will be a part of our Grand Spectacle, commencing just as soon as the enclosure is filled. Come first, come luckiest, get the best spot and see the whole show!"

As he spoke, peasants filtered into the enclosure by twos and threes, fishing in pouches hidden under their garments to produce the small coins necessary. These they yielded up to Roganthus, where he sat in the boot of the wagon. He gazed down sourly on the crowd, his sullen, hungover slouch and shapeless tunic giving small hint of his own once-celebrated physique.

As the entrants paid, they filed in beneath the hinged wagon-tongue, which was raised up like a stile by means of a rope. Normally this would have been done by the gatekeeper, but in view of Roganthus's injury, Bardolph sat near him in the driver's seat. He raised the pole grudgingly, barely high enough to let the tallest customers duck in underneath.

"Alas, that is all the circus will hold," Master Luddhew finally announced in response to Bardolph's curt, chopping hand-signal. "No more spectators will be admitted. You may return for a later exhibition—remember to tell your friends and family of these marvels, and bring them back here with you." So saying, Luddhew stepped down from his pedestal and strode toward the coarse, patched curtains.

Inside the open-topped enclosure, a framework of ropes and poles stretched overhead. The second wagon stood at the back wall of the canvas circle, serving as a stage. The space before it was clear of onlookers—kept so by the animals lurking there, chained to the front and rear wheels of the brightly painted cart. One of them was a bear, the other a black tiger. They prowled and ambled to the length of their tethers and eyed the watching peasants sullenly, as if waiting for one to step too close.

Striding fearlessly between them, Master Luddhew turned with a flourish of his cape and addressed the crowd. "Here they are, captured in the southern jungles and transported a hundred leagues for your amusement. First Burudu, a wild swamp bear from the lowlands of Kush . . . a vicious man-eater, kept tame and controllable only by this enchanted object." Taking from his belt a ceremonial flail consisting of three metal stars tied with thongs to a metal-headed stick, he waved it before him. "Burudu, up!"

The bear, lumbering on the grass, rose ponderously on its hind legs as if at the object's command, or to avoid its sting. The beast's fur was mottled golden-brown, its muzzle long and tapering, its paws broad and powerful, with black pads fringed by matted fur and large, untidy claws. In height, as it reared up off the ground, it far overtopped the circus-master, drawing a gasp of awe from the crowd. Luddhew, after scrambling up onto the wagon-bed, waved the flail again above the creature's black, snuffling nose and made it settle down on all fours.

"And here, even fiercer than the giant bear, is Qwamba—queen of all the beasts, the dreaded cave tiger from the mountains of Punt! No death is more swift or silent, as she stalks her unlucky prey through the caves and cliffs of the savage realm! Yet Qwamba, too, is obedient to the power of the magic flail."

The coal-black beast, viewed in the morning sun, was subtly patterned in silvery-black hues with faint stripes corresponding to those of a common tiger. As she paced before the brass-shod wheel, her glossy coat flickered in an eerie impression of alternating darkness and brightness. All at once, at a flourish of the circus-master's metal crop, the creature sprang up lightly and noiselessly onto the wagon-bed. There she crouched at the limit of her chain, flicking her tail impatiently as she waited at Luddhew's booted feet.

"She cowers now, controlled by the spell," he proclaimed. "But if it were not for the magic of my flail, the beast would be raging wild, scorning man's puny darts and taking her meat from field and farm. Enough . . . Qwamba, down!" With a twitch and rattle of the lash, he sent the tiger leaping away, pouring herself like a torrent of ink into her resting-place on the trampled grass.

"And now, gentlefolk of Sendaj, another natural wonder every bit as rare and strange—Conan of Nemedia, the last living specimen of a tribe of wild northerners who mated with titans! You see the result before you—a living mountain of a man, thicker and brawnier than any natural human—brutal, invincible in combat, yet able to mimic human customs and dwell among civilized men. Examine him carefully . . . but do not venture too close, for he is just as wild and deadly as these jungle beasts!"

Conan arrived on cue. Vaulting up onto the wagon-bed in a single leap, he strutted forth, hulking and posturing before the crowd. His speech, by prearrangement, was limited to a few grunts and snarls of exertion. But his talents must have been adequate; his appearance caused a murmur of comment which the bear and tiger had not—since these were country folk, after all, used to a variety of wild and domestic beasts. They watched in bemused silence as he lifted heavy-looking stones and balanced them one-handed overhead, bent a thick bronze bar in his two hands, and burst a chain that Luddhew padlocked around his chest. As he hove himself up into a handstand and managed a few awkward palm-steps across the stage, there was actual applause.

Some of the onlookers were, in point of fact, larger than Conan was, mainly by virtue of their girth around the middle or by sheer massiveness. But he, with his weight poised high in the chest and shoulders, his skin oiled and sun-bronzed, and his taut muscles standing out like ropes, awed them sufficiently. Their shouted comments were frank and credulous.

"Will he fight the tiger and the bear?" asked one small boy, seated on his father's shoulders. "To be fair, I think he should only wrestle them one at a time."

"Do you use the whip on him, too?" someone else yelled from a safe place at the back of the crowd.

"Why don't you tell him to roll over and bark?"

"Silence, all, and thanks for your acclaim," Master Luddhew said firmly over the babble. "Now comes the real test of our champion's strength and dexterity. He will grapple with any challengers among you, two at a time, one fall per contestant. Each man pays a silver shekel as his stake. If any team tumbles Conan, they will be given six shekels in prize money."

At the announcement, a murmuring and jostling began in the crowd—mostly of watchers stepping back from the open area before the stage, or placing bets. At length, a handful of husky young men gathered at one side. They whispered together, shot surly looks at Conan, and held forth silver coins that Luddhew was quick to relieve them of.

"Here we have the first team. Contestants make ready."

At the circus-master's words, Conan leapt down from the wagon, passing between the idle tiger and bear with a careless stride. Luddhew braced the two men—gangling farm-rubes dressed in worn, patched jerkins—and restrained them, keeping a hand on each one's shoulder. As Conan drew near, the Bossonian turned them both loose with a firm push. "Honest grapples only, remember," he added officiously. "No blows or weapons."

As was usual with a pair of adversaries, one of them moved just a bit faster and more boldly. This was the one Conan concentrated on; after a casual feint leftward, slowing the timid one with his eyes, he darted right and seized the leader's wrist. With his other arm he bore down heavily on the man's shoulder. Once he felt his victim's knee strike the turf, he let up and shoved him away.

"One contestant down," Luddhew announced. "Now it becomes a solo match."

"But say, I did not fall," the country lout protested. "That was no real throw!" He turned back to enter the fight again, but Luddhew restrained the man by grasping his collar.

"A knee down is a fall, by Royal Khorshemish rules," the circus-master said. "You kneel to your King, do you not? And likewise to your vanquisher." He pointed to the fresh stain of mud and grass on the fellow's sackcloth trouser-leg. "If you want a second match, await your turn and choke up another shekel. Meanwhile, wait and watch."

While they argued, the second challenger made only a halfhearted show of opposing Conan, backing off steadily. Tall and gangly as the man was, the putative offspring of mortal and titan overtopped him; and when Conan lunged forward catlike to clamp on a hold, the farmer's panicky face proclaimed that he was ready to run. Conan let his grasp on the turning man slip. At the same moment, his toe flicked discreetly sideways, kicking the fellow's sandaled foot behind his calf.

The farmer tumbled down on all fours. Conan bent and helped him to his feet, muttering a polite growl that acknowledged a fair match. With a grateful, still-frightened look, the man fled off into the crowd.

The second match started out much the same as the first. Luddhew, while initially bracing the challengers, kept hold of one of them a split second longer than the other. During that interval, Conan collided with the first and trounced him by throwing him over his hip. The second man was stouterhearted, oxlike, and every bit as large as Conan. Conan fenced with him, attempting a few unsuccessful holds and twisting out of some others; ere long he managed to back his challenger up in the vicinity of the wagon with its two fanged, clawed guardians.

As the bumpkin glanced over his shoulder to see whether the beasts were poised to devour him, Conan darted forward. Clapping a hand on the man's nape and kicking one leg out from under him, he hove mightily, playing into the fellow's tendency to move forward, away from the watching bear and tiger. The farmhand went down with a thud, but without substantial injury. In a moment he picked himself up and hobbled off, chastely silent.

"That is the last team of challengers," Luddhew announced—truthfully, since no one was now badgering for a fight except the first contender Conan had felled, and he had no luck finding a new teammate. "It is a final proof of the invincibility of our northern champion, Conan the Mighty.

"And now, from the shores of the Western Sea, comes a marvel of another kind: Sathilda the Flying Woman and her Imperial Acrobats, defying death in the sky above your very heads!'"

As he spoke, the silk-clad woman was already shinnying up a rope suspended from the timber verticals and taut cables strung overhead. Two trim young men in tights and sleeveless jerkins likewise

hauled themselves aloft. Meanwhile Conan, shouldering his way effortlessly through the crowd, laid
hold of Sathilda's rope and bore down on it to ease
her ascent.

Once the trapezes began swinging, the press of
the crowd moved backward, away from the circus's center area and out from under the threat of
falling bodies. The daredevils performed without
net or cushion, their tackles strung just high
enough to be beyond reach of the audience.
Sathilda executed agile twists and somersaults in
midair, near enough that the onlookers could hear
the slap of her hand on the flying wooden bar or
her partner's taut arm. They caught the faint fra-
grance of her sweat as she flew past, and even felt
it prickle their upturned faces. Her two teammates
performed mainly stationary roles; they gave her a
push to start her off on a flight or, at most, ventured out on a free-swinging trapeze to catch her
and bring her back to the platform.

In the middle of her act, she shifted to the taut
rope at the center; running out onto it gracefully,
she performed cartwheels and pirouettes. Twice she
made missteps, or feigned them, only to catch the
rope on the way down and swing herself back up
on the other side. Her skill and supple beauty,
adorned as she was in her skintight green costume,
held the crowd rapt. Their silence was broken only
by the skirling of Bardolph's flute and an occasional
drum-thump to punctuate a noteworthy feat. For a
finale, she returned to the trapeze; Luddhew announced that she would undertake a specially elab-
orate aerial flip and twist.

The swinging commenced, with several prepara-
tory flights to build up momentum and coordinate
the timing with her partners. Then Sathilda released her grip and arched high overhead, writhing
in the air like a silver-green fish leaping after a
dragonfly. She completed the maneuver, straightening out just in time to catch the arms of her high-
swinging helper. But there was too much speed, or
too much sweat; on the return swing, heading toward the platform, her grip on her teammate failed
and she plummeted earthward—straight into the
arms of Conan, who had moved inconspicuously
forward to catch her, letting only her slippered feet
touch the ground.

An immediate, exultant cheer went up. The
crowd surged forward to congratulate acrobat and
the strongman—without much success, for Conan
quickly bundled Sathilda over to the wagon-stage,
and up onto it to make her final bow. The circus-
goers, after the announcement by Luddhew that
her aerial show was at an end, were left to watch
the next act: sleight-of-hand and communion with
the dead, by wizard-gowned Bardolph and the
fortune-teller Iocasta.

"A solid performance, flawless as usual," the
circus-master told Sathilda behind the canopy, once
the magicians were safely under way. "That mock
fall came off perfectly—the yell those rubes gave
out should be enough to fill up the arena for the afternoon show. There is no better advertisement."

"And Conan was properly in his place this
time," the acrobat said sweetly, bestowing a kiss
on her helper's cheek.

"Yes, excellent," Luddhew said with a nod to Conan. "After only three shows, you are doing tolerably well at taking Roganthus's place."

"Filling in for him temporarily, you mean, while he recovers," Conan said. He glanced to the former muscleman where he lay on a pile of tarpaulins, lounging disconsolately and swigging from a clay bottle. It was unclear to him whether Roganthus had heard his circus-master's careless remark; but out of consideration for the injured man, Conan hoped not. Moments later, Luddhew was called aside to speak to some local visitor, a small dapper man dressed prosperously in silk fez and fur cape, along with stylish pantaloons and tassel-toed slippers.

"I am not one," Conan explained to Sathilda, "who takes naturally to strutting and posturing before an audience. Nor to playacting and deceiving a crowd of gullible peasants, and being mocked by them. But I will do it, or any other task it may take, to go on traveling by your side."

"What you do, you do admirably," Sathilda purred to him. "Better by far than any before you." Standing up on tiptoe, she pecked a kiss onto the side of his neck. "As for the mummery . . . as strange and foreign as it may seem to you, you should enjoy it and learn from it. You could be at it for a good long time," she added with a glance over her shoulder at Roganthus.

When the magic act ended and the patrons were all driven out of the circus enclosure, the principal performers sat resting on the wheeled stage. Most of the circus hands were still occupied in tents and stalls along the roadway, conducting games of chance and deception. But these notable performers would have been mobbed in the market crowd, so they took the opportunity to eat their lunch in peace. Gnawing hunks of bread, cheese, fruit, and sausage, and washing the repast down with watery local wine, they sat talking of business concerns.

"I would welcome the chance to enhance my magical skills," Bardolph was saying. "Why not learn true magic, instead of all this flummery? It is rumored that there are sorcerers in the great cities who can perform all sorts of spells and transmutations, levitate objects, predict future events, and so forth. But none of them ever displays his tricks for the public. Why is it that every traveling wizard is a sham, deceiving audiences with little better than sleight-of-hand?"

Conan glanced up from the task before him. "From what I have seen, the seers who command such skills have slight interest in pleasing an audience. They pay a heavy price for the knowledge they gain, and then use it in secret ways to win earthly power or mystic goals of the obscurest sort, beyond the understanding of mere humans." While he lunched, he wielded a light hammer, carefully tapping the single bent link from his chest-chain back into shape. "On the whole they are an unsavory lot—half-human and half-devil, often as not, from their evil dealings—"

"Yes, yes," the little man said, "but even so, a few of their showier tricks might serve us well in the circus. Real magic would draw vast crowds, spread one's fame as a performer ... and pay off doubly in my gambling concessions."

"I would not dabble in it if I were you," Conan earnestly warned him, testing the chain between his fists. "Why trouble about such things, anyway? Your act is a success, and you are guaranteed a place here, at all events—every circus needs a dwarf."

Bardolph's instant movement brought him up near Conan where he sat leaning against the wagon's bench. His bunched fist hovered opposite the Cimmerian's nose. "I would have you know, Outlander, I am no dwarf! That is not my reason for being here, nor my sole purpose in life. I am a musician, a prestidigitator, an oddsmaker and healer, no mere freak to be displayed in a darkened tent! If I happen to lack your unnatural bulk, which makes you fit for public exhibition—just remember, my size gives me certain advantages in fighting as well." He slapped the long knife sheathed at his belt. "A blow I strike is one you will long remember. So think carefully before you provoke me, Northerner."

"Enough, now, Bardolph. The man-titan meant you no insult." Iocasta came up behind the small man and laid a soothing hand on his shoulder. "The outlander is new here and does not know our ways. Let him be, now." Her careful, solicitous tone made it evident that she thought Conan the one in greatest danger.

The Cimmerian, for his part, honored Bardolph's declaration with silence. As his challenger glared angrily, then turned contemptuously away, he did not apologize or try to justify himself. The others soon smoothed the matter over by resuming the conversation.

"I myself do not crave to know the ways of the famed oracles and big-city soothsayers," Iocasta said. "Their mouthings are always so vague and full of double meanings—I am happy enough with the second-sight that has been granted me by the gods. To predict a love match, find a lost coin or bauble, or forecast the spring rains—something tangible and precise—is more to my liking than the fates of nations and armies."

"Come, now, seeress," the half-drunken Roganthus called out, lying back against a pile of sacking at the corner of the stage. "If you really believe in your own power of prophecy, you are as much a fool as the farmers! We have all seen you use the grossest deceit to put over your visions."

"What you refer to is showmanship, the merest trappings of my art," Iocasta blithely told him. "At the core of it lies something mystical, something I know to be genuine. I sincerely feel I have been touched by the gods."

"Oh, aye, surely enough!" Roganthus ridiculed, tipping his clay flask high and draining its dregs. "I, too, believed I was charmed and invulnerable ... until some hulking, careless, country lout jostled me the wrong way over a bench!" He ruefully rubbed his hunched shoulder. "Now I sit watching life go by, waiting for the gods to end their callous game of tormenting me. My fame and prowess are gone—I try to help in small ways, of course, wherever I can. But it may never be the same as it was—"

The strongman's wine-soaked lament was interrupted by a sound that quickly roused the circus folk: the din of harsh raised voices from the fairway. Bardolph and Sathilda sprang up at once and headed out through the canopy. Conan and Iocasta followed hurriedly, leaving Roganthus straining as if to haul himself upright from his bed of sacking, slowed by pain and drink.

A few dozen paces from the arena, a dense knot of onlookers obstructed the foot traffic along the village street. They gathered near a long, roped-off enclosure that served as the stall for some exhibit or game of skill. There appeared to be an argument going on at the front, to which the crowd contributed lusty cheers and raucous dissent.

"What do you mean by hurling your cloddish missiles and wrecking my display?" the stall's proprietor shouted, doubtless intending to summon aid from nearby circus cronies. "This is a knife-throwing game, not an ax-fight! See how you have ruined my target!" The huckster held up a painted wooden disk for all to see; its centermost planks were split and staved in, amid a scattering of tiny holes and splinterings made by knifepoints.

"Aye," his adversary calmly replied. "It was a true, straight cast, was it not?" The speaker, a slim, arrogant youth, glanced back to his nearest companions and the rest of the watchers. "Knives or hatchets, standing targets or running ones, I can best you or anybody in this mummers'-troupe of yours."

"Aye so, Dath!" spirited voices replied from the crowd. "We know it to be true! Give those cheap hucksters a trouncing for their money!"

The lad was obviously a local village tough, not farmlike in his dress—and no stablehand either, with dung at his heels and oats in his hair. Rather, he looked like a tavern and crossroads idler, one who made his living by no honest toil. At his belt he had rehung a brace of axes, polished silver-bright; at his back stood two younger-looking ruffians of his same sort, as well as two village girls. The whole band of them smirked jauntily at one another, meanwhile sneering at the circus crew in wry contempt.

Dath's immediate adversary in the dispute was the young acrobat Phatuphar, one of Sathilda's team who did knife-throwing exhibitions on the side. For penny wagers, the lithe young performer challenged passersby to strike a painted mark by casting two or three short, sharp-pointed steel knives. These he dispensed from a belt-pouch where he stood before the barrier. His target ordinarily hung from a post at the rear of the enclosure, backed up by curtains of tattered burlap to catch the misses.

Mere moments before, while Phatuphar went to the back of the stall to collect the thrown knives, reckless young Dath had ambled up and hurled an ax past the concessionaire's head, striking the target dead-center and shattering it in the process.

The controversy had not so far grown violent, and the circus folk who came running stood quietly around the edges of the scene—except Luddhew,

who moved to the center, still in the company of
his silk-hatted guest. The disputants now talked in
terms of a wager, and the circus-master seemed to
sense that there might be a chance for profit.

"If it's a contest you want, I would not hesitate
for an instant," Phatuphar declared. "This purse
says I'll better any toss you can make—five silver
shekels, assuming you can match the bet!"

"That should be easy," Dath replied.

The purse at the young challenger's waist
looked thin and slack to Conan's eye. But when
Dath turned around to face the crowd, a half dozen
hands rose up in support of his bid, most of them
clutching bright silver shekels. "Go on, Dath!
Trounce him well!" voices shouted.

"Give me five coppers on the Sendajan," one
eager investor cried out. "He may be an unholy
terror, but the lad can fling an ax!"

The original bet was soon covered; Luddhew
held the stakes, while the fez-hatted man, obviously a figure of some respect, vouched for his
honesty. The circus folk, knowing Phatuphar's
skill, busied themselves covering a number of side-
bets. Meanwhile the two marksmen worked out the
details. "Try any target you want," Phatuphar challenged. "I'll match or better your throw with my
knives, two for one!"

"You throw first, and I'll match you with axes,
one for one," Dath replied. "But let's liven up the
show—we need a wench for sport." He turned his
eyes to the nearby crowd. "You, Jana," he said.
"You know I would not harm you."

The girl was one of the young ones who hovered

behind him, slender and big-eyed, her hair hanging in oiled ringlets. She had dressed for the market fair in a coarse white cotton shift, and adorned herself with tortoiseshell hair-clasps and copper bangles that showed off her tan, slim arms and ankles to good advantage. She looked up at Dath and her other friends carelessly, without a flicker of doubt, before striding forward into the young man's reach.

Laying an arm familiarly around Jana's waist, Dath led her back past the barricade at the front of the stall. "Come along, circus hand," he said over his shoulder to Phatuphar. "Bring your target, and we three will give them a contest to remember."

Arriving at the vertical post, he let Phatuphar suspend the target from its metal hook at the top. Then, leading Jana up to the post, he wound a thong around both her wrists and bound her with it to the same hook—leaving her on tiptoe with arms raised against the post, facing the crowd.

The wooden disk had five painted circles: a white one at its smashed center and four red ones positioned at the top, bottom, and sides. With the girl strung up in front of it, only the red circles at either side were visible. "These will make good marks," Dath announced, pointing at each of them. "You keep still," he instructed the bound maiden. "Trust me." After conferring on her a casual, one-sided embrace and a kiss, he led the way back to the throwing-place.

"There, now, an easy enough target," he told Phatuphar, pointing at the two red circles. "Do not let your fear of striking the woman spoil your aim," he added nonchalantly. "She is but a village waif."

The market crowd looked excited and wide-eyed, caught by their own enthusiasm and their bets on the black sheep Dath. Evidently Jana's family, if she had any, was absent—there were no cheers or catcalls as Phatuphar readied his knives either, but Conan guessed there would be trouble if one of the steel spikes so much as nicked the girl. He thought momentarily of intervening, but he had been impressed by his fellow trouper's skill. Upon seeing it demonstrated, Dath might back down from his bluff.

It was a respectable distance, ten paces and more. Phatuphar frowned in sullen concentration. Slowly he drew back his sinewy arm and, with a quick lash of his shoulder, sent the metal prong spinning through the air. It struck with an audible impact, standing out from the red-painted circle a mere finger-width from the girl's armpit. There came from the crowd a murmuring sigh that sounded like relief, in spite of their bets. Then, with little warning, the acrobat drew back his arm and hurled the second knife, causing the watchers to swallow their gasps.

The second cast was nearly as true as the first. It struck at the edge of the second circle a full hand's-breadth away from the girl's supple flesh, barely inside the red perimeter. Phatuphar's nerve may have wavered, but not by much. This time a buzz rose from the crowd, not merely of relief but of eager speculation.

Dath laughed aloud. "A pathetic show! You

think I cannot place my ax between your blade and Jana's pretty flank? Why, I could shave her fair armpits if I wanted to." Reaching to his belt, he drew forth one of his axes, well-oiled and well-edged. "Nay, 'tis not enough. I prefer something of a challenge. With these two axes, I will set the girl free." So saying, he flung back his arm with blinding speed and hurled the ax, its silver blade and sharkskin-wrapped handle whirling in a sun-bright disk of speed. To throw, Dath arched his whole body, showing Conan and the rest that the cast had been for maximum force and impact.

The ax struck dead-center, embedding itself in the target post where it stood up directly over Jana's head. The whites of the poor girl's eyes could plainly be seen orbiting upward in fear, and at the physical shock of the weapon driven in between her two upraised arms. It had not touched her flesh—nor, for that matter, severed the thong that bound her wrists to the eyelet. It could hardly do so, since her wrists were tied scarcely a finger-width apart, with the metal hook interposed between them. Perhaps realizing this, she began to writhe and tug at the thong, twisting and stretching on tiptoe to unhook her wrists.

Dath, however, ignored her struggles. "A near success," he cavalierly announced to the watchers. "The waif was almost set free of her miserable bondage. Now, one more cast ought to do the trick."

"Nay, do not throw!" Phatuphar cried, lunging forward. "It is too dangerous—"

But Dath paid no heed. Even as he spoke, with

a convulsion of his arm that was almost too sudden to trace, the second hatchet left his belt, lashed backward in his grip, and hurtled through the air at the target. Seeing its flight, Jana could not help but duck her head aside and writhe violently against the post, anticipating the weapon's impact.

The movement should have cost the girl her life. Fortunately the ax arched high, almost missing the target entirely. Its blade lodged in the topmost edge of the vertical post—within easy reach, if Jana had wished it, of her fear-clenched fingers.

Once again, it did not sever the thongs that bound her wrists; nor did it lie any nearer the target-marks pierced by the two daggers. The crowd, having witnessed their hero's bluster and bravado, now muttered in doubtful consternation.

"A good try," Phatuphar grimly observed. "But a little off target, I would say. You missed both the painted marks and the thongs. The girl is not set free, either, not by any stretch of the imagination. So you can hardly pretend to claim the prize—"

"Quiet, fool! By Set's fangs, I told you I would free her!" Pushing past Phatuphar and stretching his lithe frame across the barrier, Dath straightened up holding yet another weapon—a long-handled iron hammer used by the circus crew to drive in ground-stakes and erect the stalls. Before any could interfere with him, he raised the clumsy metal implement in a two-handed grip and hurled it through the air—toward the hapless girl once again—oscillating wildly as it flew.

The watchers flinched backward when it struck, fully expecting to see tender young brains spattered across the grass. The missile hit instead with the clank of steel, striking one of the ax-heads already sunk into the post and rebounding off it, to fall down past the girl's averted face and land with a thud at her feet.

As a further consequence of the blow, the metal hook upholding the thongs loosened and pulled free of the split post—causing the target disk to thump to earth. As it did so, the maid Jana stumbled to her knees across the fallen hammer and fell forward—shaken, but evidently unharmed. At this, a murmur of amazement passed through the crowd, followed by yelps and strident shouts.

"Dath freed her, did you see? And he did so with only two ax-throws! That means we win!"

"He is a fine, clever lad! I knew he could do it!"

"A well-thrown ax can accomplish more than any dart-toss!"

Phatuphar was the first to raise a protest. "Wait, now! He made three casts, and none of them hit the target we agreed on! He cannot claim to have won—"

"Quiet, show-boy! Dath's skill is twice yours!"

"You slippery circus hucksters cannot squirm out of this one—"

With shouts and threatening gestures, the confrontation rapidly built toward a riot. The tight group of circus performers pressed in closer, watching belligerently. Conan, for one, judged that a brawl would be a safer risk now that Dath was disarmed. The wagering had deteriorated into a shouting-match centered on the tall figure of Luddhew, who held the stakes, with his fezzed visitor standing close by, watching, but evidently taking no part.

"Enough," the circus-master loudly declared to the crowd. "The terms of the contest were never carried out! Your champion chose a different target, so the bet is void. I will refund your shekels, but not pay the bet."

"Liar!" the bettors raged in return. "Lousy sneaking vagabonds! We won the wager and you know it! Render us our silver, or we'll take it out of your hides!"

Then battle was joined, with the locals swarming in on Luddhew and Phatuphar and the circus folk moving to their defense. Fists and sticks flailed; fruit and rock-chunks whizzed overhead, and striving, lunging bodies were knocked to earth, to be kicked and trampled in the dust. Conan moved furiously through the mob, snatching up town yokels and hurling them back on their fellows. Occasionally he paused to drub some particularly menacing rioter to his knees with a body-blow from fist or elbow. Repressing his murderous instincts, he did not lay hold of a weapon or lash out deliberately to hurt anyone; after all, he was new to the circus and unsure of the protocol in this type of battle. Killing and maiming customers might be poor etiquette, so it seemed to him.

Nevertheless, he bore in before Luddhew like a tornado through a woodlot, grappling and throwing aside two or three attackers at a time. The circus-master stood aloof, contenting himself with an occasional shove or kick at assailants who forced their way too near. The diminutive silk-clad visitor hung back, though he did not flee, watching the brawl with lively interest.

Dath, as Conan was surprised to note, did not take part in the melee. His two male cronies surged into the mob with knives drawn, but never got the chance to use them. One was pummeled in the face by Conan, the other in the gut and pate simultaneously by Bardolph and Sathilda, who were equally alert to the danger. Dath, whom Conan observed out of the corner of his eye, did not even trouble to rearm himself. He went to meet the girl Jana as she made her way back from the target zone, disheveled and frail, but he only briefly kissed her and patted her on the rump, sending her off. Afterward he stayed near the barrier, idly dodging bodies that were flung his way as the circus band cleared the street.

"Desist, now! Cease this unsporting behavior," Luddhew scolded the fast-dispersing throng. "Since you have broken the gods' law of hospitality, I declare all bets forfeit! Go back home, our afternoon show is canceled!"

There was little argument with this, because few of Luddhew's assailants remained standing. The circus hands, skilled and ruthless skirmishers, patrolled a lane fast emptying of frightened, limping foes. Farther up the village road the fugitives eddied and muttered together, looking as if they might cause more trouble in a while. But for now, the circus booths and concessions were clear of all but fallen and unconscious rioters . . .

And of Dath, who came strolling empty-handed toward Luddhew. "Well, ringmaster, have you seen enough of my marksmanship? I grow weary of this village and crave to leave the district. Is there a place for me in your band?"

Luddhew had weathered the riot untouched, with the forfeited bets concealed somewhere on his caped person. Now he stepped forward, beaming. "Indeed, lad, I can say we'd be happy to use an able arm like yours! There are greater things in the offing—for I must tell you all, this distinguished visitor of ours is none other than Zagar, talent-procurer for the High Court at Luxur, and he has an announcement to make." He led forward the small man, an elegant fur-clad Argossean by his look, who touched his fez and nodded around the group of circus actors.

"Greetings to you all," the stranger said with an ingratiating smile. "After seeing your various skills, I am much impressed. Speaking for my employers, it honors me greatly to invite your entire troupe to the Stygian capital to perform before Lord Commodorus in Luxur's Imperial Circus. Make ready promptly, that we may begin the journey at once."

CHAPTER 3

The Last of Rivers

The journey southward to Luxur was a long one, hot and dusty in this summer season. But it was relatively free of brigands and wild beasts, passing as it did through meadowlands settled with occasional farms and villages. The trek was by road, along the net of trade highways connecting the Shemitish city-states. Such roads provided reliable passage in most months, principally from north to south—since, of the farm and caravan traffic moving east and west in southern Shem, most was borne in wide-hulled ships along the broad black highway of the River Styx.

The circus traveled on its own power. Zagar the Procurer sat astride a richly bridled ass, with Master Luddhew accompanying him on a splendid bay mare provided as a courtesy to the circus-master.

Since the heavy mule-wagons were crammed with cordage and equipment, most of the troupe—except Roganthus, who still complained of his injuries—straggled along on foot beside the wagons. The performing bear and tiger followed, each chained securely to the rear of a wagon to prevent them from scattering the mules. But an exception was made for the big cat Qwamba; she was allowed a narrow ledge at the back of the rearmost wain, on which she might lie and doze or lazily survey the trailing humans, as she wished.

All their efforts—especially Conan's, as the strongest member of the troupe—were required when the wagons bogged down at a stream crossing or a steep hill ascent. Where there was room, everyone pitched in a shoulder to help. Even Qwamba leapt down from her resting-place to carry her own weight—while Burudu the bear, lending his strength to the task, often accomplished as much with a single impatient swipe of his paw as any trio of humans or mules would have done.

Along the way, the band stopped and gave circus performances in several market towns, not only to sustain themselves but to polish their various acts and spread word along the route of their triumphant march southward. In all, the impending honor of the visit to Luxur seemed to sharpen their skills and whet the enthusiasm of their audience. While trudging the long days away, they speculated on what their reception in the city would be, and how high fame and success might vault them. It was generally agreed that, in all the Hyborian world, no more prosperous or exciting venue might be found than glamorous Luxur.

"For you know," Bardolph assured them, "of all the fabled cities of Stygia—from ancient Eshur to hoary Pteion, from black-walled Khemi on the seacoast to Qarnak in the hazy East—Luxur is the one truly cosmopolitan place. It looks northward, openly embracing foreign customs and visitors. It is the great riverport, the trade and culture center for the rulers of the whole Stygian Empire. Long I have wished to see it."

"It goes to show," Sathilda observed, "that even the hooded monks of the South must have their amusements."

"They must, if their country is to gain a voice in the northern capitals," Luddhew declared from his saddle. "If they want to entertain foreign dignitaries, carry on far-flung trade, and keep up with events and fashions in neighboring lands, they must have a free, open city to traffic with the broader world. Luxur serves them that purpose, methinks."

"The Stygians' great allies are the Corinthians," Bardolph confidently added. "I have heard that it is they who really run things in Luxur. For you know, the folk of Corinthia are clever merchants and diplomats, while the Stygians, as a people, are preoccupied with their notions of piety and endless religious observances. By opening new caravan routes to the headwaters of the River Styx, some enterprising Corinthian traders gained the trust and reliance of high Stygian nobles and priests. Now, they tell me, Luxur is practically a Corinthian colony."

After listening patiently, Conan could not help voicing his doubts. "'Tis hard for me to imagine the gray-robed priests of Set allowing their city to be run as openly and sinfully as Khorshemish or Shadizar," he said as he ambled along between the wagons. "In Khemi, to my remembrance, they lock the city gates at night, and let the hungry temple pythons scour the streets clean of unbelievers— that's Stygian hospitality as I've known it! Are you telling me they'd let outsiders turn their capital into a freewheeling bazaar and brothel, as the Corinthians have done in Numalia and Arenjun?"

"You might be surprised, Northlander," Bardolph said. "Even Luxur's appointed ruler is a Corinthian, installed with the blessing of the Stygian priesthood: Commodorus, whose administration doubtless sent our friend Zagar scouting northward for new talent. The fellow styles himself Tyrant, and uses these public shows to enhance his popularity, so they tell me." The Kothian spoke briskly, striding along with rapid steps to match the others' pace. "I would suppose that such a one will seek even higher rank, perhaps by changing religions or marrying into the Stygian nobility."

"Trying to better himself. That is the city way." Dath, who strode along a little apart from the others, added his views. "Let us hope life in Luxur proves more interesting than in these one-ass rural towns like Sendaj. I crave excitement and challenge, especially the kind that leads a man to riches."

Since joining the troupe, the young ax-thrower had fared well. His axmanship had been made a part of Phatuphar's knife-throwing concession, and had soon eclipsed it. Dath's was now a major act of the show, announced by Luddhew along with Conan's and Sathilda's. The Sendajan enjoyed a corresponding increase in pay, while Phatuphar continued as his assistant and as a part-time acrobat.

The human target they used was still Jana, for the sultry orphan girl had decided to leave Sendaj and travel with the circus. To face death in her daily act, she was now roped by wrist and ankle to a large, spinning wooden disk—and, for a grand finale, freed from her bonds by ax-casts severing the four ropes that held her limbs.

Not surprisingly, the young woman had chosen a mate in the circus troupe. Some thought it ironic that her romantic attachment was not to Dath, but to the less popular Phatuphar. She evidently found the steady, mild-spoken acrobat a comforting and attentive lover.

If Dath minded, he did not let on. Phatuphar welcomed Jana to his bed-mat and talked of having Luddhew marry them. What his thoughts may have been as he watched the harum-scarum former boy-friend Dath hurl deadly missiles at his beloved could only be guessed.

So they worked their way, trudging or performing each day, idling, gambling, luring, and bedazzling the locals by night. But most memorable of all was that final evening they pitched camp on the edge of a fragrant, vaporous black gulf—and, by dawn's first light, made their way down the bluffs into the valley of the mighty River Styx.

The Last of Rivers, seen from the bluff, stretched away east and west like a broad belt of dark leather, girdling the earth's belly atop a sash of brightest green. To the glaring east, the water's dark surface carried a bright sheen like the scales of old Set, the serpent-god who claimed the river as his own. Away to westward, the black- and green-braided currents wound off into a gray haze, finding their unhurried way to the sea. Across the expanse of water vast green vistas could be seen, with an occasional white mound or pink buttress aglow in the rising sun: not cliffs, Luddhew told them, but massive works of man—here a great city wall, there a temple or a mighty tomb.

With the coming of midsummer, the yearly river flood had receded. Now farm fields, ruled out in orderly blocks and triangles by the surveyor's art, stretched on either hand like sections of a lattice-screen. The earth of the fields clumped rich and black, bulging with fertility and sprouting an unbelievable bounty of green and gold, rice and groats, vines and bulbs. Dark, slender-limbed Shemites, in this district indistinguishable from the Stygians across the river, worked the fields by the score. They weeded, raked, and thinned; in places they raised up water from canals in wooden swapes and buckets to irrigate the crops.

Even after the circus procession sank down to the plain, the raised surface of the road remained firm and resilient to sandaled foot, hoof, and wheel. But in spite of the slight elevation they lost sight of the river, moving instead through a hazy dream of drooping grainstalks and papyrus, slender date palms, humble dwellings raised up on stilts or stony middens, and small, neatly plowed fields of onions and cotton. The air was heavy with vapor, the heat sluggish and intense, the gnats and flies thick and relentless.

Then at once their view opened out onto an obsidian sheet of water fringed by swollen, distant greenery. The road diminished to a smelly fly-swarming apron of pockmarked mud, there to vanish into black-stained depths. Low, broad shapes came creeping toward them over the river, and a sullen chanting sounded in the distance.

"What excellent fortune!" Zagar the Argossean called out to Luddhew. "The bargemen must have seen us descending the road, and set forth to carry us across. We will not have to wait here gathering flies for long." He leaned forward to wave a hovering black cloud away from the twitching muzzle of his restless donkey. "Have your purses ready for the toll—but fear not, I'll see that they don't cheat you."

The rafts and barges drew slowly near, poled and rowed by lines of chanting crewmen stationed along either side. The craft were formed from thick bundles of reeds, which were evidently impervious to the water and more easily obtained than wood. The few thin timber limbs and laths in evidence were laid down crosswise and tied securely in place to bind the hulls together and provide a deck of sorts. The cumbersome boats moved smoothly enough through the water, grounding on the mud a few feet from shore.

The crews, wedging the vessels into place with their poles, scrambled ashore to drag ramps and log props into position for the wagons. The mules, coaxed by their drivers, were induced to slog forward a few steps through the mud of the riverbank and climb up onto the rafts. Conan, shoving and slipping at the back of the wagons, half expected the wheels or the animals' hooves to break through the flimsy bottoms of the rafts and sink them. But the makeshift vessels seemed to buoy up the weight easily enough.

The circus hands waded through the warm shallows and climbed into canoes, whose massed papyrus was bundled up out of the water into neatly formed prows and sterns. The passengers knelt in between lines of rowers, who sat on the bulging reed floats that formed the vessels' side-wales.

Only then did the haggling over fares begin. The fleet's captain, a rotund man in muddy wet clothes and a grimy turban, argued doggedly with Luddhew, with Zagar fiercely interceding. In the end the debate was resolved by the circus-master handing over a purse—not to the bargeman, but to Zagar, who passed it along after evidently extracting some sort of share or tariff from it.

Then the rowers pushed off, muttering their work-chanty in mournful voices. The sluggish boats drifted free of the mud, snubbing and scraping clear of underwater logs and weed-banks, and a slow, nearly imperceptible headway was gained through the still water. Listless breezes moved the clammy river vapor past them; tinged with its mild, sweetish stink, it seemed almost as heavy and thick as the dark water lapping beneath the bows. Even the harsh southern sun lost its power in the dank river domain of the mighty Styx.

Their way was soon lost in a maze of estuaries and islets. They could not pass straight across, for the river shifted perspective constantly by its mysterious channels and eddies. In time the water rippled deeper and blacker; then the rowers drew out their slim oars and passed them through loops of rope knotted into the papyrus, to apply leverage against the dragging currents. The downstream motion could still be traced by watching the shift of clumps of foliage ashore, but Conan found it hard to believe that they were making forward progress at all.

Strange beasts dwelt in the waters of the Styx. Gazing into the shallows, the Cimmerian spied turtles with blunt snouts and jagged, knobby shells, and giant fish whose flat heads sprouted numerous antennae. Elsewhere the scaly, saurian backs of crocodiles could be seen floating or sliding down from mudbanks. And once, just ahead of the lead barge, a giant pink maw erupted from the water, the hideous visage sprouting stumpy, razor-edged teeth that parted in a grunting, bellowing roar. It was only a river-horse, a hippopotamus of the sort Conan recognized from the western marshes. Nevertheless it frightened the mules, who bolted in their harnesses and knocked several rowers temporarily overboard.

In time, they passed through the swiftest and

deepest part of the river. Reed banks closed in once again to fringe meandering sloughs and interlinking lagoons. Only this time, it seemed, the belt of marshes was much thicker—trending, as it did, not toward valley bluffs, but into flat open plains or desert. The rowers poled through swamps for a league and more before passing into agricultural lands worked by brown, naked toilers; and even then the voyage was not ended. Some of the farm fields, at least, lay on broad, flat islands. The chain of boats followed channels for a long way before coming up to a solid landing formed of flagstones and gravel laid down over the river muck.

Here were other reed boats, rude temporary dwellings built of the same material, and the starting-point of a new highway. Lean, idle field workers swarmed down to haul the wagons off the rafts and up the sloping bank. They clamored and groveled for tips or the chance of employment as the mules were led ashore and hitched in their places.

The barge captain obstreperously demanded extra payment for an overweight load, and was given a grudging sum by Zagar. Then, having consumed lunch in the boats and drunk sufficiently of the Styx's dark water, Luddhew's circus was back on the highway.

The road here was broader, raised above field and canal; it was white-metaled, with stones and gravel that gave off a glare in the noon sun. More traffic gradually joined in from side-roads— ox- and donkey-carts heaped with the river's bounty, peddlers laden with sacks and baskets, and troops of field hands marching barefoot under the snake-headed rods of their overseers. All of the passersby eyed with astonishment the circus troupe, the colorful wagons, and the loping wild animals, although piety and the press of business kept them from clustering around and following along after. The road was wide enough in most places for two wagons to pass abreast; there were ramp bridges across the canals, and the troupe made steady progress between roadside camps. So unvarying was the prospect, however, they found it hard to recall whether they had been on the river road two days or three.

Ahead, on a low, shimmering horizon, there came into view a broad pale blur that Zagar said was Luxur. It almost seemed to recede before them from day to day—an effect no doubt of its great size and of the vaporous heat arising from road, field, and canals. As the place rose more clearly into sight, it showed them a solid, impregnable face: a high outer wall spaced between steep square-topped towers, with low hills and monumental structures rising within. The central gate, tall and imposing, faced southward toward the river—a massively buttressed arch, with glints of yellow-bronze in the gateway hinting at the grandeur of the portals.

"That great colonnaded mass on the hill is the Circus Imperium," Zagar told them, pointing ahead from his donkey's back. "It stands taller and broader than any temple or tomb in the city, even exceeding the palace of the Tyrant himself. It has all been built within the last few years, through his heroic effort, and is constantly being improved and enlarged—a splendid showplace, as you will see."

"That is where we will perform?" From his saddle, Luddhew shaded his eyes to peer at the rounded pile just visible above the walls, fringed by smaller neighboring buildings and greenery. "How soon will it be?"

"Tomorrow, if my dispatches arrived timely enough to provide for everything." The Shemite grinned blithely at the circus-master. "I will confirm the arrangements as soon as we reach the city."

"So soon as tomorrow!" Luddhew's exclamation echoed with the excited murmurs of the nearby performers. "How will we ever have time to prepare, to rehearse?"

Zagar straightened his fez with an air of utter confidence. "You have rehearsed enough, I would say. Just use the talents the gods have so generously bestowed on you, and give us your best. I guarantee that the city crowds will be delighted."

Excited at this news, eagerly planning and discussing how best to awe the crowds, the performers jabbered and gesticulated as they moved along the road. Time passed more swiftly now, until the city walls loomed high before them, still visible above the fringe of orchard trees and hovel roofs that clustered near the road. Only the crown of the Circus Imperium peaked above the walls, glowing yellowish through desert dust in the declining sun's light.

As they waited to cross a canal bridge, a caped and turbaned horseman reined up beside Zagar at the head of the party. He handed down a scroll, which Zagar unrolled and read in silence. Where Conan stood, he could see that the message was inked in upright Corinthian characters.

"Excellent," Zagar told Luddhew, furling the scroll and sliding it into his sheephide vest. "The preparations are being made for your arrival. Tonight you will be lodged outside the city wall. You can rest up for your triumphant entry on the morrow."

Word spread swiftly among the circus folk. They crossed the bridge and trundled some way farther toward the city along a cobbled lane of suburban shanties and farm sheds. Then they turned abruptly off the main road, down a palm-shaded path. It led them to a low-walled caravansary yard which housed camels as well as horses and mules.

The inn turned out to be lavish; a generous meal was soon laid for them, and soft sleeping-mats were set out on the hard-packed earthen floor. The front terrace of the place looked toward the city wall across a rushy pond, the surface of which was pooled liquid blue with twilight. The lights from lamps and torches atop the wall gave off a starlike, dreamy glimmer in the dusk.

Since the only other guests in the place were caravan-tenders muttering together in Berberish accents few but themselves could understand, the circus troupe shared their dinner alone. The old Stygian couple who tended the inn were too busy for conversation; even the agent Zagar had ridden ahead into the city to make advance preparations. So the actors lulled each other with dreams and fancies of unequaled fame and fortune in the capital as they retired wearily to bed.

Conan and Sathilda slept outside on the terrace. This was necessary due to the female acrobat's special relationship with Qwamba, the night-tiger. The circus hands who helped feed and groom the giant beast were leery of their ward, but Sathilda bore an affinity for her cat-sister. She had formed the habit of sleeping next to the animal, both for her own protection and to calm her friend's nocturnal grumblings.

Conan, mistrusting those same restless cat-dreams, preferred to sleep outside easy reach of the she-cat's claws and fangs. He did not want to wake up in Qwamba's bristling embrace, be it feral, jealous, or affectionate.

So the two humans bedded down at the limit of the creature's chain—which, in this case, was fastened around one of the stone columns of the inn's portico. The animal kept off intruders while affording them decent privacy—but it was not unusual for Conan to awaken by night and see the tiger's great golden eyes regarding him, its heavy black head nesting comfortably on his lover's thigh.

The night was pleasantly cool, in any case. The chirrup of frogs in the marsh and the occasional rumble of wheels over the bridge and cobbled apron before the city gate were restful. So, weary with travel, but faintly astir with anticipation, the three of them lay watching stars wink into existence over the Stygian plain.

CHAPTER 4
Luxur

The performers arose at dawn and commenced feverish preparations, scouring travel mud from the wagons and animals, brushing and mending costumes, polishing leather and bronze and gilt and paintwork. Luddhew assured them that the bulk of their equipment would be unneeded in the great amphitheater; the permanent showplace had plenty of ropes, canvas, and timber of its own. So the main cargo of both wagons was unloaded into vacant horse-stalls at the inn. Instead of drayage, the wains would be used as rolling stages to parade through the streets of Luxur, showing off the black tiger, the bear, and the various other performers for the purpose of luring and inflaming the crowds.

After half a morning's labor, plus a period of exercise and drill, the players grew nervous. They had hurriedly eaten their breakfast of figs, dates, dry biscuits, and tea at dawn. Now they sat restlessly juggling, repolishing the wagons, or sipping wine-scented water in the shade of the portico. The Stygian sun was already high and merciless; distant shouts, gongings, and trumpet-blasts from the city gate indicated that the day's commerce was under way. Among themselves, they questioned when and if the summons might arrive.

All at once, the scuff of hooves and jingle of harness sounded outside the caravansary. Zagar rode in and dismounted from his donkey . . . smiling grandly, though he looked flushed and rumpled from the heat. Outside the low-walled enclosure, a dozen horsemen in well-trimmed Corinthian garb straightened their ranks under the gruff commands of an officer. It was an honor guard from the Tyrant himself, so Zagar proclaimed to Luddhew and the players. The band was to proceed immediately to the Circus Imperium, there to perform before the lords and citizens of Luxur.

In a great bustle the mules were hitched, the wagons straightened, the gear and fastenings checked one final time. Then they trundled forth, with the great bear Burudu chained behind the foremost wagon and Qwamba riding regally at the rear. As they passed out of the inn yard, the cavalry officer and six of his men took the lead, the other six falling in behind—to protect the troupe from attention-seekers, as Luddhew explained, and to ease their passage through the city crowds.

The lanes leading to the great gate were broad and well-paved. They led past sunken groat-fields, farm villas, and market stalls, meanwhile crossing over the dikes and canals that irrigated the land and formed outworks of the city's defenses. The local inhabitants on the roadway looked to be slaves and farmers of much the same sort the travelers had seen the previous day. They gazed up blankly at the crowded wagons and scarcely responded to the players' cheery waves and greetings, except occasionally to extend a hand for alms. But they were country folk, as Luddhew pointed out—simple and fixed-minded in their devotion to the harsh Stygian gods. Doubtless they were also leery of the city guardsmen riding before and behind the party.

As the city bastion and giant bronze-sheathed gate loomed ahead of them, the horse escorts proved their worth. Before them, merchants, mendicants, oxcarts, and camel trains scattered with alacrity to the sides of the roadway. As the mounted troops and wagons rumbled up the stone apron toward the looming pylons, trumpets blared from the top of the wall in salute. Tall-helmeted gate guards in vests of polished link raised their bright spears up vertical, and the watching mob bellowed forth its enthusiasm. At once the circus troupe began to prance, posture, and perform tricks, some leaping from the wagons to juggle and caper in the very midst of the crowd. So disporting, they made their entry into the great city.

The sun on the valves of the bronze gate was blinding. As he passed through them, Conan imagined that he was entering some mythical paradise of blazing glory. The city walls, too, were vast and imposing, with huge defensive cranes and ramp-ways installed just inside the gates. Beyond the paved entry plaza, the city surged right up to the stone buttress in a flood of clay and stucco, a maelstrom of sights and noises and smells. The sense of confinement was immediate. It was a suf-focating hive, a teeming warren of cramped, crowded humanity, like many another city Conan had seen.

The folk within, though mostly sharp-faced, olive-tan Stygians, were unlike the country toilers he had so far seen. They wore fezzes and tight-pointed turbans, coarse sandals and tassel-toed slippers, as well as a bewildering array of rags, robes, togas, vests, silken breeches, and woven da-shikis. They jabbered in a dozen tongues, scorning the gate guards' spears and the clattering hooves of the cavalry, and greeted the circus troupe with shouts of mingled glee and astonishment. There were many other strains present among them as well—grayish-skinned eastern nomads, smoldering black faces out of Kush and Keshan, curly-haired Shemites, and, most notably, a substantial minority of pale, square-featured Corinthian types. This was a city crowd indeed—diverse, animated, and dispu-tatious.

Their rowdy enthusiasm was all the circus play-ers could have wished; even so, there was an edge to it that Conan did not quite understand. The city-dwellers, while applauding the performers and trailing along after them in droves, simultaneously seemed to regard them with derision, as something quaint, old-fashioned, and laughable. Their attitude was irksome to Conan, making him feel less inclined to go through motions he found stilted and artificial just for their amusement.

Still, their contempt toward him could scarcely exceed his for them, looking down as he did on all civilized and overly cloistered city-dwellers. Furthermore, his fellow actors did not seem to mind, and he found their enthusiasm and eagerness to please the mob contagious. So he persevered, watching the crowds thicken and the maze of roadways narrow and twist—and incline upward, as the wagons climbed toward the amphitheater that could occasionally be glimpsed on the low hill ahead.

On the wagon-bed, Conan's principal duty consisted of standing with his chest puffed out and turning woodenly to show off his physique. At times he would lift up hollow iron ingots onehanded—or bend a leaden bar into a curve, then bend it out straight again. Such stunts could be repeated, he had learned, without having to work up too much of a sweat or a killing rage. Occasionally, if the watchers seemed to demand a special thrill, he would beckon to Sathilda, hoist her onearmed overhead, toss her back and forth from hand to hand, and let her spring down in a somersault to the wagon-bed. Her supple strength made her seem featherlight, and their antics together invariably brought yells and applause.

In the aftermath, the female acrobat would launch a series of handsprings, cartwheels, and backflips, often somersaulting from the jolting wagon directly to the paved street. Dath, too, would juggle his axes, spinning them high and catching them behind his back, occasionally letting them cleave into the wagon-deck to prove their sharpness. Bardolph, gaily dressed, had an intricate jig he danced while playing melodies with his flute. Burudu the bear amused the crowd with his antics, doing somersaults on the pavement or bouncing a ball, while Luddhew managed to make Qwamba the tiger spring down off the wagon-bed and leap over an extended cane. The others of the troupe, the tumblers and mimes and jugglers, all took their turn; the only passive one seemed to be Roganthus, whose hunched-over shoulder, as he sat on the wagon-bench swigging from a wineskin and lashing the mules, served as a mute reminder of the fragility of human hopes.

As the teams drew the wagons tortuously onward, the streets opened out somewhat. Close-packed hostels and tenements gave way to gardens, courtyards, and more prosperous dwellings set back a little from the road. The view broadened ahead, exposing the massive, many-arched shell of the amphitheater at the low hill's crest.

The mobs in the street, however, did not dwindle; rather they grew and intensified. In addition to the yelling rabble who streamed alongside the circus wagons, cheering and urging them onward, there were many who already filled the street, either making their way uphill toward the hulking colosseum or idling in long lines outside it. They included scores of the better-dressed citizens, notably those with spotless, foreign-looking robes and pale Corinthian faces. These patricians regarded the passing circus with mild cynical looks and, instead of cheering or jeering, made low-voiced comments to one another.

Spurring their horses through the throng, cutting across streams of pedestrians flocking toward the stadium when necessary, the cavalry guard kept the circus wagons rolling briskly. The horsemen led the way around one end of the high oval amphitheater, along a narrow cobbled lane flanked by the iron-grilled walls of villas and estates, with their terraced upper stories almost closing out the sky overhead. Conan saw the trailing crowd dwindle rapidly and fall behind; likely this was because there was no public entrance at this end of the Circus Imperium. Instead, just ahead along the curve of the massive pile, there yawned a tall, vaulted archway whose heavy doors stood open.

The cavalry vanguard, at their commander's instruction, passed the archway and turned, forming a cordon across the street and waving the circus wagons inward. Luddhew reined his mules over toward the edifice, and Roganthus followed in turn with his team. It was here that Zagar jumped down out of the lead wagon and stood by the wayside, calling out to Luddhew, wishing him a successful performance and waving to the troupe.

As they trundled into the dark, echoing cavern, impressions were many and confused. Conan smelled manure, animals, fodder, stale torch-smoke, and sour underlying scents. He heard a low growl and saw Qwamba's neck-hairs bristle at the sudden change of surroundings. He himself glimpsed cavernous shadows, vaulting stonework, furled and stacked canopies and banners, bins of mortar and sand, piles of building-stone, chariots, harness and tackle, and masses of idle circus-type decor stored in alcoves and stalls. To his surprise, the two wagons did not stop at all but kept rolling forward.

Stadium attendants, dressed Corinthian-style in knee-length white tunics belted at the waist, lined the broad passageway. Officiously they waved the teams and drivers forward, and Luddhew, in his lead wagon, obeyed them. Conan had expected the inevitable wait, a long tiresome interlude to work out their performance with the stadium's managers and possibly set up special equipment. But the wagons continued briskly forward toward a second set of heavy wooden doors. These, operated by chains and metal pulleys, were already scraping open before them, letting in blazing daylight and loud, surging waves of applause.

"Now, fellow troupers, I want you to put on your brightest faces." Luddhew, standing up in his wagon-seat, gave the reins to Phatuphar beside him and turned to face the performers. "This is the great moment, our debut here in fabled Luxur. Remember all of your skills, be proud of your circus heritage, and do not fail to please the crowd!"

The actors around him answered with palpable enthusiasm which Conan could not help but share. He felt nervous only because of the uncertainty of it all, having no idea what sequence of acts the circus-master might plan to announce, or whether the show would have an introduction, a buildup, and a finale like most performances. He resolved just to follow along and watch the others, who now stretched, preened themselves, and grinned in anticipation. They and Luddhew were seasoned performers, after all, and must know what they were doing. For his part, he resolved to strut and posture his very best, and throw Sathilda higher into the air than ever.

The wagons rolled out onto a nearly empty sandlot ringed by stone bastions and sloping amphitheater seats. The ledged slopes swarmed with cheering, colorful throngs ... almost brimful, except for a few patches of bare stone stairstep along the top rim of the stadium. More watchers streamed in each moment through entry-tunnels spaced halfway up the inclined walls, so Conan guessed the place might soon be filled. The crowd was exuberant and noisy; as the circus came into view, their cheers rolled from one end of the oval stadium to the other in a great echoing tide.

Ahead of the wagons, across the middle section of the open expanse, the level sand seemed to fall away in a depression from which one could see the tops of bushes and trees. Presumably it was a park or a stage-setting of some kind. Above it, against the backdrop of the massive stadium and the seething crowd, Conan saw a spidery framework of ropes and timber tripods raised—trapezes and slings for the acrobats, no doubt.

The players entered the amphitheater as they had done the city gate: dancing, fluting, and juggling in their places on the wagon-beds. Any sounds they produced—along with Luddhew's imperious accents as he called out the names of the acts in

Corinthian—were instantly drowned out by roars of acclaim from the audience, many of whom leered down from the ends of the arena walls, two or three man-lengths above them at either side of the arched entry gate. Conan, hulking atop his wagon-bed and hoisting his hollow weights, wondered at the need for the high walls. It would have been easier to let the crowd swarm down into the sandy area and witness the show close-up. But then, considering the crowd's size and frenzy, he felt thankful they weren't within arm's reach.

Yet he noticed that, as the wagons circled in place, with the high-plumed mules prancing valiantly and the players going through their impromptu routines, the audience's acclaim quickly faded. After only a few moments of carnival gaiety and uproar, the tones of Bardolph's flute and Iocasta's chimes became audible again, squeaking and clinking feebly in the vast space. The loudest sound was that of the heavy doors as they scraped and thudded ponderously shut behind the wagons. Except for an occasional hoot or cry from the crowd, and the faint continuing roar of murmured conversations, the onlookers became quiet. Their silence, to Conan, seemed like one of expectancy.

CHAPTER 5
The Arena

Conan noticed a stirring of dust at one side of the enclosure, not far from the wagons. Low wooden gates in the curving wall were thrown open, and from the inner darkness came snorts, guttural commands, and the scuff of hooves on stone. Out onto the sand there issued a shaggy creature with two wide-curving horns—a wild Shemitish bull, lurching and galloping erratically into the open. He was followed by more of his kind—not cows, but bisonlike males, broad-shouldered and massive, numbering ten at least by Conan's count. They slowed to an ambling gait, half-blinded by the arena's brightness and confused by the sudden clamor of cheering that poured down from the enthusiastic stadium crowd.

The mules of Luddhew's circus seeing the massive prong-headed animals stampeding forth and kicking up a storm of dust, shied away to one side and broke their gait.

"What is it?" Bardolph yelled back from the front wagon, "a second animal act? They will upstage us!"

"Is this a circus, then, or a cow pasture?" Dath, nimbly juggling his axes, turned in place aboard the moving wagon to take in the spectacle.

"Whatever it is, it looks like trouble." Conan, setting down his dumbbells, moved forward to help Roganthus with the team. He had seen the ferocity of wild bison before, and doubted that these could be very well tamed. "We'd all better stop making noise and capering about," he announced. "Just stand quiet till this is cleared up."

"What, because of a few bulls?" Bardolph, lowering his flute, spoke up scornfully from the other wagon. "Mitra knows. we've seen enough cows in our travels, and in our camps and tents!"

"Have you seen so many at once? Or such ill-favored ones?" Conan, taking over from Roganthus, urged the mules forward as smoothly as he could, without snapping the reins or jingling the harness overmuch. Gazing back at the trailing herd of long-horns, he saw what to him were ill signs: the panting leader, quite literally, had blood in his eye. Red also oozed forth around his nostrils. The beast had been cruelly goaded and beaten, most likely to infuriate him; the other bulls likewise moved with a wary, aggressive gait. As Conan watched, the leader lowered its head and began pawing the sand of the arena with one hoof.

"Hold onto the wagon," Conan warned the others. "Be ready to run or fight if need be. They may charge us any moment."

"Well, then, we should call someone for help," Sathilda sensibly proposed, looking around the blank stadium walls. "Or else threaten to leave outright and cancel our act. Why should they allow these animals to run wild and disrupt the show?"

In answer, Conan gestured back toward the wooden entry doors, which were now shut tight. "The show, it should be obvious, is a bull-baiting," he told her. "And we are the bait."

His answer was confirmed by a new surge of cheering from the watchers—for, even as he spoke, the foremost bull snorted a spray of blood onto the sand and trundled his great bulk forward in what looked like the beginning of a charge. The other animals, obedient to the law of the herd, began to straggle after him.

Conan urged the mules along faster, turning them straight away from the mass of cattle. If he could keep their rear end toward the bulls, he thought, with the wagon's bulk between them and the mules, all would be well . . . no easy prospect in a walled, semicircular space.

Luddhew's wagon had rolled to a stop, with some kind of argument going on in the driver's seat. Now, at the approach of the bulls, the circus-master urged his team forward again, likewise turning them away from the menace. Their route diverged from Conan's, straight toward the arena wall, so they would have to turn again sooner or later.

Looking back, Conan saw the giant bull trotting along steadily behind his wagon and gaining ground, with four of his fellows following close. Three younger bulls had veered aside to follow the other wagon, while two others stood there angrily indecisive, blowing up arena sand with snorts of their broad nostrils.

Ahead, Conan's course intersected the stone wall; so he urged his team gradually aside, avoiding a sharp turn that might slow or topple the wagon. As he veered beneath the high barrier, he was aware of a tumult directly overhead and sensed a rain of small objects around him. Debris was being hurled down on him by the hostile crowd; but he scarcely paid attention, for at the same time, he heard and felt the heavy horned skull of the lead bull striking and scraping at the rear of the wagon, jolting it forward. There were gasps from the wagon-bed behind him, but all the circus players evidently managed to cling to their places on the wagon. The mules, nervous but well-trained, negotiated the turn smoothly. They came out in a brisk canter, heading for the sunken area in the middle of the arena, which Conan hoped might provide them refuge.

The depression, he saw in time, was filled mostly with water, representing some sort of artificial swamp. Its shallows and sandbars were decorated with stone-potted trees and shrubs, some of which stood up above the level of the main arena—though they did not reach as high as the rope walks and trapezes strung above the pit. The drop-off at the near and far ends of the pit was sheer, higher than a man; and at either side, the square-shaped depression ran straight up against the far higher stadium walls. There was no way for the wagons to get around it without leaving the arena.

The purpose of the watery morass was all too clear. In it, sliding and squirming in the artificial muck, dwelt reptiles: giant Styx crocodiles, some with bodies thicker than a man could girdle with both arms. The quagmire had been dug here as an obstacle, a menace to any who tried to traverse the ropes and trapezes above it, seeking safety on the vacant sand at the far end of the arena. It was another snare, just a part of the trickery that characterized this whole devilish Circus.

The trees, though . . . might they not provide refuge to any who fell into the pit? Gazing at them, Conan frowned in distaste—for, solid and well-tended as they looked, they leaned lopsided in places, sagging heavy with the weight of some strange fruit. It coiled around the trunks, gleaming in harsh daylight, and slid sinuously through the branches—snakes, tree-pythons sacred to Father Set. Any who escaped the crocodiles by taking refuge in those branches would nevertheless find themselves in a reptilian embrace—slower, perhaps, but just as deadly. Doubtless the ravening crowd would find the poor fools' deaths even more gratifying.

The pit's drop-off, an ankle-high curb of granite, converged imminently with their route. And still the bull-herd thundered and bumped along behind, having found a tempting target for their wrath. So Conan urged his team into a sharper turn, which they managed in good order, curving back inward toward the center of the semicircle.

There waited another obstacle, in the form of two ambling bulls who had not joined in the pursuit. For their sake, Conan cut his turn short. He passed as close as he dared without running afoul of their long, curving horns or letting them terrify his team. If only the mules could keep up this pace a while more— say an hour or so—they might tire out both the bulls and the crowd and win their freedom.

Yet disaster, ever in the offing, finally struck. Luddhew's wagon, pursued just as closely as Conan's and cramped between the free-roving bulls and the arena wall, essayed too sharp a turn. The vehicle did not overtopple but slowed abruptly, its front wheels skidding and furrowing the sand, its bed shuddering and jolting beneath its startled riders. The mules were dragged out of position, left straining and staggering to get the vehicle moving again at speed. As they labored under Luddhew's urgent whipcracks, the three young bulls charged around the side of the wagon. They attacked fiercely, driving their horns into the bellies of the helpless mules.

The animals' screams of agony and terror, hideous as they were, were all but drowned out by the roaring of the stadium crowd. At this first sight of carnage, the bloodlust of the city mob was shown by a frenzy of dancing, leaping, and waving arms in the stands. Meanwhile the surviving mules kicked and strained in their traces, dragging their gored, bleeding fellows after them and jerking the wagon-yoke precariously sideways.

As Conan brought his team around in a broad circle, several bulls abandoned their pursuit of him and joined in the stationary fight. They ran blindly toward the beleaguered, limping wagon, rammed it, and finally succeeded in overturning it with tosses of their thick, powerful necks. The crash spilled Luddhew, a handful of circus players, and the bear Burudu out onto the sand, scrambling to avoid the churning hooves and spear-tipped horns of their attackers.

The bear, however, did not cower meekly away. Turning and batting aside the horn of one of the bulls, it laid open the animal's flank with a swipe of its mighty paw. The bull, scarcely daunted, ducked in low and tried to bring its rapier horn up in a belly-rending slash. But Burudu closed in behind the horn and grappled with the bison, tearing at the leathery hide with his powerful claws and slavering fangs. The struggle became a blur of churning, tossing sand, out of which enraged bellows and thunderous roars issued amid the tumult of the crowd.

Conan, meanwhile, brought his wagon around the less embattled side of the toppled hulk—angling in close enough, he hoped, to keep any bulls from charging in between the wagons. He did not dare bring his team to a halt, but slowed them to a trot, letting the still-pursuing bisons bump and batter at the rear of the bed and try to gore the turning wheels. At his urgent shouts, the riders from the overturned wagon came running. They dodged past the circling, lunging bulls to clamber aboard, drawn up by eager hands.

Most of them seemed to have escaped unscathed—a blessing and a handicap, since Conan's
mules now had to labor under a double weight of
human bodies. They were helped along by the
bulls who rammed and jostled from behind—but
the wagon drays were tiring, too, and were pite-
ously distracted from their work by the slaughter
of the stalled team, which still went on with great
violence and cacophony.

All at once the shaggy lead bull grew tired of battering the tailboards. Snorting lustily, and perhaps
smelling the scent of the team through his blood-
dripping nostrils, he lunged. His great body drove
past the corner of the wagon to attack the front.

This move was evidently resented by one
watcher—Qwamba, who crouched at the center of
the wagon-bed under Sathilda's comforting arm.
Without any audible command, propelling herself
in a powerful leap that rocked the conveyance on
its wheels, the great tiger launched itself through
the air straight onto the old bull's back.

In her pounce, the jungle cat was like a black
shard of midnight crashing through pallid daylight.
The cat struck the bison's broad shoulders and
clung there, her mighty claws clenched in the
tough hide, her fangs ravening and tearing at the
hairy, humped back. The bull arched and twisted,
vainly trying to throw off its devilish rider. Sand
fountained high; from within the dust cloud, the
night-tiger's pelt shimmered and flashed like a
glimpse down a bottomless well.

The crowd went wild.

The wagon, meanwhile, pulled free of the thick-

est part of the fray. But they were by no means
clear. Angry bulls circling the carnage and wreckage were now drawn toward the furious movements of humans and mules. From either side,
outriders closed in to menace wagon passengers,
mule team, and wheels. Dath lashed out with first
one ax, then the other, retrieving them by means of
thongs looped over his wrists; but the weapons
were too light to break the heavy horn-pates of the
lunging behemoths. He had to content himself with
wounding them and driving them back from the
wagon tail and wheels.

Conan, seeing several bison closing in on the
team, gave the reins over to Bardolph and climbed
back into the wagon-bed. Taking his leaden bar
and bending it through the ring of one of his iron
weights, he formed a mace of sorts, massive and
square-headed. He dragged it forward and, bracing
his legs against the wagon-bench, swung it over his
head at the nearest bull that harried the team.

The force of the blow almost toppled him from
the wagon; he had to let go his weapon and grab
the footboard for safety. The mace, striking the bison on the nape, made the animal stagger against
the front wheel, nearly tumbling beneath it and
causing a wreck. But the bull kept its footing,
slowing abruptly and falling away behind the
wagon in a broken gait.

Again the edge of the crocodile-pit loomed
ahead. Conan shouted at Luddhew, telling him to
turn the wagon short ... toward the center, near
the ropes and beams of the aerial riggings. With

the bulls closing in, there might lie their best chance for safety.

But the team would not turn. Hemmed in by wild bison on either side, with hot breath on their fetlocks and sharp horns goading their flanks, the mules raced mindlessly on toward the precipice. Luddhew lashed his whip, and Conan took his turn hauling on the reins, all to no avail. In moments they would reach the stone edge and be flung into a seething morass of flesh-eaters, fanged monsters that made their present pursuers look benign.

Conan dropped to his belly in desperation and, leaning down between the mules' lashing tails, groped for the harness chain. Shading his face against sand churned up by flying hooves, he found the chains' taut connection and, with a well-timed turn of his wrist, unhitched it.

The effect was immediate. The wagon, its wheels lagging in the soft sand, hung back ... while the mules, pulling forward steadily as the chain worked free of its eyelets, broke loose from the wagon-tongue in pairs and ran free.

Unburdened, they gained instant speed and left the pursuing bison in their dust. Three of the four sets of mules veered aside, kicking up their hooves in brisk flight. Only the last pair—held back too long, and goaded too urgently by bulls on either flank—failed to win clear. Lunging desperately, they ran straight forward into the pit. One of the enraged bulls followed straight after them, disappearing in a din of bellows and shrieks.

As the wagon lost way, the bounding wagon-tongue caught and furrowed sand, causing the front wheels to veer sharply aside. With its last lurch of forward motion, the vehicle tipped over and spilled its riders into the open arena.

This time, the whole troupe found themselves staggering and scrabbling for any available safety. There was precious little of it to be had, for the overturned wagon was already gouged and battered by the angry horns of pursuing bulls. From the level sand, above the stone curbing at the edge of the pit, two wooden tripods stood up tall and fragile. These offered scant protection from the bulls; from each apex trailed but a single knotted rope, offering a precarious way to the top.

The first tripod, which had appeared from a distance to anchor a stout cable, actually supported a slender balance-beam—a wrist-thin plank of wood mounted to the tripod with its narrow side facing up, for strength. Even so, it was so frail that it sagged visibly in the middle. It stretched unsupported from the timber apex overhead to another tripod on the far side of the pit . . . some twoscore paces distant, farther than a man might fling a stone.

Atop the second of the tripods was a narrow perch, barely wide enough for two people to stand side by side. To it was tied a trapeze, the first of several that hung down from overhead cables, leading across the pit at regular intervals to the farther side. Provision had been made, then, for the acrobats of Luddhew's circus—if they were willing to perform for a crowd over a pit full of voracious monsters.

Between the two sets of tripods, a third way across the pit existed—a bridge made of thin planks, laid transversely across two ropes that were bolted into the stone curbing scarcely a half-stride apart. The laths looked frail and loose, bound in place only by coarse twine. Worse, there were no railings or guide-ropes alongside the sagging span. In the middle, the bridge hung down almost to the waters of the artificial swamp—shallow waters that roiled and surged with the passing of reptilian bodies.

The clamor from the nearer edge of the pit soon ceased—the terrified braying of the mules and the fallen bull's bellowings replaced by coarser grunts and tail-thrashings as the carnivores fought and tore at the carcasses. Along the sand rim of the arena, too, things had grown quieter. Some of the bulls yet lingered near the first abandoned wagon and its slaughtered team, while others charged off in pursuit of the free-running mules. For the moment, only three bulls bedeviled the fugitives, making short charges across the sand and hooking their long horns at human targets who dodged and scurried before them.

"Up, then, and make your way across!" Conan called to those who swarmed behind him. "Onto the ropes and trapezes, if you can, or else across the bridge! We fighters can hold off these brutes yet awhile." He turned to swipe a sandaled foot at the head of a bull that had moved in menacingly close. "Dath, fellow, over here . . . can you spare me one of your axes?"

Before the ax-fighter could reply, he was set on by one of the bulls, a red-eyed behemoth that lumbered belligerently forward and drove him back toward the edge of the pit. The Sendajan cut and hacked at the scything horns without visible result;

then he scored a good cast with one of his tethered axes. It smote the animal between the eyes and made it stop in its tracks, shaking its head dazedly.

"Good, lad!" Conan shouted. "Now, in for the kill!"

But even as Dath moved, the beast regained its wits and lunged forward, swiping its horns beneath its attacker's legs and knocking him prone. But as the bull capered forward to trample the youth, Dath rolled clear, escaping injury from the thrashing hooves and his own ax-blades.

From just behind Conan came an outraged, frightened yell; turning, he saw the limping Roganthus caught on the horns of a second charging bull. The bison gave a heave of its mighty neck and shoulders, and Roganthus was flung through the air, to come down on the stone curbing at the very edge of the pit. Striking with an audible thud, he lay groaning, and barely kept himself from rolling over the side.

"Crom and Mannannan!" With an angry oath, Conan ran at the bull and seized it by the horns. The animal drove its hard-plated head at his midsection, but the growling Cimmerian leaned forward and thrust back, his feet sliding in the loose sand. He used the long horns for leverage, twisting the massive head down and aside and forcing the beast to stagger sideways to keep its balance.

The test of wills was intense—a struggle hailed by thunderous cheering from the arena crowd. Meanwhile, as the two strove and grappled, other circus folk ran to the wood pylons and the hanging bridge and began their flight to safety. Sathilda, after making a foray hand over hand all the way across the pit to test the trapezes and get them swinging, returning to her embattled friends.

Arriving at the near tripod and clinging to one side of the narrow perch, she sent off the less skilled aerialists with perfect timing, then caught the fragile trapeze as it swung back. One by one the young athletes, males mostly, swung out over the pit, passing lithely across to drop on the sand at the farther side.

On the balance-beam, those who lacked aerial skills but were still fairly fit tried their luck. Phatuphar chose to lead Jana by that route, holding her hand as they inched along, although it was yet unproven that the narrow timber would support one person, much less two. When they were safely across, Bardolph went running nimbly out across the void, scarcely looking down. Others followed one at a time, while their companions anxiously awaited their turns.

For those who, like Luddhew and Iocasta, lacked acrobatic skills, and for any players lamed in the wagon wrecks, only the rope bridge was left. Those few survivors began parceling themselves out onto the treacherous span; anxiously they called back to their fellows not to crowd on too quickly, less the frail ropes snap. The bridge, with its loose laths bending and cracking underfoot, was almost as much of a balancing-act as the wooden beam. As Luddhew and Iocasta approached its center, the frail planks hung literally awash in the lizard-infested bog, nosed at and tested by crocodilian snouts. Yet as more refugees ventured onto the span to escape the bulls, the swaying and sagging actually diminished. As the ropes tautened, the leading couple safely gained the upslope.

Conan, meanwhile, continued to grapple with his bull in a roaring, cursing frenzy that caused other bison to turn aside from the fight. Wrenching the black-tipped, blood- and sand-crusted horns relentlessly sideways, he forced the animal almost to the stone curbing; then, with a savage heave, he threw it over onto its flank, where it landed with a ground-shaking impact. Fallen, the bull flailed its hooves angrily a moment and, with a forlorn bleating, slid slowly into the pit. The splashings and bellowings that ensued were soon drowned out by the roar of the appreciative audience. But the tumult did not serve to keep loose bulls from straying near and veering in toward the fight, and Conan was soon menaced again.

The she-tiger Qwamba had long since crunched the neckbone of her victim and finished lapping up her fill of the bull's thick blood; Burudu, too, had survived his battle, whether by victory or standoff none knew for sure. Both animals came loping back over the sand to their human keepers, and their presence, with sullen growls and flashing, red-rimmed fangs and claws, surely helped to fend away the bulls' charges. Now, with only a handful of circus folk left at the edge of the pit, Sathilda leapt from her perch and gave her attention to the animals.

"Poor dears, we must save them, too," she announced, moving her gentle touch from the bear's lumbering rump to the tiger's dusty sable. She gestured toward the half dozen surviving bulls that slowly but steadily converged on the spot. "Qwamba can make it alone, she is an excellent swimmer, but Burudu will need our help. You must guard the bridge, Conan, till everyone else is across."

"What? A bear three times my size needs me to guard its tail?" Conan, now armed with one of Dath's light axes, glanced behind him over the bridge with its scatter of individuals teetering, limping, and creeping across to the farther side. "Leave the wild beasts to fend for themselves! They have a better chance than we ever did."

"No, they are our partners. They rely on us, and we them. Qwamba, up!" At a snap of her fingers, the night-tiger obediently sprang up one leg of the tripod, raising splinters on the wood surface with her razor claws. From there, the black cat flowed smoothly up onto the balance-beam, which now was empty of human traffic, and ran forward.

The wooden stringer could not by any stretch of the imagination have supported the immense bulk of the tiger near its centermost point. But such was the motion of the cat, so uncanny its speed and balance, that it ran straight across without ever stopping or resting its full weight on the frail timber. Like a flicker of night-cloud it passed overhead and, with a fluid leap, bounded down to the sand on the farther side

"There, you see?" Sathilda demanded exultantly of Conan. "Dath, Roganthus, you go next, and hurry! We cannot trust Burudu's weight on the bridge till everyone else is off. Dath, you help Roganthus along."

"Nay, I can do it myself," Roganthus called

back, setting forth on his own in a fairly erect posture. "That bull that threw me did not hurt me much; in fact, my leg works better now." Crouching low, his hands almost grasping the bridge-planks for safety, he made good progress. Dath followed him without a backward look.

"By Crom's scratchy linen clout! How long do we have to dawdle here, woman?" Conan, swinging the ax furiously against three encroaching bulls, fought to keep himself, his bedmate, and her pet bear all from being crowded over the pit's edge at once. His blows connected; he even sheared the tip off one bull's horn, but the light throwing-ax was never made to shatter the thick skull of a wild ox.

"They are nearly halfway across," Sathilda replied anxiously. "Burudu, fight!"

At her commands and emphatic gestures the bear lunged forward, swiping aside one of the three horned heads with a blow of its paw. The insulted bull snorted and bore in angrily, but could not make any headway against Burudu's fur-clad bulk. Meanwhile Conan jumped clear, as two more young bulls shouldered in and clashed horns irritably with the pair he had been battling.

"That's it, then," he declared, seizing the girl's shoulder in his thick, grimy hand. "Go now, onto the bridge."

"Burudu, here!" Giving way reluctantly at Conan's shove, Sathilda paused to coax the bear after her. "Come along, Burudu, follow me!" And Burudu, turning at the sharp sound of her voice, abandoned combat readily enough and followed.

Conan was unsure whether he preferred to be in front of the lumbering brute, like Sathilda, or behind it on the narrow bridge. Lacking any choice, he pressed after the beast's brown, rumpled hindquarters, feeling bull-horns graze and prod his own back.

No sooner had the span taken on the combined weight of the two humans and the bear than it gave way beneath them. Fortunately it parted behind them, where the ropes crimped through the eye-bolts at the pit's edge; just as luckily, both the ropes gave way at once, so they were not dumped sideways into the teeming quagmire. After a sudden dousing and a desperate scramble, they found themselves slogging through thigh-deep water over sand hummocks and the backs of slow-moving lizards, following the treads of the bridge that stretched before them to the far edge of the pit.

Sathilda, splashing with all her acrobat's strength, managed to stay ahead of Burudu, whose ponderous weight served to hold the bridge-ropes taut for her. The bear smashed and splintered the planks as he went, but also mauled some of the crocodiles severely and fended them back with ill-tempered swipes of his paw. Conan was left to follow as best he could, smiting behind him with his ax and avoiding the scissoring jaws of the smaller, quicker crocs.

In that way, speeded by peril and without fear of losing their balance, they made it rapidly through the center of the reptile-pit. Those others who had been caught on the fallen bridge, including Dath and Roganthus, appeared to be making the climb safely to the farther side.

Only one of the python-draped trees loomed near enough to their path to pose a threat; and Conan, leaping up and swinging his ax, split the head of the thickest serpent before it could drop down and snare one of them in its coils.

Amid a converging formation of snapping, lunging crocodiles, the Cimmerian managed to stay upright and unscathed. Finally, after the remains of the bridge span had been splintered and demolished by Burudu on the ascent, Conan hauled himself hand over hand up one of the dangling ropes, to join his companions on the far rim.

They stood clustered together, welcoming their friends up onto the bank but looking somewhat unsure. Before them stretched another expanse of sand as large and empty as the first one, leading to no evident exit or open doorway. The only thing before them that was any different from the farther side was a low wooden trestle piled with leaning spears, halberds, rusting swords, and dented bronze shields—a weapons-rack. The roaring of the crowd, which had swollen to a frenzy as Conan hacked his way through the lizard-pit, now fell back to an expectant murmur.

A chorus of trumpets sounded, echoing sourly across the sprawling stadium. At a far corner of the arena, low wooden doors opened wide. From them came pouring onto the sand a troop of warriors, nomads of the eastern desert. Whirling curved swords overhead, the warriors gave tongue to wild yells and charged.

CHAPTER 6
Sand and Steel

As the circus troupe stood gaping in shocked silence, Conan shoved forward between them. "Come, then, and arm yourselves! If any of us survives this, it will be by weapons-play! Here, grab a spear and form a phalanx."

So saying, he strode to the makeshift arsenal. The stoutest-looking sword he snatched up and slid beneath his thick weight-lifter's belt, letting it hang heavy at his side. With the thonged ax dangling from his wrist, he gathered up swords and pikes and pressed them into the hands of those crowding close behind him. "Here, Jana, this javelin ought to be light enough for your arm! Phatuphar, take this, but I hope you brought your throwing knives along. You, Roganthus, are you sure you can swing that?"

In reply, the ex-strongman raised the longsword he had chosen, flexing his arm freely. "I can, indeed. By Mitra's mercy, the hurt you so carelessly gave me is gone!"

Amid the clank and scrape of weapons, Conan moved around to the front of the arms-rack. The yelling bedouins had a long sandy space to cross, but now they drew near. Numbering two score and more, they spread out widely and broke into a full run . . . already in spearcast range, Conan saw. Reaching behind him, he drew a light javelin from the untidy pile, balanced it in his palm, and hurled it.

The sound of a steel-tipped shaft driving into a human chest was never a pleasant one. Nor was the scream of a crowd that watched in frenzied exultation, maddened by the sight of the first human blood shed that day.

Yet over the unholy clamor the charge continued, even as the circus folk straggled out in a line to meet it. Conan dipped into the pile of rusty weapons; he hefted and threw again and again, until every unclaimed spear found its home in the vitals of an attacker. Others cast their weapons with less effect—except Dath, who flung his ax and split the face of an attacker at ten paces, the full length of his thong.

Phatuphar's hurled knives could wound but not stop the nomads, who wore thick robes. They appeared to be wild bandits, rounded up on the Stygian frontier and ordered to fight for their freedom. Conan had killed countless such marauders in the desert and did not qualm at killing more of them here.

The battle-lines met abruptly, with shrill cries and the clashings of long, curved *yataghans* against the coarser steel of the arena blades. The circus players' line held against the attack, bending back slightly at either end but standing forth at the center. There Conan swung his notched sword one-fisted, and parrying the nomads' slim blades with Dath's light ax held in his off-hand.

Conan fought and slew lustily, hacking through leathery necks and wrists and skulls—or else, where his worn blade could not cut the tough woolen folds of their garments, clubbing his victims with the dull steel and breaking their bones. Repeatedly he stepped forth out of the phalanx, letting nomads surge about him. Where their wickedly curved blades struck and clashed together, Conan was not—time and again he eluded them, only to dart back an instant later and wreak new death and mayhem on the return pass.

The players backed him solidly. Fighting close, they choked up short on their spearshafts to thrust and jab at the enemy, or at the very least held their shields and points firm to fend off the assault. Of the other circus stars, Bardolph and Roganthus fought most exuberantly, each one holding up one flank. Bardolph thrust and chopped with a halberd, a weapon long-handled enough to compensate for his short reach, while Roganthus swung his sword in great swaths, flailing and beating aside the attackers with his newly recovered strength. Dath, however, slew more than both of them combined;

plying a battered shield, he had a sly way of darting in under his enemies' swordstrokes and dispatching them with a quick upswing of his ax.

The back of the phalanx was guarded by the circus animals. Any nomad who sought to outflank the troupe and slaughter them from behind was confronted by Qwamba and Burudu pacing nervously in the rear, a daunting sight; after one interloper was severely mauled by the bear, and another disemboweled by the tiger, the rest gave second thought to trying.

Then, almost as suddenly as the battle had joined, it was over. The sand lay strewn with woolcloaked bodies, to which Conan's last lunging foray had added several more. On finding their number thinned to a mere handful, the survivors broke and ran away, some staggering from wounds, the rest throwing aside their weapons. Conan started after them with his sword raised and a feral snarl in his throat . . . but then he thought better of it and turned back to his companions.

Among them he moved half-dazed with battle lust, stepping over dark-cloaked bodies. He let his bloody weapons drop into the sand, the better to clasp and embrace his friends' shoulders. To his numb astonishment, he learned that not one of the whole circus troupe bore any wound more serious than a mere gash. None had died except the mules; not even the jungle beasts looked sick or scathed.

"Indeed," Roganthus exulted, "I am better off than I was!" The strongman waved his sword exuberantly on high. "Praise be to Mitra for sending a mad bull and a flock of brigands to cure me!"

The din from the cheering onlookers gradually beat through to their distracted senses. They glanced up to see the audience in turmoil, waving, capering, and crowding against the stadium rail. The beaten nomads had retreated to the side of the arena, where they now were allowed escape by the same door through which they had entered. No new threat was evident ... yet the players had learned to mistrust the Circus Imperium. Rearming themselves and moving in a tight group with their animals trailing behind, they went toward the hoped-for exit.

As they came near the arena's high wall, individual outcries emerged over the general uproar, and distinctive figures could be seen—red-faced men waving both fists high overhead in frenzied salute, oddsmakers arguing and scuffling with bettors, and town women leaning out wantonly over the rail, baring their breasts at the victors and licking their painted lips. As seasoned circus hands, the performers had seen this sort of thing before. But the scale and intensity of it here were astonishing and more than a little frightening.

Above the nearest fringe of maddened spectators, moving through the middle of the stadium's riot, there seemed to be some kind of procession—a flock of notables dressed in robes either pure white or pure black, passing from an area of privileged, stone-carved seats at the center of the arena, moving along an aisle to the far end. As the players came up before the low wooden postern, which now was shut tight, and balked at coming any nearer to the raving mob atop the wall, the dignitaries were led through the crowd directly before and above them. Then a voice, issuing from a liveried herald stationed over the archway at the end of the arena, rang out in clear, understandable Stygian.

"All hail the lords and priests of Luxur— foremost among them Commodorus, our city's Liege and Tyrant, and Nekrodias, High Primate of Set's Temple."

The herald's shout, carrying as it did across a good part of the stadium, resulted in a slight and momentary increase in the cheering. Meanwhile the aristocratic procession, pushing forward steadily through the mob, arrived at a level, balustraded terrace just above the terminal archway. And the doors in the arch, as massive and impregnable as the ones through which the circus troupe had entered, began to grate inward.

"Victors of this noble day!"

The speaker was a pale-skinned, white-robed, athletic-looking man with a bushy wreath encircling his curly blond brow. Stepping forward to the carved balustrade, he declaimed like a trained orator with one arm graciously raised. At the sound of his voice, the crowd's babbling actually diminished somewhat.

"O happy victors! Seldom has our Circus Imperium witnessed so proud a performance as yours . . . so complete a triumph, and won at such a small cost! We hail you as heroes, we officers and nobles of the city and church of Luxur. I, Commodorus, exalt and salute you above all other citizens! I know that the elders of the city temple must do the same."

At his latter statement a black-robed figure, the thin vulpine man who had moved up beside Commodorus, nodded tersely. Meanwhile he kept a fixed public smirk on his otherwise sour-looking face.

"Therefore," Commodorus resumed, "we welcome you to Luxur, and extend to you all the bounties and delights of our great city! Welcome, victors . . . may your lives be long and your fame eternal! Before we resume the games with our afternoon combats—I decree a public triumph in your honor!"

As he finished, to a new thundering of cheers, the heavy doors beneath him thudded open and a festive cavalcade emerged. Children, wagonloads of flowers, fair young men sitting bareback astride white horses, and capering slave girls wearing little else but bows and garlands . . . here, for once, was nothing fierce or sinister or dangerous. As the circus troupe moved impulsively toward the exit, a rain of blinding colors sprinkled down from the stadium seats: flower-petals, they were, wafting and shimmering gaily on the sunlit air. Whole wreaths of flowers, bright coins, kerchiefs, and women's dainty garments fell at the heroes' feet.

Meanwhile, on either side of the stadium, venturesome spectators were starting to lower themselves down the arena walls. Males and females alike, descending by means of ropes and slings, dropped onto the sand to pursue the illustrious ones—a fact that made the players press forward all the faster into the bosom of the procession that issued forth to meet them.

As Conan pushed through the throng, he felt a hard, heavy blow strike his shoulder. Looking about him to find the culprit, he discovered what had been thrown—a purseful of thick coins amounting to a small fortune in gold.

Even as he tucked it away out of sight in his belt, he felt a soft hand settle on the same throbbing shoulder. A young maiden, clad in a flimsy diaphanous tunic, made him an offer of a wineskin, by the wordless expedient of thrusting its horn-spigot up to his lips. Accepting it, he drank greedily, pumping the cool liquid out of the goatskin into his dry gullet. Once he finished, he surrendered the depleted skin, his brain reeling from the heady liquor.

He saw his companions similarly greeted, by servants who succored them with food and drink from waiting carts. Others lent their scrubbed shoulders to support the dusty, weary victors, asking in sympathetic Stygian accents about their aches and their exploits. Moving as a group, the players followed along the cool, perfumed tunnel toward a garden that shone sun-drenched through the farther archway.

Then, for a sudden brief moment, roars and outcries echoed fiercely in the tunnel. Stadium attendants, holding forth joints of raw meat as bait and using long, noose-ended sticks as goads, had tried to divert the tiger Qwamba and the bear Burudu down a side-passage toward some unknown destination. Just as swiftly as the ill-tempered beasts lashed out, the animal-baiters scuttled clear to avoid injury. An instant later Sathilda came running forward to stand protectively before the growling beasts.

"Thieves! Scoundrels! Do not try to steal our pets, or they will rend you bone from tendon!" The female acrobat stepped back to stand calmly between the bristling animals. "Whatever ill-fate you intended for our friends will be visited on you tenfold!"

"Come now, lovely maiden . . ." An officious, violet-togaed male servant, clean-shaven and youthful but already bald atop his head, bustled over to calm things. "Surely you do not think we mean any harm to these brave, noble beasts—"

"Nay," Conan put in, "any more than you meant to harm us by throwing mad bulls and madder bedouins at us in the arena!" Shouldering his way over to join the dispute, he took a place before Sathilda and glowered ominously. "Why on Crom's earth would we or these animals ever dream of trusting you?"

"Sir, most noble hero—Conan, is it? I am Memtep, chief eunuch in charge of hospitality at the Circus Imperium. I am aware that there may well have been some slight error, alas, in the booking of today's performance. But I assure you, nothing ill was intended, and we thank all the gods that no harm came to you. Regarding these beasts, we only want to provide them safe and comfortable lodging for the night—the same as we would hope to furnish you and your companions, by way of expressing our sincere apology."

"Spend the night here in Luxur, with more of your so-called hospitality? And with that sorry sculp Zagar, who sold us down the River Styx as slave-fighters?"

"If we stay, the animals must remain with us," Sathilda declared firmly. "They are accustomed to sleeping at our side. After today's events, I do not think they would take a separation well."

Conan looked dubiously at the others. Luddhew, who stood nearby, gave a quick nod of assent. The hair at the back of the beasts' necks had smoothed somewhat, and the other players were gnawing loaves and joints of fowl, obviously accepting the idea. Feeling a wine-bearer jostle his elbow, Conan seized hold of the flask. He drank deep before proceeding down the tunnel.

He found a cartload of dates and sweetmeats that appealed to his belly, which had known no food since morning. He felt uncertain about the situation here, and vaguely resolved to get his friends free of this fools'-pageant soon. But for the moment, perhaps it made sense to rest and restore the troupe's strength. Meanwhile, the food-cart contained hunks of braised meat he found spicy, so he sought out another wine-bearer and guzzled her flask near-dry.

The garden, as it happened, led them to a broad marble pavilion enclosing a lavish public bath. The great pool was unoccupied as yet, its waters clear and steaming; but white-clad attendants waited to strip away the victors' garments, lave off the crusted sand and blood from their limbs, and usher them into the limpid depths. And, after their day's ordeal, the circus players were loath to pass up such an opportunity. After all, it was better than group-bathing in some cold Shemitish brook or a muddy farm sump. So they lay down their weapons, abandoned their gory costumes, and ventured in.

As Conan reclined in the tepid water with his purse of gold looped safely around his neck, he must have dozed. He drifted fitfully in and out of awareness, to the sound of yelping and splashing as Roganthus sported with the slave girls in the pool. Then, some distance away, voices were raised in irritable disagreement—familiar voices, whose accents jolted Conan awake.

Splattering scented water, he mounted the steps, dodged the attentions of towel-bearers, and strode across the marble tiles toward the ornately carved benches. There sat Luddhew in a Corinthian-style toga, expostulating angrily with someone about the cost of circus wagons and mule teams. And there opposite him sat a smaller figure, clad in a bright silk blouse, embroidered vest, pantaloons, and a tasseled fez: Zagar, the deceiving Argossean. Conan's voice grated in his throat.

"Now then, you perfidious whelp, some questions will be answered."

Leaning forward to seize Zagar, the Cimmerian was for once taken by surprise as the spry procurer turned to him with a wide-eyed expression, sprang up from the stone seat, and clapped his small hands on either side of the larger man's neck. Beaming delightedly, the Argossean planted two swift kisses on the outlander's astonished face, one on either cheek.

"Conan, my brightest star," Zagar crowed for all to hear. "Our troupe's mighty champion, the deadliest fighter ever to grace the Circus Imperium! How wise I was to discover you and bring you here from that little Shemitish village ... Sendaj, was it? And now, what wealth and honors lie ahead of us! We have business matters to discuss, my brave fellow! Great prospects indeed!"

"What are you babbling about?" Though flushed and taken aback by Zagar's display and suddenly mindful of his own undress, Conan still felt a vengeful impulse. His hand, which had darted out to shove the fawning Zagar off him to arm's length, now knotted and twisted in the Argossean's silk collar. "Lying churl, you dumped us here in the arena and left all us to die—"

"Now, now, my dear boy! Nothing happened after all, and you were a great success!" Zagar squirmed futilely in Conan's silk-tearing grasp. "Do you really think I would be so inconsiderate? ... I did not know, not any more than you did, I assure you! It was all a mistake, some whim of that great fool Commodorus, perhaps!" The Argossean's face reddened, his voice rasping hoarse and desperate due to the gradual constriction of his air supply. "But you were well able to handle anything that came your way—I saw that from the start, when I watched you tossing those bumpkins around the village street! You are a natural fighter, the best thing to come to the Circus in years! And

I am the one who knows how to make it pay, for all of us . . .

"Listen to what he says, Conan." Luddhew, reaching forward to lay a hand on Conan's half-crooked arm, spoke in quiet earnest. "Zagar knows this town, and he has the connections to shape our future here."

"What?" Conan demanded, giving Luddhew an incredulous glance. "You think there is some future in being torn apart by wild animals? Or diced by nomads, for the enjoyment of a mob? A great lot of good this scalawag's Corinthian gold will do you, once you are writhing in a crocodile's jaws—"

"Nay, Cimmerian, 'tis not so! A fine circus like yours and Luddhew's should never again have to vie in the arena!" Zagar, still in Conan's loosening grip, squirmed and spoke volubly. "That was a mistake, a sad injustice that I swear will never be repeated! There is much to do here at the Circus—I can win you concessions that will fatten your purses and make you all lords of Luxur!"

"There now, Conan—release him, and let us hear him out." The circus-master, with patient persuasion, untwisted Conan's fist and drew it clear of Zagar's collar. "Having seen the worst of this city, we may now be in a position to enjoy its best—but without any more trickery or foul-ups, mind you," he scolded the talent-procurer.

"Nay, I would not dare." Muttering thankfully, Zagar made a submissive, smiling bow to Conan. "There are sideshows, intermissions, courtyard acts, and vending concessions," he enumerated.

"After your exploits today—which were well-nigh the grandest in our arena's history—every Circusgoer will be eager to meet you and bring business your way. I can arrange it so that all you tumblers and mountebanks will want for nothing." Addressing the small, towel-wrapped crowd that had gathered round, Zagar drew interested looks and murmurs. "As for you, Conan, a fighter of your prowess—there is no limit, the folk of this city will crown you in white gold and make you a demigod.

"Of course"—he glanced to the onlookers—"there are others here who can fight, and who acquitted themselves nobly." He did not mention any names, to Roganthus's visible disappointment. "You will be pleased to know that not every arena contest is to the death, and not every fight has a totally unforeseen outcome." The Argossean smiled. "We try our best to manage our athletes for the greatest satisfaction of the Circus patrons. So there may be rich opportunities for each of you, without undue risk."

Luddhew spoke up unexpectedly. "If Conan fights for you, he should be able to keep the bulk of what he earns." He laid a fatherly arm across the Cimmerian's broad shoulders. "There is no point in his continuing to give a third of his salary to Roganthus."

"No, I should say not!" Roganthus said indignantly from the pool shallows. "I have no more need of it, and would not want it. In fact, I am his tutor and his better." He flexed his arms and shoulders massively to show off his state of health.

"So then, he may keep it all, except for the one-third portion that goes to our circus administration." Luddhew nodded in judicious approval. "But of course, he should fight only if he feels certain that he wants to take the risk," he added considerately.

"I have nothing against fighting," Conan declared. "But I hate to see my innocent friends endangered." He looked around to the others, and felt Sathilda's hand come to rest lightly on his other arm.

"Never fear, O warrior." The talent-procurer smiled. "I think we can reach some satisfactory agreement." So saying, Zagar resumed his private negotiations with Luddhew, a heated interchange that lasted many minutes before they finally struck a bargain. Meanwhile, Conan stretched himself out on a raised marble slab—where, enjoying the attentions of a skilled masseuse, he once again fell asleep.

CHAPTER 7
The Heroes

That night the players were housed in lavish apartments adjoining the baths, which appeared to have been part of a temple residence at one time. Wine aplenty was provided, along with various musical instruments suitable for strumming and piping late into the evening. Conan and Sathilda ended up sleeping on a cool marble terrace overlooking the city, sprawled on a silk-covered divan with the tiger snoring at its foot.

When Scorphos the sun rose out of the yellow eastern haze, Sathilda merely groaned and burrowed deeper under the pillows. But Conan soon was up and dressed in the large-sized, gilt-embroidered tunic his hosts had provided, foraging for his breakfast and exploring the Circus grounds.

The noise of wild animals roaring and bellowing

led Conan to an expanse of pits and pens screened
off by tall cypresses from the back of the colosseum. The Circus menagerie was vast, with brass-
barred cages for the lions, massive leg-manacles
for the jungle elephants, and tanks dug into the
stony earth to house the crocodiles. Bullpens, stables, and carriage works extended down the hill,
along with enclosures full of sheep, goats, and
chickens fated to nourish the flesh-eaters. The
feeding was even now under way, carried out by a
host of slaves who went busily about their duties
and scarcely glanced at Conan.

"A formidable task, beast handling. The mule-
meat from yesterday is already consumed." Behind
Conan, cheery-voiced Memtep approached from a
hay-strewn alley. "The Circus Imperium has a
wide assortment of animals from every corner of
the empire—mainly the fierce and freakish kinds,
of course, for the public's tastes. A noisy lot at this
time of the morning." He paused to listen to the
chorus of roars, squawkings, and howls that issued
from the pens around them. "And what of you,
Master Conan? Have your cravings for bread and
flesh been satisfied?"

"I have slept and eaten," Conan replied. "But if
you remember, there are two good-sized jungle
beasts in our crew that will require feeding this
morning. Unless, that is, you expect them to make
a meal of one of your attendants."

"Ah, yes, the bear and the tiger. They will be
seen to, do not fear. Meanwhile, let me give you a
tour of this place." Memtep waved an arm at the
towering stadium and its lavish outworks. "It is

splendid in its way, one of the wonders of modern Stygia."

"It wasn't here when last I passed through, some years ago," Conan remarked.

"No, indeed," the eunuch said, leading the way between bins of rotting vegetables and reeking pens full of hairy, long-tusked boars. "It was begun with the advent of the current Tyrant, Commodorus, with the blessing of Temple Primate Nekrodias, and only completed four years past. Temple land was used—all this was formerly a snake garden adjoining the main worship complex, yonder." He waved at squat green-domed buildings that rose above the sheds. "The actual planning and administration of the Circus was left to the Corinthian Trade Delegation, comprising some of the richest and most highly cultured citizens of Luxur—the same ones who built the great aqueducts that promise to double our city's extent. Their talent and vision, combined with the vast resources of the Stygian realm, have created something truly noteworthy—"

"Who pays for it all?" Conan asked. "And to what purpose?"

"It is a joint venture, and it pays for itself many times over, in many ways." Memtep waved vaguely. "There are the admission fees, of course, and the flourishing trade in betting. Foreign merchants and emissaries are drawn here, to our city's greater good, and our Corinthian and Zingaran allies are made to feel at home." He led the way out of the animal-pits into the shadow of the towering stadium. "Most of all, the public spectacles uphold the prestige of our state and church, and keep the city-dwellers respectful. They teach essential moral values, such as hard work and fair play." Coming to a tall wooden gate, Memtep pushed it open and led the way into a walled enclosure. "Work and practice, as you must know from your own circus, are the source of all achievement."

The spacious dirt-floored area was tented over with a screen of coarsely woven cloth—transparent from within, though it dimmed the bright daylight. It likewise served to mask the area from prying eyes, particularly from the back rim of the stadium, which loomed just overhead. The space was an exercise yard with hay-bales and vaulting horses, stands of blunt mock weapons, and practice targets suspended from cranes and posts. Only three or four athletes were present at this early hour, exercising in silent concentration, but the place was obviously the main school annex to the central arena.

"Our real fighters prepare themselves here," Memtep said. "There are plenty of others—condemned criminals, slaves, and war prisoners like the wild Rifs you fought, who abide in prison-pens farther down. But the true lords of the Circus Imperium, our featured gladiators, enjoy comfort and prestige such as few citizens can ever hope for. They are encouraged to practice and exercise." He moved to an arm-long wooden beam that hung on a chain suspended from an overhead crane, bearing a dented shield at one end, with a blunt metal rod projecting from the other end like a sword-blade. "Some have trainers as well, ex-mercenaries and military officers who teach them fighting skills."

Conan, taking up a wood-padded metal brand from underneath a bench near the gate, advanced on the hanging target. Raising the mock sword, he struck the copper shield a blow that bent it almost double. The reaction was immediate, the beam leaping and gyrating on its chain so that the sword-end came flailing around; only by ducking low did Conan avoid a near-lethal repayment of his own stroke.

"That is no way to swing, leaving yourself wide open," a deep voice remarked. "Here, let me show you!"

Edging away from the still-oscillating weapon beam, Conan looked around. Memtep had scurried well back at his first stroke, but a black-skinned, leather-kilted figure, a broad-shouldered Kushite by his look—came over raising a sword-stick of his own. Conan watched with interest as he strode around the opposite side of the target.

"Greetings, Muduzaya!—known to his arena fanatics as Muduzaya the Swift, until he won the title of Swordmaster," Memtep added for Conan's benefit. "This is Conan—already called the Slayer for his triumph here yesterday." The eunuch did not venture to touch the Kushite or clasp his hand, any more than he had Conan's, but stood a respectful distance from both men.

The newcomer did not seem overly fierce. As he squared off before the sword-beam, his slow, confident manner belied any claim of swiftness. He was a fighter, to be sure . . . bearing scars, though not from any arena skirmish. The pale scarifications on his cheeks Conan recognized as the ritual markings of a tribal officer of southern Kush. Yet when he moved, he glided silently and innocuously as his own flitting shadow. Muduzaya's face wore a dreamy, contemplative smile as he raised his steel cudgel in a massive fist.

"See, now," he declared, bracing to swing, "before you ever strike, be ready with your backswing." Blunt metal resounded as Muduzaya's mock blade struck the hanging one, then clanked in a quick rebound against the circling shield.

The effect of his blows, besides fending away the beam, was to drive it crookedly at Conan—who, rather than stepping back, lashed out and struck twice in equally swift defense.

"Ha, you are not so sluggish, after all!" Stepping forward, Muduzaya commenced a series of powerful forehand and backhand blows. His strokes drove the target dummy relentlessly at the Cimmerian, the fixed shield and sword veering in wild alternation both left and right, at crotch and crown. Conan surrendered no ground, dodging or parrying each swipe of the rough metal and occasionally sending the dummy back at the Kushite with equally daunting force.

"By your unusual speed you break many rules," Muduzaya observed. He meanwhile readied a two-handed overhead stroke that, when delivered, sent the beam's blunt sword-tip swooping straight at Conan's breadbasket.

"I make rules, too." Fending aside the blade, Conan pivoted on one foot and gave the beam a well-placed kick that sent the jagged shield straight at the Kushite; to dodge it, Muduzaya had to shift his feet in an agile but less than dignified way.

"Well-done," the black man allowed with a nod. "Remind me not to go up against you in the arena. Not, at least, at the end of a long, weary day." He put out his big hand and caught the beam on its backswing. "Enough now, I would not want to wear you out." Muduzaya himself as Conan saw, scarcely breathed fast and bore no sheen of sweat.

"Agreed," the Cimmerian said, stepping clear of the target. On an impulse, he tossed aside his cudgel and put out his hand. After a brief glance into Conan's face, his adversary did likewise and returned the handclasp—using the legionary grip, wrist-to-wrist, each man's hand clamped about the other's forearm. It was a greeting most frequently shared by troops and mercenaries of the eastern desert, wanderers all.

"Peace, then." Nodding. Muduzaya turned and strode away. The other athletes in the compound, though they had looked up and observed him taking Conan's measure, did not interrupt their routines to greet either man. As potential competitors and potential slayers, they preferred to keep to themselves.

"If your popularity persists and grows to match Muduzaya's," Memtep observed, "very likely you will be pitted against him. The public has a craving to play off their heroes against one another."

"And such a fight draws lavish bets, I would guess." Conan nodded contemplatively. "Still, some accommodation can be made, mayhap."

They passed through the practice compound into a spacious shed—an armory, barnlike and musty with the smell of rust and old blood. The equipment set out in racks and bins varied greatly, some of it polished and well-kept, some battered and almost laughable in its shoddiness.

"These helmets are ungainly, having such broad visors and bills," Conan observed. "Why would a fighter burden himself so, at risk of straining his neck?"

Memtep smiled, venturing to touch one of the helmet-rims with his slim dark hand. "With afternoon sun burning down on the white sand and bouncing off the marble walls, a gladiator will risk quite a bit for some shade, so you'll find. If a wide-brimmed casque keeps you from being blinded by the glare, or by a flung handful of sand, then it's well worth the weight."

Conan grunted in understanding. "And this dross over here is reserved for your less favored contenders?" He moved among the bins of rusting, broken arms.

"Exactly." Memtep led him over to a heavily barred door in the farther wall. Unlatching it, he pulled it open onto a dank, smelly passageway. "Through here are the slave and animal holding-pens. This entrance to the arena is known as the Convicts' Gate."

Turning aside, Conan walked along the cobbled tunnel toward the bright, glaring light at the end. Gazing out through the half-open portal into the vacant stadium, he was astonished to see scores of workmen installing heavy timbers and partitions in what formerly had been the crocodile-pit, erecting a level floor across the two-man-deep depression.

"The arena surface is usually flat." Coming up beside the Cimmerian at the drop-off, Memtep answered his unvoiced question. "The understruts and floor segments can be rearranged in countless ways, so as to form hidden pits, mazes, raceways, or whatever might be required. There is even a plan to divert the main aqueduct and flood the whole great oval."

Conan said nothing, watching the antlike labors of the men in the pit. It was now clear of reptiles, and nearly so of water, except for broad sandy puddles that remained in the depths. He was thinking how the whole place must have been specially readied for the arrival of Luddhew and his troupe. Yet he saw no point in belaboring Memtep over it, since it all seemed to be working out satisfactorily.

"The Circus Imperium is in a constant state of change, forever being improved and enlarged upon." Memtep pointed to other work crews who were replastering the stadium walls, repairing the benches, and installing what appeared to be a canopy or balcony over the privileged seating. To erect pillars, the workmen were pouring troughs of sludgy gray flowstone into wooden forms. "Our craftsmen work under the most advanced designers and foremen from far-off Corinthia," Memtep added, "so there is no limit to what can be done."

As the eunuch spoke, he turned and led Conan back along the tunnel; but the Cimmerian stopped to look into an archway from which the stench of death emanated. In the dark, cool interior, several steps down, he saw corpses lying on straw pallets on the floor. They were the desert nomads who had been slain the previous day—a few of them, anyway, their twisted bodies looking pathetically ragged and frail in their slack robes. A male slave, white-robed against the chill, sat in attendance on a wicker seat; he eyed Conan incuriously, apparently oblivious to the smell.

At the far side of the sunken chamber was another heavy door, which scraped open. From behind it emerged two men—red-robed, priestly-looking types, their heads shaven under the loose cowls of their robes. Without even glancing at Conan, they nodded acknowledgment to the seated slave, who made a mark on a wax tablet in his lap. Then, stooping at either end of one of the bodies, they lifted it smoothly up on its sagging pallet. Moving silently and expertly, they bore it away through the open door, which thudded shut behind them with the rattle of a latch.

"Who are those men?" Conan asked, turning to Memtep. "What becomes of the bodies slain in the arena?"

The eunuch answered as if reluctantly, leading Conan off down the corridor as he spoke. "As I said before, the Circus Imperium was built on hallowed ground, with active support from the Temple of Set." He looked back at his listener with solemnity in his eyes and with what might have been a glint of superstitious fear. "As you may know, a large part of our religious faith here in Stygia deals with death—that is, the fate of the soul, or *ba*, once its mortal husk collapses and fails. It has been revealed to us that, to ensure eternal life, the bodies must be preserved—bodies of lords and lowly ones alike, so they may continue to rule and serve in the Afterworld. Do you understand this?" Memtep, leading Conan out into daylight between barred sheds and cages, looked inquiringly at his guest.

"I know that you Stygians are great mummy-makers and tomb-builders," Conan replied.

"Precisely. To sustain the spirit in the afterlife, the body must be correctly prepared and preserved. As a condition of the Circus's establishment in Luxur, it was agreed that every man or sacred beast who happened to die here would be granted mummification rites, and guaranteed a place in eternity. The red-robed acolytes you saw are special trainees under Chief Embalmer Manethos, who answers directly to the Temple Primate himself, Nekrodias. The Temple maintains an embalming-crypt here, adjoining the Circus." Memtep nodded toward the farther end of the stadium's rear area, which they had not visited. "In that way, the proprieties of our worship are maintained in the face of foreign customs."

"So the arena's dead are all mummified?" Conan asked, shaking his head in uncertainty. "Even if their own beliefs differ?"

"Not all receive the same honor," Memtep said, ignoring the second part of Conan's question. "The arena's most famous fighters, by popular demand, are immured—entombed right here in the walls of the stadium." He pointed to one of the shallow alcoves under the series of arches that held up the curving vertical wall. "Of course, all the death-shrines so far have been installed overlooking the street. They do a fine job of it, embossing urns and wreaths, with sculptured flowers and testaments inscribed in Stygian and Corinthian text. Atop it all is the death-mask of the hero, set intaglio with gemstones in the eyes, so that they seem to follow you. A champion's place in eternity is well-assured."

Conan kept silent, deciding to ask no more questions. Himself, he thought little of death. His own beliefs, shaped by the preachments of austere northern gods such as Crom and Mitra, placed little importance on the fate of the mortal body after its extinction. Even so, the notion of being gutted and stuffed at some future time when he was helpless—spiced liberally, and wrapped and propped up in a niche for public inspection—made him queasy. He had seen sorcerers, rank necromancers, perform unspeakable tricks with the reanimated bodies of their victims. Was it possible that Set's priests might truly enslave his soul with their embalmings, and hold it in his body to rot, dooming him perhaps to wander forever as an outsider among prating, praying ghosts in their dim Afterworld? He did not like to think about it.

Memtep led him by a semicircular route back to the apartments, where his companions were just now arising and partaking of fresh viands. They were enthusiastic about what had turned out to be, after all, their great success in Luxur. After break-

fast, Memtep took them to the rear of the compound and showed them their long-term lodgings:
a row of humble priest-cottages that, in point of
fact, promised to be more comfortable than the
temporary suite of rooms. Bardolph and several
others were eager to go immediately with Luddhew to fetch the troupe's personal belongings from
the caravansary with the replacement wagon teams
that had been made available. Some of the players,
including Sathilda, wanted to prepare the quarters
for the humans and animals and work out details of
their new acts.

"As for me," Dath announced, "I would like to
see the town."

"I, too," Conan said. "I have never yet had a
good carouse in Luxur."

"That sounds like a pleasant way to spend the
morning," Roganthus joined in, flexing his shoulders. "Let us see what damage we can do."

Securing an advance on their pay from Luddhew, the three set out. Though refusing Memtep's
offer of a slave guide, they made note of his direc-
tions to the Corinthian Quarter and the Canal
Wharf—said to be the most hospitable sections of
the town. Conan told no one of the purse of gold
that had been flung at him, but kept it safe on a
thong around his neck.

They made their exit by way of the carriage
yard, which did not take them past the stadium and
the hill-front with its fashionable dwellings. Even
so, within a dozen strides they were recognized
and set upon by a band of ragged street urchins.
The children pestered them for alms and, receiving

none, made scurrilous references to their life-and-death skirmish of the previous day.

"These are the country louts, are they not?"

"Yes, the yokels who tried to entertain wild bulls with their dancing and juggling!"

"I did not know a country circus bred such fighters." The ragamuffins' obvious leader, a scrawny copper-skinned boy, centered his impertinent attentions on Conan. "Are you attacked much by bulls and bandits, out there in the rural mudflats?"

"We know how to deal with nuisances of all kinds," Conan answered meaningfully. "Now, begone."

"You did not learn to swing a sword like that in a medicine show," the youth persisted. "Are you a mercenary, then, or a gladiator from one of the Hyborian cities?"

"Why should you want to know?" Conan countered. "Do they let babes like you witness the carnage of the arena? If so, 'tis a grave error."

"I see more, and know more, than any ten adults in this city," the cocky youth replied.

"Oh? What is your name, then?"

"I am Jemain," the lad proclaimed, to the respectful silence of his fellow ragamuffins. "And you are Conan the Slayer, the next great hero of the Circus Imperium."

"A public sensation," Dath the ax-juggler put in at Conan's side with a knowing smile. "And a great betting favorite, no doubt."

"Yes, more surely, someday," Jemain answered with a wary look at Dath.

"And what of me?" Conan's other companion demanded. "I, Roganthus the Strong, discovered this oaf. He learned what little he knows about circusing from me." His voice was only half-jocular, containing a real note of vulnerable pride. "Tell me, young ruffian, is there any glimpse of me in your soothsayer's crystal?"

Jemain's sly young face flashed a cynical smile. "Yes, surely you have a place. The Circus Imperium welcomes all, and puts each to his best use. A skillful fighter can win great wealth in his time there."

Roganthus seemed to accept this; the others lapsed into grateful silence. Most of the street urchins had fallen away, with only Jemain dogging the three men. Likely he still hoped for a handout or at the very least, marketable information.

The cobbled alleyways they followed from the arena compound led downhill, angling into a broader thoroughfare in a valley between the stadium and the taller, less densely built hills to the south. Passing between shops and tenements, they came into the shadow of a series of high stone arches that marched above the rooftops, spanning whole buildings at a single stride.

"Here is the tallest of the aqueducts Commodorus built," Jemain said like a diminutive tourguide. "It has made life easier in the city and allowed the rich to improve their estates on Temple Hill."

"Water runs atop that?" Conan asked, squinting upward into the bright blue.

"Yes. In a roofed shed, to keep out the bird-droppings," Jemain explained. "It comes from streams in the southern hills. The Corinthians brought a thousand engineers and stonemasons to Luxur to build it."

"But the heavy lifting was done by Stygians, I'll wager." Conan brushed his hand against the chest-sized blocks of stone as they passed one of the pediments of the arch that spanned the street.

"Yes. The Temple Primate decreed a labor draft from the farms, as they always do with the great tombs and temples. And for the stadium itself—but the Corinthians are good bosses." The boy smiled. "Not many of the workers died, except from falls."

Conan grunted, noting how well-fitted and dry was the masonry that held up the skybound river. "And this all has been done under Commodorus's rule?"

"Oh yes, he is the most popular Tyrant ever, especially for his pranks in the arena." Jemain waxed visibly enthusiastic. "It is said that the army will someday throw off church control and declare him Emperor of Luxur, or even of all Stygia."

"Oh?" Conan asked skeptically. "And what do Set's priests say to that?"

The boy shrugged, obviously not intimidated at the mention of his country's all-powerful serpent-god. "Old Nekrodias is crusty and not well-liked, not even by his own younger priests. In the countryside they still believe all that old-fashioned stuff, but here in the city we are more enlightened. We know and understand foreign ways, especially the Corinthian ones."

Indeed, as he walked on down the avenue,

Conan was impressed by the free, cosmopolitan atmosphere of Luxur. In this neighborhood at least, it did not have the watchful, shut-up air of other Stygian towns. Doors and windows were open and unshuttered, with awnings strung out against the midmorning sun; proud men and unveiled women moved freely down the well-paved streets, where tradesmen trundled barrows and hawked their wares from open stalls. There were no armed priests stationed in kiosks or patrolling in bands, and no religious shrines and four-headed snake totems at every crossroad. The military was not in evidence, either, though Conan recalled that the circus wagons had passed barracks on entering the city, near the main gate. It was almost like being in Tarantia or Belverus, he decided, though not nearly so free as wild Shadizar.

Along the way the three circus performers were recognized and hailed, all the more frequently as they descended into common, congested quarters of the town. Pedestrians greeted them from afar, or pressed near to clasp their hands for luck. They were offered fruit and buns by shopkeepers, and drink by a wine-vendor; and more than once a tradesman came running with a damp clay message-pad, begging to press Conan's palm into it to make an impression of his swordhand. He consented, understanding that these imprints could later be baked hard and sold to fanciers and collectors, or even duplicated and counterfeited. One merchant made a point of obtaining handprints of all three men; this circumstance soothed Roganthus's pride, though

Dath's head did not seem to be turned by all the attention.

In all these proceedings the scamp Jemain did his best to appoint himself the group's unofficial guardian. He chased off bands of smaller children who tried to gawk, retrieved uneaten morsels and secreted them in his shirtfront, and gruffly demanded payment from those who wanted palmprints. He offered the athletes his services as a guide to taverns, gambling dens, and bagnios, meanwhile trying to extract information about the men's physical condition and fighting skills. In general he made a nuisance of himself; but he was a keen observer of character, and knew when to shut his mouth.

With his unasked help, they soon found themselves in a bustling foreign quarter whose shopstalls were decked with exotic foods, fabrics, vessels, and personal adornments from far-off Hyborian lands. Much in evidence were the goods of Zingara, Argos, and Asgalun, carried here by ships plying the Western Sea and the River Styx. But the majority of tradewares were obviously Corinthian and Zamoran, brought here via Koth, Khoraja, and the deserts of eastern Shem. Corinthian brokers had succeeded well at using camel trains as desert-ships, and the Styx as a cheap trade conduit, floating their wares in disposable reed barges downstream from the river's inland reaches.

The city's craving for foreign goods was obviously great. Aside from the scattering of pale-featured northern colonials doing their daily shopping, supplying themselves and their larders as if they were at home in Corinthia, Conan saw prosperous-looking tradesmen and expensive women—the wives and concubines of church and civil officials, with their litters and covered chariots waiting—adorning themselves in the jewel bazaar and trying on fashionable garments behind the flimsiest of curtains in tailors' stalls.

Women of other sorts noticed the athletes, too, calling out to them seductively and venturing forth from doorways; but it was obvious that business was on their minds, and Jemain did his best to shoo them off before his sightseers could be tempted.

As they came in sight of the city's East Wall, the street took on the appearance of a pleasure-district. Numerous taverns, stables, hostels, and less orderly establishments offered their business to the camel-riders and bargemen who brought wares from abroad. By night, Conan guessed, it must be a lively quarter indeed, with one or more ships or caravans always newly arrived from sea and desert expanses.

But the real squalor lay outside the city's East Gate. Luxur's builders had evidently been reluctant to open their town to naval invasion by letting the broad ship canal pass inside its defenses. Instead, they left a narrow strip of land lying undefended, outside the city wall but overlooked by it, where river ferries and barges as well as easterly caravans might be unloaded. The Canal Wharf, so-called by respectable city-dwellers, had grown into a teeming slum of sheds, warehouses, nomads' tents, and vendors' ramshackle stalls. It lay outside the domain of the church wardens and customs-takers, who collected their due in the shadow of the city gate. Therefore, the place enjoyed a thriving commerce in tariff-free and black-market goods, heathen idols, condemned and unfit slaves, and other wares that might fall short of the city fathers' high standards. Most of it, of course, ended up inside the city anyway, smuggled in by private dealers and enterprising citizens.

Having come thus far, to the very river-bottom —where unpaved streets ran foul with muck, and wayside lurkers beckoned to passersby and called out in strange languages, making even plucky young Jemain look ill-at-ease—the threesome decided to seek refreshment. They found their way into the only public-house that advertised itself here: a cavernous, many-pillared building, obviously converted from a stable and still smelling like one. The Pleasure Barge—as symbolized by a crudely carved and painted boat-silhouette nailed over the door—fronted on a muddy, reedy wagon turnaround. A mere dozen paces away half-sunken flatboats sat moored in stagnant canal water.

Boisterously the gladiators ordered their drink out of casks and jars set in the back of the shanty, across a plank that was laid over two barrels. The publican was a one-eyed, one-armed river pirate; he delivered them beverages in gourd-sized palm-nut halves that served as noggins, then greedily plucked up their copper coins. The boy drank watered wine while the three men swigged sour *arrak*, fermented palm-sap from the southern plantations.

"What are the odds in the next arena meet, then?" the barkeep asked in a rasping, Shemitish-accented voice. "Are you lads assigned to fight on this coming Bast Day?"

"We might very well be," Roganthus answered, obviously flattered to be recognized. "They have not told us so as yet."

"You lot are newcomers," the barman said, "untried in the public's eye. But there will be a fight, you can be sure of it . . . and keen wagering, too." He squinted his one eye critically to examine the three. "You are all feeling well, then—no injuries from yesterday's affray?"

Roganthus snorted. "Hurt? Rather the opposite, I would say! I seem to thrive on that sort of thing. And it works up a powerful thirst. Here, fellow, another of those sour beakerfuls," he said, slapping more coppers onto the rough plank.

"If you want to gain valuable inside information on these future champions, I am the one to ask—I, Jemain, of Tanner's Warren!" Inflamed by his weak wine, the boy crowed grandiosely across the bar. "I am a faultless oddsmaker, and a star-caster as well! I have rare intuition none other can match!"

Conan, who had learned to put small faith in the mutterings of touts and tipsters, was nevertheless impressed by this city's continual fervor of betting speculation. Now he leaned over to catch the barkeep's one watery eye. "I know not if you were at the show, and saw my party almost butchered alive by wild beasts and brigands." At the barman's wary headshake, he continued, "Yet obviously you know of it. I ask you, would you truly lay money on the outcome of such a mad spectacle?"

"I? Why, indeed, I had a silver shekel riding on it. Nothing personal, you understand."

Since the man did not say he had won any shekels, Conan assumed the bet had been against himself and his friends. He frowned. "But tell me, why would you risk money on a bout that has no whit of sense or fairness to it?"

Speaking authoritatively from below, Jemain chimed in. "Everyone knows the fights are unfair. It's just a matter of finding out which side the advantage is on and fixing the odds accordingly."

"Myself, I follow the arena fights regularly," the barkeep said, ignoring the urchin's babble. "After all, it was there that I left this arm and this eye, all on the same day! In time, with Set's good grace, I shall win back enough to compensate me for the loss."

"By all the gods," Conan avowed, sipping his *arrak*, "that will take a cartload of silver! To suffer those grievous wounds all at once, and yet survive—"

"Aye indeed, 'twas not easy," the man said bitterly. "I myself, if the truth be known, had to fight all the harder after my parts were hewn away. I came within a hair being packed off and stuffed by the Morgue Priest Manethos's embalmers, whether breathing or not! Beware of them, my friend . . . not every injured fighter is so lucky as I was!"

While Conan, Jemain, and the barkeep exchanged stories, and Roganthus became better acquainted with his *arrak*, Dath drifted away. In the half-open porch of the tavern, among the various indolents and beggars, there lounged a group of four shabby-shirted, underfed youths who had followed the gladiators down from the town . . . casually, but with a wistful eye to a robbery, so Conan guessed, once their targets should become well-oiled with drink. Dath, sauntering up to these ruffians and braving their initial scowls, fell into low-voiced conversation with them. Soon after that, he and they disappeared from view.

But Conan was not overly concerned; Dath was, after all, of their age and general type, and less a foreigner here in Stygia than he himself or Roganthus. With quick wits and a smattering of Stygian, he was well able to take care of himself, and would probably turn them aside from their hunt.

Even so, none of the three had brought along a real weapon—nothing more imposing, at any rate, than a mere foot-long dagger. Conan therefore resolved that he should be cautious, and avoid confounding his wits with too much drink.

No sooner had this resolve been formed than he was interrupted by a wharf-rat, one of a pair who had been idling, already drunk, at the front of the inn. The bare-chested, oversized Stygian looked as if he could pole a barge single-handed to Khemi or, for that matter, float there himself. Blessed with overkeen hearing, the fellow broke in on their conversation.

"Namphet, I have heard stories of your arena days till I want to puke! As for you outlanders— you should learn that there are those of us who could match your feats of derring-do! And far surpass them, too, if we did not have honest work to occupy us!"

Roganthus, idling over his drink, was quick to take umbrage. "Say now, fellow, do not dismiss us unfairly! You may not know that we are trained professionals, devoted to physical culture and the mastery of our athletic skill. Not many men could stand up to us in a head-on grapple—"

"I, for one, see little to be afraid of." The Stygian glanced around at his companion, a taller and thinner but equally ugly stevedore who pressed up close behind, wearing a bucktoothed sneer. "Weight-lifters, are you? I lift more weights in a day, unloading cargo barges on a morning shift, than you do in a summer's tour of Shemitish cowtowns!" He guffawed and belched simultaneously. "Fighters, you claim to be? Well, Lufar and I have ended more fights right here on the canalfront than any ten oiled, pampered pups like you in the arena! And we're ready to show you how it's done . . ."

Conan was already edging aside for space, planning to break free of the ramshackle confines of the bar and find room to maneuver in the street. The wharf-elephants moved aggressively to cut him off—but just then, help arrived from an unexpected quarter.

Dath and the street idlers had suddenly reappeared to enclose the two drunken marauders in a businesslike semicircle. Without threat or preamble the blows were driven in, low and fast—darting so swiftly, Conan could not tell if they were struck with bare fists, brass cesti or, hopefully not, knife-blades. The longshoremen battled vainly for a moment, then turned and stumbled away through the tavern's open barn doors. They were pursued a few steps by their vanquishers, who gave them parting kicks and then returned, laughing cruelly among themselves.

"Most efficient." Conan, who had never even had the chance to land a blow, gazed solemnly at Dath and his newfound friends, the four street rogues. "You, too, could just as well fight for pay in the arena."

"One or more of them will, if I have any say in it," Dath replied frankly. "They are good steady fellows."

"I still think we could have beaten them without any help." Roganthus, rising belatedly from his keg-seat, managed to look morose and disappointed.

"We had best go, in case they return with the wharf guards. They are few but troublesome." Jemain, who had evidently been the one to run and fetch Dath in the first place, beckoned them outside, back toward the city gate.

As they downed their drinks and went, eight in number now and enough to face down any marauders, Dath sounded well-pleased.

"I tell you, Conan, I am glad we traveled here to Luxur. Already I feel right at home!"

CHAPTER 8
Battle Practice

In the days that followed their Circus debut, the players worked hard at learning Luxur's ways and polishing their acts. A new arena spectacle was proclaimed by Commodorus, droned forth by criers from the temple porticoes and announced in red-clay daubings on public notice walls. It was scheduled for an imminent date, a few days hence, a special extra showing to be wedged in before the traditional Bast Day exhibition.

This news caused a pleasant flurry of expectation among the populace. The pace of renovation on the stadium was stepped up accordingly. Even Conan, caught up in the general fervor, undertook a program of physical training to master the ways and weapons of the arena.

When not battering at the various dummies in

the exercise yard, and doing severe damage to their
cantilevered limbs, he resorted to human sparring
partners. Some of these were from a special class
of arena slaves, adept at holding up wooden
swords and shields and dodging the trainees' over-
eager blows.

But Conan preferred working with his real fellow gladiators, closely observing their moves and
timing. Most often he sparred with Muduzaya the
Swordmaster, learning respect for the black warrior's subtle misdirections and the swift, powerful
sweep of his mock sword. He sustained frequent
scrapes and bruises, and dealt out some others
himself, yet considered it a small price to pay for
the useful drill. It said much about the ease and affinity of these two men that their practice, with all
its thumps and abrasions, never crossed over the
line into real, murderous combat.

In the evenings, after long days of exertion, some
of the warriors found themselves drawn with Conan
to the disreputable surroundings of Namphet's pub
in the Canal Wharf district. In spite of the poverty
and filth of the wretched neighborhood, the place
somehow felt congenial. It catered to foreigners, for
one thing—to barge-polers and camel-tenders laying
over from Shem and the eastern deserts. There in
the shantytown, a fighter could guzzle his native
brew and share gossip with visitors in familiar dia-
lects. Then, too, the publichouse stood well outside
the fashionable city quarters where the athletes were
recognized and tiresomely fussed over by adoring
Circus fans.

It was not a stylish place, the Pleasure Barge,

but it was run by an ex-gladiator. The toilers and farm types who frequented it would either challenge a man openly or let him drink in peace.

Some few of the fighters, and especially the circus players, actively sought out the city's accolades; Luddhew, Bardolph, and Roganthus boasted of being wined and dined nightly by rich Corinthians and civic officials. Conan guessed that Sathilda might secretly crave such distinction; but for the time being, she was content to crowd in with a pack of cursing gladiators, aboard chariots commandeered from the arena stables. Often as not, the big cat Qwamba was left behind to guard their love-nest while she and Conan thundered off to carouse nightlong outside the city wall.

"Do you know what events are slated for this upcoming show?" Conan asked Ignobold, one of the older gladiators, over drinks at Namphet's. "Will it be wild beasts again, or single combats? Surely they cannot find another group of foreigners as gullible as we were, to be lured blindly into the arena."

Ignobold was a swart, black-browed Ophirean. He had wandered southward guarding a caravan and found Luxur and its bloody Circus Imperium to his liking. "I heard they caught a troop of marauding bandits from Khauran," he murmured over his cupful of *arrak*. "Military renegades . . . you can expect to meet them in the killing-pit this time around."

"Is that so?" Conan turned to Sathilda at his side. "Khauranians are good fighters," he frankly told her. "They should make worthy adversaries."

One of the older and more battle-scarred heroes, revered by the city fans as Halbard the Great, leaned over his bench. "I was set to fight Saul Stronghand this time around, man-to-man, for high stakes." The rival he named, one of the younger gladiators, was not present at the pub. But even so, Halbard spoke in a gruff, confidential tone to the handful seated around the table. "I did not fear the contest in the least—no, indeed, that Stronghand is a raw upstart, cocky and overrated, if you ask me." He shrugged his massive shoulders, his callused fingers tugging at one battered ear. "But that weasel Zagar, the so-called talent-procurer, came creeping up to me the other day. He wanted me to lose the fight—take some small wound, he suggested, and go down in the sand. My life would be spared, so he assured me—and I would receive a share of the prize money in secret." He frowned and shook his head in sullen disapproval.

Listening closely, Conan leaned forward. "You refused him, then?" he asked.

"Refused? Why, I offered to flatten his nose for him and tamp that silken fez down about his ears!" Halbard shook a scarred ham-fist and thumped it down on the keg-top. "I would not sacrifice my reputation that way, not for any mere passing gain—my good name is my livelihood, my one true possession! I told him, lay your crooked money on me instead, Zagar, for I will fight Saul Stronghand and trounce him well! Now there is some talk that the match will be canceled—not if I have anything to say about it!" He shook his jowled, battle-scarred face in indignation.

Muduzaya, who had been listening from an adjacent keg, now spoke. "Have a care, old friend. These bettors often try to sway the outcome of the contests. They go against a fighter's strength and popularity if possible, just to promote their own long bets. They would make our reputations rise and fall like a juggler's batons if they could." With one large hand he clapped the battered warrior on the shoulder. "You will have to fight all the harder these next few games to keep your standing."

"Indeed," Conan added, intending to comfort the melancholy man further. "Just stay alert and lucky. I would guess there is a rich, easy retirement for a fighter as well-beloved as you."

While Conan waited, the other drinkers said nothing. At their too-conspicuous silence, he felt compelled to press home his point. "Is that not so? Do most of the successful gladiators live out their days here in Luxur, or do they travel home in glory?" He spoke low, trying not to let his question carry to Namphet, who struggled to fill beakers and keep track of payments with his one remaining hand and eye.

"Yes, well, that was my plan," Muduzaya said. "I always intended to save my pay and my wagers and retire after a few years in this business, Set granting me some good luck." He shrugged apologetically. "But you must understand, Conan, we gladiators are not the best and wisest at keeping money. If we were, we would be temple coin-changers instead of man-butchers."

"To be sure," Ignobold put in, "a man has to keep up appearances and be generous to his friends and concubines. It is hard enough to live decently on the pay they give us for risking our lives, believe me! And these oddsmakers—if you can turn a profit against them, even betting on the surest outcome, you are a soothsayer indeed!"

"In truth," Muduzaya said glumly, "I cannot think of a single noted gladiator who has kept his place in Luxur over these half dozen years. There are those who departed for Corinthia and the Hyborian cities, of course—and Commodorus himself, who they say was an arena fighter in his early days. But as a rule, our sort does not know how to handle business affairs."

"That is why a wise gladiator has a business advisor," the ragamuffin Jemain piped up from the end of the table. "If you want, Muduzaya, I'll be your handler."

Conan could almost imagine taking him up on the offer himself—though, on further consideration, he guessed that the brassy urchin might prove no more wise or honest than Zagar and the rest.

Of all the gladiators and circus folk, the one who appeared to have the most business sense was Dath, and he was in their midst ever less frequently. He seldom troubled to attend practice sessions—though the two street ruffians he introduced, Sistus and Baphomet, turned up regularly and trained with cool energy. Born fighters from the city's outlying slums, they were quick to master the subtle tricks of the arena.

But while Dath was on good enough terms with the eunuch Memtep to get them into the job, he himself kept busy with other things. Driving to the tavern with Conan and friends, he would share no more than a single drink and be away, slouching off with shady characters to roam the nighted alleys of the Canal Wharf. Among these low sorts he made fast friends ... and dangerous enemies, as one incident showed ...

It was a late-night homecoming in three chariots, rumbling in a staggered line through the dark, cobbled streets. Conan, Dath, Baphomet, Sistus, and Halbard, with Sathilda and three or four other lively females, were crowded on the platforms in a fairly riotous state, clinging to the bouncing chariot-rails. Suddenly, a few street-corners past the wide-open city gate, a band of dim figures blocked the moonlit lane. It must have been well-planned, for, as the horses shied and the chariots slewed to a halt, a dozen roughly dressed attackers moved out of the nearby shadows bearing swords, axes, and clubs.

Dath, less drunk perhaps than the others, was quick to bark out orders. "Form a square back-to-back," he snapped. "Don't worry about defending the chariots, they're after us!"

Conan saw the wisdom of his words. Had the horse teams been battle-bred, it might be possible to break out through the converging attackers. But these animals were tame city drays, and the only weapons their passengers carried were shortswords and paltry daggers. As he took a place in the circle, drawing Sathilda in behind him, he heard Dath sound three blasts on a wooden pipe he'd drawn from his cape.

"Keep in formation," Dath said coolly, his voice

steadying the intoxicated crew. "Just hold them off as best you can—no heroics, your arena fans aren't here to watch."

The notion of a raw street youth issuing orders to a band of trained fighters was peculiar—but the strangeness was soon forgotten as the attack began. Rocks flew; Conan felt a jagged chunk clash off his swordblade and strike his bare shoulder, numbing the bone and drawing forth a trickle of blood. He saw Halbard take two high hits from heavy stones and stand before them, shaking the dizziness from his shaggy head. An instant later the silent attackers struck, and the bleary, ill-armed gladiators were hard put to hold their ground. Conan made his dagger keenly felt, downing his first assailant with a low swift thrust. Even so, the need to stay in line and avoid striking his comrades in the darkness hampered him.

Of them all, Dath fought best. He was best prepared, and the flash of his two wicked axes, darting out against flesh and bone and leaping back on the ends of their thongs, set the tempo of the fight. The metallic clanks, crunches, and moans of fallen victims were the only sounds, aside from low muffled curses and the snorts of the frightened horses. From time to time, a window-shutter was heard to creak in the narrow avenue, and a slit of lamplight hinted at spying eyes. But no civil alarm was raised, and no voice dared call an end to this sullen warfare in the bosom of the sleeping town.

Then, even as the battered, dazed gladiators were forced back on themselves, there came an interruption. From the direction of the city gate, scuffing, slapping footfalls announced the arrival of more fighters. They came in a mob, panting and cursing in the dark, and fell immediately on the ragged horde of attackers.

The pressure was off the gladiators; Conan and the others were free to break rank and pursue their enemies. But there was no sure way of telling one shabby band of street fighters from the other—except, Conan belatedly saw, by the dark headbands the friendly ruffians wore. In moments, both groups had scattered in the darkness, disappearing like rats into the city gutters. The avenue was silent—though in the distance the clanking and shouted commands of a late city patrol could now be heard.

"It's over," Dath's firm voice called out. "Back in the chariots, quick now, and home to the arena! There will be no more trouble this night."

Dath, though, did not accompany them; he went off afoot after his street harriers. Conan and the others were left to flee, salve one another's wounds, and, early the next morning, explain to Memtep how the group of gladiators had beaten off a band of robbers in the countryside. The eunuch was obviously displeased, in his officious way. He warned them sternly against forays outside the city, and threatened to rearrange their fighting schedules. Conan, though it pained him, kept his sore shoulder a secret. It was not his sword-arm, so he did not think it would cause problems.

When next he saw Dath at the inn, he pressed him for an explanation. The young fighter took Conan and Sathilda aside from the other gladiators at the Pleasure Barge, likewise abandoning his own gang of toughs. Sitting opposite them over a small cask, he addressed Conan in his cool, cynical way.

"Here in Luxur, to improve their efficiency, the street thieves, petty gamblers, and loan-enforcers have the habit of banding together. They keep each other informed that way and come to one another's aid against civil authorities and outsiders."

Guardedly, Conan nodded. "I have been in cities such as Arenjun, where there were thieves' guilds," he admitted.

"In a city as great as Luxur," Dath explained, "criminals organize themselves according to what quarter of town they operate in. That tends to separate them by nationality as well." As if painting a map, he swiped his hand broadly across the barrel-top before them. "The Stygians always controlled the heart of the town—here, near the main gate. Migrants from Corinthia have since come to dominate the area just inside the East Wall." He flicked a hand in the direction of the nearby city gate. "The Circus Imperium, now"—pointing to the middle of the cask—"comprises the richest section of the temple quarter, on high ground. So it is fiercely disputed territory."

"And what of this foul slum we now wallow in?" Sathilda, watching Dath, seemed to follow his account with wry clarity.

Dath arched one hand sidelong at the rim of the cask, calmly turning his gaze up to her. "The Canal Wharf is just now gaining influence as a full-fledged city quarter, with strong ties inside the city wall. It is made up mainly of non-Corinthian foreigners—desert tribes, southerners from Kush and the other black kingdoms—Shemites like us, too." He smiled. "I have made some boon friends in the slum-dwellers' ranks."

Conan grunted in understanding. "So what we went through the other night was a gang war against Corinthian hoodlums—just because we come down here to Namphet's, to swill a few with you and your friends?"

Dath half shrugged. "There is that, and more. The street fighters like to line up behind certain champions in the arena games—they bet on them, wear their colors, and so forth. In our group, which includes Luddhew's circus, we have a large share of foreigners—yourselves, Muduzaya, Roganthus, Ignobold there, and various others like myself. But no Corinthians, or only the occasional one. So we are no favorites of the East Quarter lads."

"Hmph." Conan shook his head. "And to prove it, you are telling me, they will try to butcher us in the streets, before we ever get to the arena?"

"They may have been after me in particular," Dath admitted. "What matters it, anyway? As I said, the danger is past."

"I, for one, don't pretend to understand," Sathilda declared. "Here is a teeming, prospering capital with all the comforts one would wish and the blessing of a stable government. Why would anyone carry on such a war in the city quarters?"

Dath tossed down his drink. "True enough. As I tell them, the fighting is best kept inside the arena. Of course, they have to get their practice somewhere. Most of these lads grow up yearning to fight in the Circus. For them, it is the only conceivable way to gain money and respect."

"There are plenty of other ways to succeed in the poor quarters of the northern cities—by theft, gambling, smuggling, arm-twisting, skull-cracking." Conan nodded critically at the ill-clad group idling watchfully together near the door. "I don't see what these ruffians of yours lack that other bullies have."

Dath smiled. "You are right, those things all exist here—and better opportunities, too, such as the graft on temple, tomb, and aqueduct-building. But you must see, the Circus Imperium is at the heart of things—everyone here respects it, or at least pays attention. It's what Luxur is all about." He laughed suddenly at his own eloquence. "You have to forgive me—though I'm a foreigner, I love the place as if I was born to it!"

"You've certainly made friends here. They came swiftly to our aid the other night." Conan glanced at the band of toughs who stood by, guarding their leader.

"Yes, well, they stand ready to protect us if the Eastsiders make another move—though matters are settled for now." He glanced around the squalid interior of the tavern. "In time, maybe we will take our pleasure in a posher part of town."

In light of the ambush and of that conversation, Conan and Sathilda took care to travel armed and in company. They were not attacked, though they heard rumors of more skirmishes between the various street mobs. Now, when passing through other districts of the town, they were conscious of some watchers observing them with expressions other than fatuous hero-worship.

Of all the admirers and acquaintances they met, one proved to be of special interest. This was a courtly, dissolute northerner named Udolphus. His slumming frequently took him, with a pair of young companions and bodyguards, to Namphet's pub. As a Corinthian noble, he was out of place there to begin with; his noisy manner made him stand out all the more. Before long he was lavishing his drink and wit on the gladiators, most particularly Sathilda—though Conan, seeing his mate's reaction to the nobleman's thick black beard and sagging shirtwaist, did not regard Udolphus as serious competition.

"Well, my lovely girl," he saluted the acrobat, "are you prepared to exercise yourself before the Circus crowds tomorrow? And you, mighty Slayer," he added to Conan, who stood looming over them, "are you feeling of a temper to fight? The entrail-readers give good augur to our new champions on the morrow, so I am told. Can you handle a troop of Khauranian renegades?"

"Khauranian cavalry troops are crack fighters," Conan avowed earnestly. "I look forward to meeting them." He took a long pull from his beaker of *arrak* to avoid any need for further commentary.

"I understand," Udolphus told him good-naturedly. "Like any true athlete, you would rather not discuss your performance in an impending event. The pressure can be worrisome. But, no matter, you look to me as if you can handle all comers. I hope you are wise enough to take an easy victory when it is offered you." Reaching up, he clapped Conan on the elbow and squeezed his firm thews. "But come, take a seat here. What is your opinion of Commodorus, that sorry excuse for a ruler? Do you think our citizens should overthrow him, as some would like to do?"

Conan remained silent, already half regretting that he had settled onto a keg. He kept his face blank and, for a distraction, invited Sathilda to sit on his lap. He knew little enough of Commodorus and had no wish to enter into slanderous murmurs against the local ruler.

But the boy Jemain, who had begun turning up at the public-house in the early evening hours to pester Conan, seemed positively taken aback by the nobleman's words. He stared in dismay at Udolpus, until the Corinthian finally grew impatient.

"Close your mouth, lad," the noble rebuked him, "before your thoughts all tumble out. Here, young ragamuffin, take this and begone!" Reaching into his toga, he withdrew a clinking purse and tossed it at the boy. "If you know what is good for you," he called after him, "you will not interfere in the business of your elders."

Shaking his head, Udolphus turned back to his guests. "A tiresome youth—Jemain, is it? Anyway, as I was saying, some think our Tyrant Commodorus a great buffoon, strutting and posturing before the crowd and claiming to be a gladiator himself." He punctuated his sedition with a long pull of *arrak*. "But on the other hand, he has his backers high up in the army and elsewhere. There are some who think he will not stay Tyrant, but will challenge the traditionalists and the church to declare himself Emperor He has won a following among the gullible populace, that is sure."

So Udolphus carried on, speaking with aristocratic, drunken abandon of the most dangerous rumors and scandals. He asked others for opinions but seldom paid attention to their guarded answers, rambling on heedlessly himself as his two young retainers watched sober-eyed.

"What of the individual combat at tomorrow's meet?" he pressed on. "The odds have not been laid—I do not think the schedule is even finalized. There was to be an epic fight between two great champions, but for some reason it has not been announced."

"Myself, I cannot say," Conan admitted. "But I would bet sparingly on such a match if I were you, knowing the sly ways of these oddsmakers." He could not resist giving that much of a hint, based on his inside knowledge.

As it happened, no announcement of the matches was made before the spectacle itself. Matters were complicated—or, perhaps, made simpler—by a sad event that occurred, or at any rate was discovered, in the small hours of the following morning. The body of Halbard the Great was found outside the gate of the Circus compound, slain evidently by thieves.

CHAPTER 9
Blood Sport

The day of the spectacle dawned clear and bright. The crowd gathered early in the shadow of the stadium's western side, buying warm tea and buns from street vendors, murmuring and wagering together based on reports of the combats to be held. The murder of Halbard was kept secret to avoid a riot, the body brought in a covered cart through the rear of the arena grounds.

After the mob had loitered an hour or two, gradually filling up the street before the colosseum, the outer gates were opened. Within them, between the ticket stalls and the still-barred tunnels slanting up to the stadium seats, concessions and sideshow acts flourished. Here knelt veiled Iocasta on her gold-fringed carpet embroidered with bright celestial symbols, telling fortunes from a smoky crystal and predicting the outcome of the day's fights. Here Bardolph sat behind a broad table, conducting his gambling games with painted cards and bone dice. Here in a screened enclosure, for entry to which a fee was charged, the black tiger and the performing bear were shown off to patrons. And high above, on taut ropes and booms strung outward from the stadium's street-front, Sathilda and her acrobats performed their tricks. In all, Luddhew's circus actors enjoyed a major portion of the crowd's business, drawing in the city rubes and a steady flow of silver pieces.

Conan watched briefly from the arena's topmost bench-row, looking down over the edge of the stadium at graceful Sathilda. He saw carnal lust and bloodlust alike flicker in the upturned faces of the mob. Boisterously they threw coins into Jana's tambourine, bidding in hard cash for Conan's mistress to perform ever more perilous leaps and flips.

As the bright sun rose past midmorning, gilded litters and lavishly teamed chariots arrived from stately villas, some located only a short walk away. These conveyances bore rich, privileged seat-holders; guaranteed choice spots, they did not have to arrive early and rub shoulders with the common herd. Conan watched them—prosperous Corinthian traders, gray-clad clerics, and military officers with their glittering women, escorted through the crush by officious guards and servants.

Then there sounded in the arena below a single trumpet-blast, the traditional signal for gladiators to get ready for their performance.

Preparations were few; Conan had not instructed

Memtep to set aside any armor for him, other than a kilt of steel leaves to protect his vitals. The usual precaution, in lieu of armor, was to apply a thick layer of oil to the hair and body, to prevent adversaries from getting a firm grip and doing damage. This process was aided by servants who oiled the fighters from earthen jars or, alternatively, helped to strap them into their armor plates. Memtep himself sought out Conan and forced a broad-rimmed metal hat onto his head, assuring him that he would value it more than his steel kilt.

All this was done in the exercise yard, where the twenty or so gladiators sullenly prepared. Even friends like Ignobold, Roganthus, and Muduzaya had little to say to one another before the event.

Within moments, a triple trumpet-blast drifted up from the arena, the signal for the stadium doors to open to the general public. There followed a pervasive, steadily growing sound that filled the stadium grounds and made the animals restless— the scuff of thousands of feet on worn stone, combined with the babble of ten thousand voices exclaiming, cursing, and shouting to friends in a mass effort to find suitable viewing spots.

The din leveled out and did not subside, vibrating instead in the stones of the colosseum and the very earth underfoot. Meanwhile, as new, intricate flourishes commenced from the sour-toned trumpets, the gladiators marched in through the main tunnel to witness the dedication of the day's games. The arena had been refurbished in recent days; its floor was now uninterrupted by any pits or raised structures and covered evenly with fresh sand.

The gladiators filed through the Gate of Champions out into the blazing sun and murmurous roar. A cheer of anticipation sounded from the crowd, which was still spreading upward to fill the highest reaches of the stadium. Then they fell silent as short, imperative trumpet-blasts heralded an announcement by some high official.

"Citizens of Luxur, I welcome you to this special day of games. Decreed by me, this proud spectacle is intended as a tribute to honor the mighty heroes—both the new and the well-known champions—who have anointed our arena with their honest sweat and sacred blood. I am gratified to see how many citizens have chosen to attend."

The speaker was none other than the Tyrant himself, proud Commodorus, standing at ease on his platform at the end of the arena. His shoulders were draped in a toga of gold-fringed white, loosely hung to show off his trim physique. Beneath it he dressed in battle-gear—greaves up to the knee, a bronze chestplate, and an armor-scaled skirt with a shortsword strapped at one side—a costume no doubt chosen in honor of his boast of having once been a gladiator himself.

"As to the scheduling of today's events, I regret that the final roster of games was not displayed before this morning. I hope you all had the opportunity to place your wagers on those contestants you deem worthiest. Some of the delay, I regret to say, resulted from the death of one of our arena's bravest heroes, the champion known to you all as Halbard the Great."

At this eulogy, a loud murmur went up from the

crowd—not truly a sound of grief, but a collective acknowledgment of unexpected change, disappointment, and the passing of familiar things.

Conan, where he and the other gladiators lined up to wait in the last vestige of shade along the arena's eastern wall, took the opportunity to scan the benches as the audience sat in relative calm. The latest improvements to the Circus appeared to be complete, he noticed—in particular the high-arched stone terrace that sheltered the lower sections of the privileged on the west side of the oval stadium. Peering up into the shaded area, Conan made out a familiar group from Luddhew's band, including Sathilda, still in her costume. The acrobats had been invited in, then, to keep company with the rich and powerful during the main spectacle. The crowd fell silent again as Commodorus resumed speaking.

"Setting aside the untimely loss of a hero, we still have much to celebrate—such as the brave young fighters who have newly proven themselves, and the skilled seers, acrobats, and exotic beasts of Luddhew's circus who have extended their stay here to entertain us further. Our fondest welcome to them all," he proclaimed, speaking between bursts of applause.

"Furthermore," he went on, "we are privileged this morning to entertain a guest. In addition to all the celebrated divines and military commanders, the nobles and luminaries who regularly grace this arena with their presence, I am honored today to enjoy the boon companionship of High Prefect Bulbulus. As we know, Bulbulus is an honored appointee of city and church, the chief administrator of all the civil guards and magistrates. Welcome, Bulbulus!"

At his sweeping gesture, a small portly man came forward from the balcony seats. Purple-togaed and crowned with a gilded, high-crested helmet that wobbled visibly on his balding brow, Bulbulus gave the impression of being a reluctant bureaucrat rather than a staunch civic authority. He did not try to address the noisy crowd, but waved dutifully and lingered in the Tyrant's shadow.

"Forward, then, to our spectacle," Commodorus declared as the Prefect Bulbulus retreated. "But first, citizens, let me ask, what think you of armed brigands? I refer to military renegades of a foreign kingdom, who enrich themselves by preying on the free commerce between mighty Stygia and our beloved sister-state, Corinthia. What is your opinion of such marauders?"

The crowd's view on the subject hardly remained a secret; a tumultuous roar shook the stadium benches, with thousands waving their fists in wrath.

"Do you think," Commodorus demanded of his subjects, "that any such raiders from the eastern mountains—cowardly Khauranian deserters, vicious as they are—can defeat the champions of our Circus arena?" He folded his arms across his chest. "Keeping in mind, as always, that if they do triumph they will go free?"

The latter part of his question was all but drowned out as the watchers shrieked and clawed the air, some rising to their feet and almost tumbling forward into the arena in their frenzy of bloodlust.

"Well enough, then," Commodorus proclaimed. "Silence now, for the prayer and invocation to be pronounced by our Temple Primate Nekrodias. Then bring on the captives, and let the games begin!"

As the bald old priest rasped forth benedictions in unpronounceable High Stygian, there was a bustle of preparation from the far end of the arena. This door, by which Luddhew's circus had entered on the first day, was known to the public as the Challenger's Gate. Now it opened, letting an ill-assorted crew on foot and horseback issue forth.

They were tall, straight-nosed warriors dressed variously in desert and mountain garb, most of it ragged and soiled. A common hue among them, nevertheless, was the yellow-brown of Khauranian military costume. Most of them retained some piece of standard armor, its silvering largely worn away—either a helmet, shield, or hauberk, supplemented occasionally by metal gauntlets and greaves. The only weapons in view were swords and daggers, with no sign of the lances and bows such cavalry troops would usually carry. Indeed, of the score or so captives, only a half dozen were mounted. Some of the few horses looked bony and overworked, while the fresher ones moved skittishly, as if ill-trained and unfamiliar with their riders. The troops themselves were underfed and abused; yet they were fighters undeniably—lean, hard men burned deeply brown by desert suns.

As they moved out into the arena, spreading in

a rough formation with horsemen grouped at either end, the gladiators likewise formed a line. Among the Circus heroes were no mounted men; but from the sides of the arena came two chariots, each with an able driver and a four-horse team. Each chariot took aboard two of the gladiators to wield sword and lance from the fighting-platform. Muduzaya and Roganthus alike jumped up onto chariots, but Conan stayed afoot, preferring to keep control of his own movements.

As the battle-cars rolled wide to maneuver, there was a general stirring in the gladiators' ranks. The arena fighters grunted, snarled, and yelled abuse at their opponents as they swung swords overhead to limber up their muscles. The Khauranians, for their part, came forward silently in a well-drilled military phalanx, with horses on either flank. Conan could see that they would make formidable foes, as he had expected.

The stadium fell silent. Only scattered shouts of encouragement or long-winded abuse burst forth from the benches as the two lines converged. The fighters squared off, sizing one another up and choosing targets.

Then, of a sudden, horsewhips flailed and the two chariots swooped inward. The flanking Khauranian horsemen spurred forward, and the lines of foot-warriors charged together in sudden violence.

Along the center of the line, steel clashed fiercely and angry yells volleyed forth. The horsemen closed in from either side, but were scattered by the bulky speed of the chariots, which the ill-conditioned cavalry mounts could not face. The

Khauranians closed their line expertly, standing firm before the gladiators' onslaught; but the chariots wheeled near with swift, close passes, one passenger swinging his sword while the other hurled javelins from short range. The force of these attacks were too much for any line of foot-soldiers. In short order the mountain men were menaced afore and behind, forced to flee or shield themselves from hard-thrown shafts. Their formation broke, and the yelling gladiators surged furiously through their ranks.

Conan faced off against a swart, broad-faced campaigner whose upper lip was already cleft by an old, sloping scar. The Khauranian fought skillfully, using a rusty steel buckler to ward off Conan's strokes and slashing back with his own curved saber. The man would have been far more deadly in a saddle, Conan guessed; his footwork was slow, perhaps from overlong marching or illtreatment. A sharp kick to the back of one knee served to trip him up momentarily; by batting his helmet forward with a resounding stroke, Conan edged behind him. His point then found the lower edge of the Khauranian's armor backplate, and he ended the man's life with a swift upward thrust.

Even as Conan dragged his sword free of the slumping body, a horseman thundered down upon him. His blood-smeared blade came up tardily; but it mattered little, because the skittish cavalry mount swerved aside a hand's-breadth early. The rider's stroke whirred high, sliding off Conan's point. The horseman cursed and wheeled the reluctant beast around, raising his sword for a killing-

stroke. Conan let the man come, crouching low to
make him lean outward; then, instead of parrying
the blow, he darted inside, close enough to be
lashed by the horse's flying mane and tail. Springing up and seizing the man's taut descending wrist,
Conan wrenched him sideward out of the saddle.

The Khauranian, to his credit, did not stay prone
on the sand for long. He rolled, keeping hold of his
sword. As he leapt to his feet, he lashed back at
Conan with a frenzy of swordstrokes.

But he was outmatched. His blows lacked force,
due perhaps to his fall from the horse or some
earlier injury. Leaving a false opening, Conan
dodged and let the cavalryman overextend himself
and stagger in the loose sand; then he darted back
in with his blade, finishing the man with a quick,
merciful thrust.

In spite of the howling and clangor on all sides,
Conan imagined he heard an extra pulse of cheering when the horseman died. His ears traced faint,
shrill ravings nearly lost in the din. "Conan!" the
distant worshipers cried. "Hail, Conan the Slayer!"
Raising his ungainly helmet, he shook off the
praise with the sweat of his sodden mane.

Of the broader fight, little remained. The scattered Khauranians, if not trampled by the chariot
teams, fell prey to the more concentrated force of
gladiators. The horsemen, rallying to support their
comrades, were soon battered or speared out of
their saddles, and the unmounted raiders were
gradually run down and hacked to pieces. Most of
the renegades died fighting in the middle of the
arena; only two threw down their weapons and ran

for the gates—which, in spite of their yells and
thumpings, remained shut. The charioteers soon
overtook these last fugitives and finished them,
mere paces away from the savagely cheering onlookers.

Conan did nothing more to dispatch the already
beaten foe. Surveying the scene, he felt vaguely
disappointed. The Khauranians, galloping free in
their foothills, would have been superb fighters.
But here in the Circus, after being starved and
scourged across a hundred leagues of desert and
sold downriver, they were broken men. It seemed
unfair, an artificial display.

Every last gladiator was still on his feet. None
of them as far as he could see, had worse than a
creased limb or a split scalp to show for the battle.
As the red-robed priests came out with their hooks
and barrows to drag away the dead, the arena
fighters re-formed their line. Beneath thunderous,
echoing waves of applause they walked abreast toward the Tyrant's viewing-perch.

"Splendid," Commodorus declared, pacifying
the crowd's tumult with broad sweeping gestures.
"A fitting end, one that must have been decreed by
the gods, and a tribute to our champions' prowess." With a stately wave he returned the salute of
the gladiators, who stood with swords upraised below him. "Heroes of Luxur, we hail you!"

The cheer that followed his words, augmented
by fierce stamping on the stone ledges, exceeded
anything that had come before. It shook the stadium, making the very sand shiver and leap under

the warriors' feet like water a-simmer in a copper kettle.

"Now for a lighter undertaking," Commodorus resumed when the feverish energy had died down. "Our honored guest, the Prefect Bulbulus, has consented to partake in a public demonstration with me. To do so, we will descend into the arena."

At this there was a new surge of cheering and stamping, combined with hoots and jocular noises. Evidently what Commodorus proposed was familiar to the patrons, well-received, but no great surprise. Preparations were already under way at the end of the stadium; a great ramp, gilt-railed with carpeted stairsteps instead of treads, was brought into the arena. The twenty or so slaves who manhandled it obviously meant to set it in place beside the exit door, known as the Gate of Heroes. Down it, the Tyrant and any others could easily walk into the arena from their viewing-stand.

Meanwhile, the gladiators proceeded to a row of benches and tables along the arena wall, where slaves waited with drink and light foods. Using pitchers and sponges, the handlers laved sweat, blood, and sand from the fighters' sunburned limbs and helped them wipe their weapons and armor clean.

With the day's heat growing intense, some of the warriors shucked off hot metal plates and heavy protective garments, letting whole pitchers of water be dumped over their heads. This was done to admiring cries and bawdy exclamations from the spectators just overhead. Most of these were females, prosperous-looking Luxur wives and buxom maids who draped themselves forward none too decorously over the stadium rail. From this spot, Sathilda was no longer in sight; Conan hoped it was plain to her that neither he nor Roganthus had been hurt.

In the middle of the arena, where attendants with donkey-carts, rakes, and shovels hurried to scrape up the blood and horse-droppings and smooth the sand, new preparations were under way. A long crimson carpet was unrolled, leading from the foot of the temporary stairway to a spot near the center, where two soft divans and a small table of beverages were set forth.

Then, to a flourish of trumpets and a rattle of drums, two figures descended the staircase. Commodorus strode briskly and proudly, with a bow in one hand and a full quiver of arrows over his shoulder. Paunchy Bulbulus, walking beside him, moved with a somewhat comic air of reluctant uncertainty. He was burdened with a long spear, far too heavy and ungainly for him to cast; to the crowd's amusement, he seemed to have trouble even holding it upright on the steep stair. Both men also wore swords belted around their waists. Behind them followed two palace guardsmen with long halberds. But near the bottom of the staircase, these two, on the Tyrant's brisk command, halted themselves at attention and did not follow their masters into the arena.

Commodorus, with his prefect barely keeping up to him, strode boldly onward to the table and divans that made a little island of luxury in the sea of sand. The two did not take seats but stood in watchful expectation. And, after the applause and general levity at the two ill-matched figures, a similar hush fell over the crowd.

In the far end of the arena a door opened. It was the wide low portal next to the endmost one, known as the Beast Gate.

From the darkness of the tunnel emerged shaggy, formless-looking creatures—steppe-lions, three in number, tawny beasts with bushy black manes and dark-tasseled tails. Even as they crept into view together, they darted and twisted with ill-tempered growls, swatting at one another and at the unseen keepers who goaded them forth. The rearmost creature batted the next down onto the sand in a whirling, snarling frenzy that echoed across the arena like ripping canvas. The fight was ended by a deep, full-throated roar from the leader, and all three animals stalked forward, scanning the flat expanse before them with beady eyes well-accustomed to searching southern grasslands.

They did not linger long at the far end, for they were jeered and pelted by the crowd above the entry gate. With irritated snarls they came forward at a slinking run, fanning out swiftly to hunt the only prey that recommended itself in the vast pit: the ruler Commodorus and his portly prefect, where the two stood waiting at the arena's center.

The jungle beasts were starved, Conan could tell even at a distance. Their ribs showed up as faint lines on their sinuous flanks, along with other marks and scars of their capture and transport. The Cimmerian had seen larger bush-lions, but never more single-minded ones; they crept forward by rapid turns, evidently intending to confuse and distract the quarry until they had worked close enough to pounce.

Commodorus watched them with a show of calm unconcern; he even turned to the table to pour himself a goblet of refreshment from one of the pitchers. Bulbulus, for his part, looked ill-at-ease—or rather, frozen to the spot. He clutched his oversized spear two-handed, with its butt dragging in the sand. The jerky motions of his ungainly crested helm as he scanned the approaching carnivores betrayed undignified alarm. With a nervous headshake he refused his host's offer of a drink; and he could not resist a longing glance toward the carpeted stair, which brought a murmur of contempt from the crowd. His gaze was soon drawn back to the stalking predators as they moved dangerously near.

Conan, where he sat beneath the arena wall, could hear isolated remarks from the crowd. "Run, Bulbulus, you quivering fool!" one heckler called. "Scurry off home before you soil your toga!"

"Who ever appointed you to command our city's guard?" another jeered. "Watch out, the lions are closing in!"

"Look at him, he's shaking in his sandals," a disdainful female voice cried. "What if the nomads were battering down our gates? Look at Commodorus, now. There's a man who knows how to fight!"

As she spoke, the Tyrant drew his heavy bow and let fly the first of his arrows. It struck the lion creeping up closest on the left, making the beast leap up in surprise and bat its own flank in baffled rage.

Responding to this distraction, the other two animals loped forward toward their prey. Commodorus's second arrow smote the foremost lion full in the chest. The strike caused it to halt in its tracks, then topple over dead in the sand.

Amid the crowd's lusty cheering, the flank-grazed lion bolted forward as suddenly as if it had never been wounded at all. Bounding to the edge of the carpeted sanctuary, the beast compressed its wiry body and sprang straight in toward its enemies, hurtling over a silk-lined divan.

Commodorus's hasty bowshot appeared to strike the animal in midair. The bright-feathered shaft lodged in its throat, yet in no way turned aside its momentum. The convulsing body of the mortally wounded lion passed between the marksman and his fleeing companion; its death-throes knocked Commodorus down and clawed the bow from his grasp, sending it flying end over end, the bowstring shredded.

That left the third, uninjured lion loping smoothly forward, gathering itself to pounce. Bulbulus, still holding his useless weapon upright, was caught crouching off balance in the sand. He was afraid to turn his back on the menace and bolt for the stair, which was impossibly far away.

Commodorus, always quick to act, regained his feet. Snatching the heavy spear from the witless prefect, he swung the gleaming point around and butted the near end firmly in the sand. The lion, springing with a thunderous roar that same instant, hurtled straight onto the steel blade. Its body was impaled on the shaft, which bent and skidded in the sand but did not snap.

Once again the stadium reverberated with wild cheering. Commodorus raised his arms and saluted the crowd, calm and unruffled in his role as champion. The Prefect Bulbulus backed away from the slumped carcasses of the two beasts, then turned and limped gracelessly toward the stair, obviously having no other thought in his mind but to leave the arena. His host, after some moments of posturing with his foot on a lion's carcass, turned and strode dutifully to catch him. Rejoining the guards, the two mounted the stairs to the arena's rim.

"Thus does our Tyrant win the worship of his people," Ignobold remarked at Conan's side. "He saves all the easy fights for himself and humiliates his political foes and flunkies in the bargain. They fear the scorn of the mob if they refuse to join him in the arena, even more than they fear the ordeals he will put them through."

As the staircase was lowered and the dead lions dragged out by horse teams, the first of the afternoon's single combats was announced. Conan had not seen the morning's postings or heard what fights were planned. He was interested nevertheless to see Sarkad, one of the established sword-champions of the arena, pitted against a new and unknown fighter, a foreign wrestler dubbed Xothar the Constrictor.

The two met at the center of the arena, since Xothar, not having participated in the morning's combat, entered through the Champions' Gate. He

was built short and squat, olive-skinned like a Tu-
ranian, with his brutally thick neck and upper body
bare in the sun. He exercised himself as he walked,
putting his chest and arms through snakelike con-
tortions, whether to impress the crowd or loosen
himself up for the fight it was hard to say. Sarkad,
his opponent, was not very likely impressed, since
he bore a sword, and Xothar's only visible weapon
was a short-tailed flail tucked into his waistband.

Yet the sword was heavy and long, Conan noted,
more suited to hacking through a coat of mail than
pinning down a near-naked adversary. And Sarkad,
though he cast off his buckler and helmet, retained
a shirt of chain links that must have burdened him
considerably. Evidently he anticipated the fight
never coming to grapples.

After saluting in Commodorus's direction, the
two came together. As Conan foresaw, the nimble
wrestler was able to dodge the mightily swinging
swordblade . . . twice, thrice, and then dance inside
its arc as the swordsman fought to bring it scything
back. Xothar's flail swung useless in one hand . . .
till it flew with a quick toss up into Sarkad's face,
momentarily blinding him. By then it was too late;
the wrestler snaked one arm around his opponent's
neck, while his other fist knotted itself in loose
mail links.

Sarkad sank to his knees. His sword swung, faltered, then flipped free as he was borne down onto
the sand by Xothar's more purposeful, concentrated weight.

The crowd's roaring filled up the long moment
that ensued. There was mad waving, rhythmic

stamping, and an eager flow of bodies through the stands as patrons swarmed to place their bets—or collect them, Conan thought to himself, since surely the loser had been held down long enough to qualify Xothar for a pin.

After a moment the Constrictor broke his grip and stood up, alone. His opponent sagged limply onto the sand, pale and unmistakably dead. A puzzle, that, since no knife or flow of blood was in evidence. Conan had heard no bones snap, nor seen Sarkad convulse in death-agony. Sitting there in the sun's blazing light, he felt an eerie night-chill creep down his neck. Never in all his battles had he seen a man throttled so swiftly and efficiently.

Xothar, prancing and flexing his cablelike arms to the applause of multitudes, strutted from the arena. The next fight was slow to be started, because of the crowd's pleasurable excitement bubbling over from the first.

This combat pitted Sistus, one of Dath's nominees from the wharfside alleys, against another relative newcomer named Callix. For this encounter, Sistus played the traditional role of a dock fighter or fisherman, taking a fishfork, weighted net, and gutting-knife as his only weapons. Conan had watched him train; evidently he had prior experience angling in the river-shallows, or perhaps fighting on the docks.

Now his net whirled and billowed in the air without any awkward entanglements, weaving a formless web of danger for his opponent. Young Callix possessed helmet, spear, shield, and sheathed sword. Yet, once battle was joined, he found that he could not maneuver safely in the net's reach, and was forced continually to give ground.

His mistake was in casting the spear, which was all that kept wily Sistus at bay. The lithe street fighter easily ducked under the cast, moving up close while the other dragged out his sword. Callix parried the first sweep of the net with a swing of his short blade; then, on the recoil, he was struck unprepared by the massed leaden weights of the net, which slammed into the side of his helmet with a dull clang. Staggering backward, he soon tripped in the net's toils. Mercilessly the long, barbed trident jabbed home, skewering its human target as effectively as any flopping fish.

In his triumph, Sistus was calm and stony-faced. He dispatched his victim with a quick stab of his knife, then untangled his weapons. Scarcely looking up to acknowledge the avalanche of applause, he exited via the Gate of Heroes.

"A splendid victory," Commodorus said from his viewing-porch. "And now for our third and final combat." Pronounced by the Tyrant, the words were repeated by criers stationed around the arena wall. "In salute to the heroes of Luddhew's circus, our new performer Conan the Slayer will fight our acknowledged Swordmaster, Mudazaya the Swift."

To Conan the news came as a grim surprise. He had half expected to fight again today, to be sure; to avoid troubling over it, he had not sought to learn the postings in advance. But to go up against Muduzaya, of all his fellow gladiators—so soon, with no chance to make changes, or plans . . .

Many of these swordslingers were boon fellows, surely enough, but the Kushite was the one he held closest to a kindred spirit. That moment he resolved himself not to kill or gravely wound Muduzaya, whatever the cost.

Walking out to the center of the arena, strapping on his ungainly helmet for the shade and concealment it offered, Conan tried to catch his friend's eye. But his opponent went resolutely ahead, plodding straight on without looking up. A pair of arena slaves scurried alongside the Kushite, on the pretext of polishing his black-enameled shield and touching up gold highlights of his broad metal waistband—a harmless bit of showmanship afforded the reigning champion. But Conan received an odd impression—that the two were actually guiding the warrior along, coaxing him to his place of combat, perhaps because he was incapable of getting there himself. Their solicitous attentions lasted all the way to the arena's center, where the white sand was newly raked, and no trace of blood remained. The two even helped him to turn and raise his sword to the Tyrant—according to custom, as Conan likewise did. Then the slaves were gone, scurrying back to the rest area.

Facing Muduzaya, Conan could see that it was true. The midnight-skinned warrior was stupefied—drugged, no doubt of it, by something put into his refreshment jar. Though the fellow held his sword at the ready, there was a dull sluggishness in his face, an opaque barrier between thought and action.

Experimentally, Conan crossed swords with him. Everyone in the front rows must have heard the dullness of the clanking riposte. The Kushite was all but paralyzed, scarcely able to fight.

Someone had sought to weaken Muduzaya, Conan guessed, to take the edge off his superb swordsmanship. But why? ... Thinking back swiftly to Halbard's recent complaint, and to his subsequent death, he saw the answer. After all, Muduzaya was the favorite, the Swordmaster. Surely he was the object of countless high-odds bets in this battle against a relative newcomer, a mere upstart from Luddhew's mime-troupe. For the champion to lose this fight to Conan would be an upset—it would reverse the odds, and reap the oddsmakers a sizable fortune. It was as the Kushite himself had warned: those who rose to popularity and prominence had better beware.

The crowd grew impatient at the standoff, seeing no bloody action and hearing only occasional list-less scrapes of the warriors' slack steel. "Fight, you overblown cowards!" hoarse cries began to echo across the stadium.

"Slay the Slayer, brave Kushite, and get me back my money!"

"You two were put here for butchery, not a dancing contest!"

"Show us some blood!"

Along with the exhortations, stones and bits of nameless rubbish began to pelt the sand around them. Conan saw that they had better fight or risk being mobbed by patrons who no longer wished to remain spectators.

"Come on, move," he told Muduzaya, smiting at the big man's sword with his own blade. "Snap out

of it, fellow! You must put on a show of fighting
to satisfy these jackals."

He ducked and lunged, making a pretense of
agility. Beating the Kushite's sword to one side and
then the other, he watched it drift back vaguely to
its central position before Muduzaya's face.

Conan's efforts drew only jeers. "Go on, slaughter him," the onlookers called. "If he will not fight,
the Circus has no use for him! Or are you, too, a
man-loving coward?"

Sweating with heat and exasperation at the
center of the vast empty arena, Conan felt helpless, like an insect caught on a blazing hearth.
"Muduzaya," he challenged, "come on and fight!"
To get the Swordmaster's attention he smote
soundly at the man's helmet-rim with the flat of his
blade, once, then twice. "Come on, then, you great
oaf! Are you as worthless as the rest of your cowardly brothers from Kush? Stand and fight, or I'll
kick you back to your stinking jungle wallow!"

Between the clanging blows and racial epithets,
something in the black man's expression changed.
His eyes behind the nosepiece narrowed, and his
nostrils flared. Then at once, his great sword began
to cleave and flail, ringing off Conan's blade like a
hammer on an anvil. From the crowd, a roar of
bestial frenzy suddenly erupted.

"That's the way," Conan encouraged him, "give
them a real show for their pennies! Then one of us
can feign a mortal wound."

A moment later, taxed by Muduzaya's vigorous
attack, he rasped out, "Good, man, that's enough!

You can let up a little—I don't want either one of us to be killed."

But the drugged champion, well-launched in his berserk attack, obviously did not hear or believe. He kept up the assault, driving Conan back with every swing of his whizzing sword.

"Stop it, you great buffoon, I did not mean what I said before!" Conan was growing weary. He doubted how long he could keep up this fruitless parrying and dodging. "Feign a low cut, and I'll take the fall—*oof*!"

Before the words were well out of the Cimmerian's mouth, Muduzaya's sword came shearing in waist-high. Conan's blade was caught in an awkward cross-body guard; it deflected Muduzaya's blow with a ragged rasp of steel, but its near edge was beaten into unguarded flesh, causing blood to welter down the pale-skinned fighter's chest. Stumbing off balance in the soft sand, he was thrown headlong.

"Aii, Muduzaya!" bettors roared from the benches. "Carve the upstart northerner into bloody gobbets! All hail our Swordmaster!"

Conan, afire with pain and unsure himself whether his fall had been real or feigned, had a sick sense of what would follow. He saw his fierce adversary looming tall and dark above him, eyes flashing beneath the ugly helmet-visor. He saw the great sword swing up overhead, as the crowd's roar climaxed. He raised his own sword in uncertain defense, making ready to kick a leg out from under his would-be slayer if chance permitted.

Muduzaya swung his sword down at a broad angle, battering Conan's blade flat onto the sand. The victor's big sandaled foot shifted and came to rest on Conan's elbow, pinning down his sword-arm. The crowd went mad with cheering.

"All right, fellow, you've made your point!" Conan muttered, watching for any warning of a killing-stroke. "Now get off me, and I'll play dead! Act as if you won the fight." He supposed that his wounds, though largely superficial, made his carcass resemble a vulture's feast.

Muduzaya lowered his sword and laid its point against Conan's chest—close enough to chill the skin, close enough to be smeared with the blood that seeped from the open wound. Then he raised the reddened blade high, to a convulsion of cheering.

"That will teach you to watch your Cimmerian potato-mouth," Muduzaya muttered.

From the Swordmaster's faltering step as he removed his weight, Conan could tell that he was still unsteady on his feet. Yet he made an adequate show of conquest; he threw off his helmet and, with sword raised high above his head, turned slowly in place.

The stadium's uproar flowed into motion. Alive with enthusiasm at the end of the program, citizens were rushing to collect their bets, swarming to the front rail and the exits, even dropping down the sheer wall into the arena to mob the surviving gladiators.

The pair of attendants from the rest area returned for Muduzaya, looking doubtful about the battle's outcome. Then at once they were overtaken by running, shouting fanatics who swarmed around the Kushite ... and carelessly kicked sand onto Conan's inert body. Laying hold of their hero in a mass, they hoisted him up on their shoulders and paraded him in circles around his supine victim. Muduzaya sat atop their shoulders unsteadily. But he was well out of reach of the two dubious-looking slaves, who soon gave up and retreated.

The worshipers would take good care of their idol, Conan guessed. He assumed that any ill-effects of the drug would soon wear off. In another moment or two, he planned to jump up and lose himself in the growing crowd.

Then he felt a nearby presence, hands tugging at his limbs. Unslitting his sand-caked eyes, he turned to see two figures stooping over him: red-robed priests, young and grim, with a hand litter waiting behind them.

"Off, wretched ghouls," Conan snarled at them, trying not to curse too loudly. "Greedy Set-spawn, wait until I die before you make me a mummy!" He hauled himself up to his feet, abandoning his sword and helmet, holding one arm close to protect his flayed chest.

Shrugging, the pair of morgue priests turned and bore away their litter. Only a few onlookers showed surprise at Conan's sudden reanimation; to escape them, he shoved away into the milling crowd.

Suddenly Conan thought of Sathilda. If she was watching from the stands, she must imagine him dead or severely wounded. Looking up, he could not find her. The row of privileged seats where she had

been before was empty. Trying not to make himself
overly conspicuous, he scanned the front row all
around the oval, but did not see her gazing down.
He had been too preoccupied during the fight to notice whether she was still watching.

The flow of the mob was toward the Heroes'
Gate. This part of the arena floor, where the gladiators had been seated, contained the greatest crush
of people. Eager spectators had lowered rope ladders and were swarming down to mingle with the
champions. The crowd included as many women
as men; hoping to find Sathilda among them,
Conan pushed ahead.

"For a corpse," someone said to him, "you look
preoccupied. The dead are supposed to be free of
mortal cares."

The voice was sultry and deep, a red-haired
woman's. Conan tried to dismiss her with a sullen
glance. But one glance entailed another—such
were her lush good looks, sheathed in clinging silk
bound with gemstones and golden clasps. Her yellow pantaloons and scanty blouse were but a single
twist of fabric, taut as a second skin over her supple charms; and her face, painted and crowned
with hennaed ringlets, was a mask from Ishtar's
temple. Ageless and timeless, she presented herself
as an expensive bauble in a costly if sparse wrap-
per.

"Not so dead, after all, perhaps . . . do I detect a
stirring of life?" The woman came near in the
throng, frankly examining Conan from head to
foot.

He glanced down at himself—gory and crusted

with sand, sweat-runneled, the blood from his chest now mostly dried or stickily oozing. His only garments were his bronze weight-lifter's belt and his kilt of metal leaves. "Do dead men strike your fancy, then?" he asked, looking back to her.

"I breathe life into them, on occasion," she told him. "Short of that, I give them reason to stay alive in the first place." Taking his arm, she led him only half resisting through the Gate of Heroes. "Come along, we can bind up these wounds of yours."

"What is your name, then—and tell me, do you take such an interest in all the gladiators, or only the losing ones?"

"I am Babeth. And of all the champions in the arena, Conan the Slayer is the one I would least expect to see vanquished. Unless he wished to be."

"You have watched me closely, then."

She draped his arm across her pliant shoulders as she led him down the tunnel, though he had no real need of support. "It is the custom of some noble Stygian matrons—if they have idle time, and no other pressing obligation—to select a champion among the arena fighters, and to favor and promote him." He felt her draw in a deep, decisive breath under his resting arm. "They might choose to encourage him in any number of ways—such as by throwing him a purse of gold the first time they saw him."

"So." He nodded in understanding. The gold he had been given was not with him at the moment, but hidden at the cottage, his and Sathilda's. "A little like backing a prize racehorse, you mean. So tell me, Babeth, what do the noble husbands of Stygian matrons think of their wives' interest in arena fighters?"

Babeth smiled, taking the opportunity to draw his arm down more snugly on her shoulder. "My husband takes little interest in such matters. He is a Corinthian merchant, and so is gone a year at a time on caravans to his home country. It leaves me ample energy for diversions."

"I see." Lacking more to say, Conan went with her through the garden, through whose shade other men and maidens passed arm in arm. Some gladiators already paused to embrace one or two ardent admirers, and to swill wine that was shared out from flasks and skins.

Adjoining the baths was a roofed pavilion which served as a dispensary and dressing-room. Here were massage tables and benches, hot and cold soaking-tubs, and salves and ointments dispensed freely from stone jars by slave physicians. The place was filling fast with athletes and their guests, as were the tepid baths; Conan had hoped Sathilda might await him here. But she was nowhere in sight, and Babeth's demands on him were insistent.

"Sit on this bench, stay quiet, and I'll bring water with an infusion of fir-sap. That will soothe your wounds and prevent festering." She went to command the physicians and, after a few moments, returned with an aromatic, steaming basin. "Here now, lie down and let me wash away this grit." Her soft hands moved gently over his midsection, spreading the warm, tingling medicine. "The cut is not deep, thanks be to Set."

Patiently she laved him and scrubbed away the sand and dried blood, careless of splashing and staining her own silken garment.

"Here, you have no more need of all this tinplate," she said, attacking his armored kilt. "Off with this pathetic rag, too. It's in the way."

She worked gently and tenderly near the cut edges of flesh, though he gave no signs of pain. When the long, shallow gash was well-cleansed and rinsed, she bound it up skillfully with an herb-salve poultice and a cotton winding-ribbon, which she anchored across his neck, chest, and waist. "There, now, you should have no trouble getting about as you ordinarily do."

"I see you have made me only half a mummy," he said, looking down at his array of bandages.

"A good deal less than half," she observed. "Now, roll over on your belly. Those great thews of yours must be sore from battling; a neck-rub will do you good. Here, I have some medicated oil from eastern Shem—sweet-smelling, is it not?"

As she straddled him and set to work, he noticed how festive the gathering had become. From the bath pavilion there came frenzied splashings and laughter, high female tones, and the gruff shouts of gladiators. In the dressing-room, most of the benches and tables had been taken over by athletes and their flirting, teasing female worshipers. Some nooks and corners of the place were mere knots of writhing, gasping bodies; elsewhere revelers ran lewdly free and unclothed.

"Doesn't that feel better? Now turn over, you must surely have other complaints that require my attention as well. This ointment is good for all parts. It strengthens the muscles and rejuvenates the flesh—"

"Conan, have you been hurt?"

Coming across the room, Sathilda interrupted Babeth's ministrations. "I did not think you would fight again," she said, coming nearer, "so I left the games early with Lord Alcestias and his household. Then, when I saw your name posted with the others, I had to come back."

Loosening her clutch on Conan's oiled flanks, Babeth turned and regarded Sathilda. "You are the acrobatess, are you not? No wonder Alcestias has an eye for you. He favors thin foreign types."

"I did not go to his villa, or even into his sedan," Sathilda said. "I was too worried—Conan, are you all right?"

"He is not hurt badly," the matron insisted, standing up to block the other woman's way. "I have already dressed his wounds. Now he must rest, and perhaps take a curative bath—"

"Babeth, Sathilda," Conan said, standing up from the bench. For modesty's sake he buckled on his armored kilt. "Thanks, both of you, for your kind attention. In truth I am weary, and would just as soon leave this turmoil." He gestured at the orgy in full swing around them. "But if you really want to care for the sick, I see one way you could help."

He was gazing across the room toward a tall, muscular figure seated on a bench near the door. It was Muduzaya, brought here by celebrants from the arena. Where he sat, staring blankly, half-clothed houris paused to admire him and stroke his burly limbs. When he did not respond they moved on, assuming he was drunk.

"Our friend the Swordmaster has not recovered from the drug he was given," Conan said, leading the way toward the helpless man. "It must have been a powerful draught. We should get him out of here and see to his recovery. If we take him to the circus quarters, Bardolph or Luddhew may know what to do."

CHAPTER 10
"O Gracious Tyrant"

According to long-established custom, a funeral was held the day after the arena games. Murdered Halbard, falsely said to be the victim of a training accident, was interred in the same niche with the newcomers Sarkad and Callix; thus the two lesser-known warriors were fortunate enough to gain a degree of final prestige they might not otherwise have achieved.

The crowd that assembled in the early shade on the west front of the amphitheater was a sparse one, even so. Weeping relatives, Memtep with a small band of arena functionaries, a few bookmakers and some local widows who habitually wailed at every public funeral, all clustered in a crowd beneath a stone-faced archway that was to be filled in once the mummies were hoisted up.

Conan, arriving late with a handful of gladiators, caused a stir among the watchers . . . in large part because Sathilda came, too, leading her night-black tiger on a golden leash.

Yet Conan himself did not go unnoticed. In particular, he saw the oddsmakers examining the cut of his bandages to gauge the extent of his injuries. The rest of the gladiators did not look any too healthy either, because of the lateness of their previous night's debauches. But Swordmaster Muduzaya was on his feet at least . . . gruffly tolerant of Conan, and actively seeking those responsible for his drugging during the games.

"Where is Zagar?" Conan muttered, gazing around the forlorn crowd. "Why is he not here? He was Halbard's procurer, was he not? And the one who tried to make him throw yesterday's match."

"When you find the little weasel," Muduzaya rumbled ominously, "save him for me. I, too, have questions for him."

Behind the stadium fence, a gray-clad Priest of Set droned on interminably and unintelligibly, pronouncing a prayer in High Stygian. Halbard's mummy, with the gaudy brass hilt of an ornamental sword exposed atop its chest-windings, was just now being raised up on a rope. From the mummy's trim, athletic shape and the ease with which it was hoisted by the two workmen on the scaffold, Conan could tell that the Red Priests must have subtracted quite a bit of Halbard's weight.

The workmen below were a few of the same crew that did renovations on the arena. Conan spied one of the louts making ready to piss into the vat of mortar that would be Halbard's tomb, and stopped him with the force of a malevolent stare. The man betook himself hastily away, muttering the lame excuse that "it helps the concrete set."

When all three mummies were placed upright in the alcove and a screen of withe and sticks was installed, the cement was troweled in over them. In front of each hero's face was inlaid a plaster death-mask taken from the corpse, a perfect likeness; afterward, their names were imprinted by fast-working artisans, along with decorative reliefs of crossed swords and coiling serpents. Although this particular tomb was set too high above the level of the street to be clearly visible, it was there for all to admire, alongside the niches of a hundred other dead champions.

Of all the funeral celebrants, the only visitor who had worldly knowledge and seemed inclined to share it was the portly, bearded nobleman Udolphus. Standing at the fringe of the gathering with his two bodyguards, he greeted Conan and their mutual friends with wry good humor. He looked fairly fresh; evidently the previous night's revel had not exceeded his usual degree of debauchery.

"And so three more faces ornament the Tomb Wall," he observed with a cynical smile. "Three more lives go as grist into the giant money-mill known as the Circus Imperium."

"Three more failed attempts at fame and fortune," Sathilda echoed him, stroking her tiger's neck.

"Halbard had plenty of fame, and plenty victories, too," Muduzaya declared. "But his success brought him no luck outside the arena . . . likely just the opposite."

"Alas, that is often true of winning gladiators." Udolphus shot a meaningful glance at the Kushite. "Their far-famed skills are a liability in the real world, and get them into trouble with the wrong people."

"What trouble was Halbard in, I wonder?" Conan asked. "And with what people? Something to do with rigged bets, I would guess."

"Those oddsmakers over there would tell me nothing," Muduzaya reported to Conan, indicating the swiftly departing touts. "They plead ignorance, and would probably lower my rankings if I were to rap their skulls together."

"Somebody knows something," Conan grumbled with a contemplative glance at Udolphus. "It's just a matter of finding out who."

The nobleman's guards edged forward at Conan's pointed remark, but Udolphus shrugged them back with an easy smile. "One who might have some useful answers for you," he suggested, "is your young friend Dath. The lad has ears in most every pub and alleyway in Luxur—through his age-mates, who regard him as their leader."

"A good idea." Conan nodded. "I'll be sure to ask him."

The ritual keening and breast-pounding that marked the end of the ceremony were well under way, and most of the gladiators summoned by Conan had slunk off to their beds. Muduzaya, who still felt weak from his poisoning, expressed the intention of doing the same. But Udolphus, seeming remarkably alert for the early hour, drew Conan and Sathilda aside.

"Look here, you two, I am not about to crawl back to bed and sleep till noon. 'Tis a new day, and a mere change of garments will do for me. If you would like to accompany me home, see my villa, and partake of a late breakfast, you would be welcome. Come along, I will be honored by your company . . . all three of you," he added, indicating the tiger.

After glancing to one another, the couple did not demur. Conan, for his part, did not feel threatened by the noble and his two guards, and he knew that Sathilda could take care of herself. With the she-tiger along, in any case, there would be little danger.

Udolphus led them briskly down the avenue that curved around the Circus Imperium. Farther on past the Convicts' Gate, the lane continued downhill between wrought trellises and garden fences. But just there at the turning, one of Udolphus's guards produced a key and opened an inconspicuous back gate.

Inside, lush vegetation crowded near a spattering tiled fountain. All around lay marble benches, mosaic tables, and gilded terrace doors opening on a lavish dining chamber furnished with priceless art and artifice from faraway lands. It was but the merest corner of a palatial dwelling that rose in three or four tiers above them. The gilded bars on the windows by themselves, Conan guessed, were more valuable than the whole treasure-troves of some wealthy estates.

Udolphus led them to an inner parlor whose fittings were just as ostentatious, though less formal. Motioning his guests to sit on a velvet-cushioned dais—Qwamba the cat choosing instead to lie down on a zebra-skin rug before an alabaster hearth—the nobleman shucked off his soiled cape into the arms of one of his attendants.

"Now at last I can relax and be myself." Reaching under his silken tunic, Udolphus pulled out a thick swatch of padding, rendering his swollen belly suddenly flat. Then, leaning forward before a polished mirror, he unstuck the straggling black beard, wig, and thick mustache that had screened his features, and cast them down on the tabletop. When he turned to his guests, the square Corinthian face and fair, curly locks of the man before them were revealed. They belonged to none other than the Corinthian Commodorus, the far-famed Tyrant of Luxur.

The tigress must have sensed the faint alarm of her mistress; she raised her night-black head where she lay and purred a low, stuttering growl. After a few uneasy moments, Conan spoke up.

"Let me understand: You go in disguise into the worst dens and gutters of your kingdom. You rub elbows there with low-class foreigners, and the poor and powerless, and preach sedition against yourself."

Commodorus smiled disarmingly. "What better way to find out how things really stand, instead of hearing it distorted through temple spies and fawning, ambitious toadies?"

Sathilda spoke up. "Do you not fear that others will give ear to your discontent and start a movement to undermine your rule? Or do you spy out any such whisperers and send your guards to drag them off to prison?"

"It matters little." Turning, the Tyrant stepped momentarily behind an inlaid wood screen to change. In a moment he emerged with a clean knee-length toga draped across his athletic frame. "Dear woman, do not suppose that a few stray mutterings in some tavern can endanger my rule. I have wellsprings of power—the love of my people, lofty alliances and treasury sources that a newcomer could only guess at." He laughed, displaying strong white teeth. "But come along, I promised the three of you breakfast. I generally take my morning meal under the gazebo."

Dismissing his bodyguards and issuing instructions to a turbaned, tasseled manservant who had appeared in the doorway, he took them into the interior of the great villa. After conducting them through the spacious gallery at its center, he led the way up a spiral staircase, past gleaming mezzanines and the open doorways of lushly furnished chambers. At the top, passing out underneath a broad crystal sun-dome whose tinted panes were set in mullions of polished silver, they emerged onto the roof—which was itself partly roofed and vine-shaded, an open terrace furnished with cushioned divans and chairs. Awaiting them there was a table laid with fruit, exotic cheeses, spiced meats, and baked delicacies. At the Tyrant's invitation they settled themselves to dine, with a view of the massive stadium and of Luxur itself outspread before them. Qwamba was content to lie prone, cracking fresh eggs and licking them up off the polished mosaic tiles.

"There lies my domain." Propping himself against the carved stone railing of the roof, Commodorus indicated the walled, hilled expanse of city that was just beginning to shimmer under the day's sun. "And here beside us is its center." His courtly flourish turned their attention to the massive, foreshortened curve of the Circus Imperium, whose high wall crested little more than spitting-distance from where they sat. "In many ways, though it may not be evident to all, it is the fulcrum of my power. It is by building and improving the Circus over the last half dozen years that I have established myself here."

Sathilda, nibbling a fragment of honeyed pastry, spoke up politely. "That has been almost the entire length of your appointed reign, has it not?"

Commodorus flashed upon her his dazzling smile. "Seven years ago this coming Bast Day, I was named Tyrant of Luxur for a seven-year term. I was then all but unknown to my subjects, chosen mainly for my standing with the Corinthian merchants and envoys. I was little more than a diplomatic pawn of the Stygian Priesthood, really—a way for the decrepit rulers to upgrade their standing in foreign capitals, gain diplomatic leverage, and spread their benighted religion by way of spies, assassins, and secret cults." He shook his head in wry, amused recollection. "But since that time the city has prospered—foreign trade is multiplied, our defenses are improved, and our zone of tribute is extended far to the southward. I am acclaimed among the greatest leaders Luxur has yet known, be they kings, princes, or tyrants. And the folk of the city know and respect me on a personal basis—all of them, from high deacons to low guttersnipes—because of the face-to-face contact they have had with me in yonder Circus arena."

"You promote the Circus as a political tool?" Sathilda asked in surprise.

"To be sure, I do. Look at the very shape of the place—it is a trumpet, a vast megaphone—a fertile valley where I can broadcast the seeds of my support. You see before you the greatest instrument of political power ever conceived . . . with the exception, possibly, of the corn dole. The crowds who flock here, week in and week out, do so for the satisfaction of mere animal needs, the ancient craving for excitement. But when they leave, they take with them something more—an idea, a name, a face. The arena has carried me into every household in Luxur. The priests and nobles will have no choice, this coming Bast Day, but to reappoint me Tyrant . . . this time for an indefinite term."

"Doubtless," Conan observed, "it comes in handy to be able to throw your political foes to the wild beasts."

"Nay, nay, dear Slayer," Commodorus corrected him, "I find it far more effective to humiliate my enemies . . . and my weak political allies as well, such as the Prefect Bulbulus. You saw our little display yesterday?" He paused, smiling, for their affirmation. "Doubtless you have heard them say that I was champion of the gladiatorial arena in noble Corinthia, long before I ever came to Stygia? Well"—he winked slyly at them—"do not believe all you hear. Still, I was a cataphract of the Royal Corinthian Guard and can handle myself well enough to thrill these city types. Violence is what impresses them most, and I am capable of dishing it out in adequate measure."

"Indeed," Sathilda affirmed with guarded admiration, "they enjoyed your hunting exhibition. I wish I had drawn so much applause with my own act."

"You will someday." The Tyrant's good wishes seemed sincere. "But for now I need all the crowd's attention for myself ... in view of my pending reappointment, and certain steps I will be taking to consolidate my reign. I want them to stand behind me, the Imperial Army in particular. In every arena show, the high officers come and applaud along with the rest, or instruct their concubines to do so. By showing my mettle, I have won their respect. The local nobility as well." He waved a hand at the lavish townhouses immediately around them. "They are weary of being repressed and disciplined by the stodgy priesthood. Their thirst for foreign goods and Corinthian freedoms reflects a forward-looking, internationalist spirit. I've done my best to cultivate that along with the support of the Corinthian migrants ... the merchants and craftsmen, engineers and administrators, who have come here to cater to them."

"What about the common people?" Sathilda asked. "Do they support you?"

Commodorus smiled. "Since Luxur was opened to the world, life here is much improved. New converts flock to the temples to Mitra and Ishtar. And the same engineers who built the Circus, working under my direction, have also reared the aqueducts, new defensive works, and the finest civic and private buildings in the land, greatly improving the commoners' lot. No native Stygian craftsmen could have achieved these marvels . . . for, huge and impressive as they are, Stygian monuments are usually just dense stone piles with tunnels hewn inside them, lacking the fine points of true architecture." The Tyrant shrugged. "Of course, it's hard getting local laborers to follow through on all the necessary steps, and keep them from skimping or stealing the materials." He flashed his guests a rueful smile. "Details like that have kept me busy these last few years—but I think the results have been worth it.

"You see, it is the common folk most of all who have been transformed. Through the Circus, and through a thousand smaller details of everyday life, we change their expectations. They can never be made to go back to strict orthodoxy under the Priests of Set, the barren lives they once led—or rather, were led into. They crave a broader range of experiences, and free contact with foreign customs and values. I have brought them too far already to ever go back—now I can be sure they'll support my rule over that of the theocracy."

In response to the Tyrant's grandiloquent speech,

Conan grunted. "The country folk are still faithful to their ancient god Set, from what I see."

Commodorus nodded impatiently. "Yes, true. And fitting enough for rural peasants." His sun-brown hand gave a broad flourish, off toward the misty expanses beyond the city wall. "Every great city must rule a vast hinterland of such benighted souls to furnish grain and tribute—and their own healthy bodies, of course. I would not tamper with their primitive belief, not as long as it keeps them peaceful and productive. If they choose to worship low animals—cats and serpents and storks—then let them, even though such customs are laughable to anyone who has knelt before our Hyborian gods in their humanlike shapes." He laughed in fond reminiscence. "We had a problem in the early days of the Circus . . . some priests objected to the slaughter of animals in the arena as being sacrilegious. Fortunately reason prevailed; now the Luxurites are so well accustomed to seeing their totem beasts slaughtered by mortals that they can never quite regard them as holy again, I am sure. Thus the old childlike beliefs will always give way to modern, enlightened ideas.

"So, in answer to your question," Commodorus said, "changes in the city do not have to entail changes in the countryside. The Priests of Set will always have their place here. The essential nature of the city remains the same . . . you know what it is, do you not?"

In response to Sathilda's inquiring look, the Tyrant spoke matter-of-factly: "The city is a dying-place. Whenever there is a flood or famine, or in the normal course of their overbreeding, country people travel here to die. They expect to make their fortunes, of course, or at least beg food from the vast granaries they have sent their produce to over the years. But on the whole they will die, from all the usual causes—starvation, disease, crime, suicide, war, human sacrifice, military and labor conscription—or in the Circus, of course— or, if they are less lucky, from the crowding, and the wasting ills that plague the poorer quarters.

"By the thousands and tens of thousands they flock here . . . all the raw, hardy surplus of Stygia's vast croplands and orchards, all seeking to crowd within a walled, cramped space that does not normally grow by a thousand dwellings in a century! Wherever do they think they will fit in? A few lucky ones manage to displace others, and some may even win high status. But as a rule, they die. Thus it has always been." The Tyrant spread his hands.

In the aftermath of Commodorus's dismal speech, neither Conan nor Sathilda seemed to have much to say. So their host, picking up a sphere of ripe fruit and gnawing on it, resumed speaking. "No need to feel glum, 'tis not so bad as it was. In the days before my reign, the Set Priests would turn pythons and leopards out into the streets after dark each night. Any poor soul who could not find shelter would be devoured, to become an instant sacrifice to the god Set. After some controversy with the priests, I put an end to the custom." Commodorus tossed his fruit core off the roof. "Which reminds me, what think you of this new wrestler Xothar, whom they call the Constrictor? He put on quite a show this last time out."

"I have not met him outside the arena," Conan avowed. "And I surely would not want to meet him in it."

"He was nominated to fight in the Circus by the High Priest Nekrodias," Commodorus said in distaste. "This Xothar is a great favorite of the priestly lot. The tale is, he was trained to wrestle using the secret disciplines of some monastery far off in the eastern hills. His victories are all supposed to be sacred deaths, sacrifices to his god, like a killing by the temple serpents." The Tyrant shrugged in impatience. "He is fast, but a ritual slayer is bound to have his blind spots. I am no mean wrestler myself, and I would venture to say I could best him. What about you?" he asked Conan. "Do you think you can?"

Conan, like a true wrestler, avoided any trap. "I hope never to find out."

"That ties into something I have been meaning to ask you." Commodorus kept his gaze on the two of them. "I have seen you fight, Cimmerian. I know few in the arena, if any, who can match your speed and skill." He smiled. "It was perfectly clear to me, for instance, that you were toying with the Swordmaster in yesterday's match, and did not truly suffer the defeat you pretended to." When Conan looked as if he would interrupt, the Tyrant waved him to silence. "Yes, I know. He was not fighting his best, quite obviously. You are loyal to a friend. I see that and value it. But what I mean to say is—I myself would like to take a more active part in one of the upcoming games, and perhaps fight in a mass combat alongside other gladiators. That would crown my arena career"—he smiled in deprecation—"and quash any jealous claims that I am a mere dabbler or a show-off.

"That done, I could retire from the Circus once and for all, a move that is wholly in keeping with the more exalted rulership I plan to assume. But to do it—to go safely among the armed arena warriors—I'll need someone at my back. A skilled fighter, one I can count on to guard me from a random mischance or a traitorous stroke—but one who will not come off looking like the true champion, or overshadow my fame with his own."

Conan nodded, following him. "You think that I am that man."

Commodorus smiled. "Indeed, Conan. No slight was intended. But you are a foreigner, unfamiliar to our citizens and untouched by our factional rivalries. Your fighting skills and techniques are not yet well known to the handicappers; you have taken a defeat, by your own choice, and suffered a wound. So at present, you could play an inconspicuous role on my behalf . . . for a considerable reward, I might add."

"You want me to guard you in the arena . . . but not too obviously." Conan knit his brow in thought a moment, then shrugged. "In truth, I cannot see a fault in your plan, or a reason to refuse." He gazed up amiably at Commodorus. "Though you are a Tyrant, you do not seem a harsh one to me. You give your people what they want, and it brings them prosperity. And you are no blind minion of the snake-god Set. Tell me, what payment do you have in mind?"

So their negotiations commenced. After several moments' dickering, a price was struck, and Commodorus passed a sizable purse to Conan as his advance payment.

"When I am ready to fight with the gladiators," Commodorus said, "I will tell you what to do. It may be during this next spectacle or the one after. For the time being, take care of yourself, and let your wound heal." After seizing Conan's hand firmly in the legionary grip, the Tyrant released it. "Now, if you three would be so kind as to excuse me"—he seized Sathilda's hand, pressed its smoothly callused palm to his lips, and let her go—"I have neglected the daily concerns of state too long already. My man will let you out the back way."

Not many evenings later, Conan found himself at the Pleasure Barge soaking up cheap *arrak*. His wound had healed, enough so for him to lash a chariot team down the jolting, cobblestoned streets to the muddy wallows of the sin-district. The tavern was nearly empty till well after sunset; then a band of street toughs trooped in, accompanied by some of Conan's brother gladiators. Thumping impatiently on the planks, they ordered and stood swilling like men who had just been engaged in thirsty work. A few of them sported fresh-looking welts and bruises, while others wore garments that were slashed or shredded. A bit later Dath strode in and called noisily for a toast.

"A tot of your best poison all around, Namphet! Savor it well, lads, and say your farewells, for we may soon be moving uptown!"

Seating himself near Conan and Sathilda, he nodded to them and took a measured sip of his drink. "It was not much of a fight," he half apologized. "I did not ask you to join us, Conan, since you are still mending."

"Whom did you fight this time?" Sathilda asked. "It appears as if you were the victors."

"It was a joint skirmish with the Gatewatch crew against the Eastsiders. An ambush, really, to repay their attack on us. It looks as if we have won ourselves a tract of territory inside the city wall, extending right up to the Temple Hill." Dath straightened his disarranged hair. "Barring some sneaking betrayal, the Silver Trident Pub will be our meeting-place henceforth."

"Your lads will move with you, then?" Conan asked. "They don't feel overly bound to their home district, I take it?"

"Who would cherish this?" Dath glanced around the shabby, disreputable tavern. "Anyway, we'll retain our control of the Canal Wharf. The traffic in contraband goods and condemned slaves is too valuable to let go. But in the city proper, there'll be a much richer set of gambling accounts to collect. We'll have the street merchants to offer our protection to—and, in the sector I have claimed, there are a good many civil construction jobs we can administer. The pickings should be rich."

"You mean, you will have a hand in the building of churches and aqueducts?" Sathilda asked.

"Why, yes. The crews are all picked men." Dath shrugged a little guardedly. "It is mostly temple money anyway, so it scarcely matters who spends it."

"Mayhap you're right." Conan nodded, dismissing the topic. "Dath, there is something I have been meaning to ask you. Before Halbard was killed, he complained to us about being told to throw a combat. He refused the offer—do you have any idea who was behind it?"

Dath shrugged. "These oddsmakers all crave inside information. That includes rigging the occasional match. Heaven help the gladiator who gets too deeply in debt to them."

Conan scowled. "It was Zagar the procurer who pressed Halbard to do it, and he has stayed out of sight ever since the killing. I would like to know who he dealt with. Memtep swears it wasn't one of his eunuchs."

Dath nodded, considering. "I have not seen Zagar. But I assure you, I will put out a watch for him. Whatever information he has could prove useful."

Conan grunted. "Muduzaya was drugged before his match with me, likely as a last-minute substitute for Halbard. I refused to do murder, and took the fall instead." He scratched under his loose bandage. "The slaves who did the drugging have been sold out of Luxur, so I am out of leads."

"Such things aren't that uncommon in the Circus, from what I hear." Dath sipped his drink.

"Muduzaya could have drugged himself by accident, after all, and Halbard's slayer might well be a jealous husband." He smiled. "But I'll see what I can do, in honor of our old times together in Luddhew's troupe." He turned to Sathilda. "I understand the circus players are all doing well?"

The acrobat beamed. "Luddhew says our last show brought in as much as any six market fairs in the country. The fortune-castings and Bardolph's Lotus Root Potion yielded good profit—and my trapeze act did, too, mainly from the betting. The crowd wants more risk, though—for this next meet I will perform over a canvas vat full of vipers."

Conan stirred in irritation. "Is that really necessary, Sathilda? You are an artist, as much as any temple dancer, but these low city-skites have no appreciation of it. I know civilized types too well, they crave only death and suffering. Mark my words, one of them will saw through your ropes for you!"

"I check my equipment," the woman said haughtily. "And I do not nag you about your exploits in the arena." She shook her tightly bound hair. "Anyway, the courtyard of the Circus Imperium is made of flagstones. A fall there means death, or worse, crippling. There is no safety net. Isn't a pit of deadly serpents better than a lifetime of creeping beggary?" Turning to see her lover's dismal look, she softened and leaned across to him, speaking more quietly. "Do not fear, Conan. These rubes have no way of knowing which snakes are venomous. And the vat is going to be specially made—I would just as soon have a layer of tautly stretched canvas between me and the pavement to stop my fall. Maybe even a cushion of serpents as well."

Dath laughed, then shook his head. "Do not worry, I won't breathe a word. And remember, if any of the others need favors, I am now in a position to deal them out." Arising from his seat, he rejoined his lieutenants.

They stayed late, for it was still two full days until the Bast Day spectacle. Returning home, their chariot was packed with three extra riders, gladiators still boisterous from the street skirmish. Conan was pleased to have them along in case of an ambush, even though on the uphill slopes they had to dismount and stumble along behind the chariot.

The streets were quiet—unusually so, as if news of Dath's victory had brought a lasting peace to the cobbled battleground. They encountered no difficulties until they were nearly home. Then it was passive trouble that found them, lying slack in the roadway: the body of Zagar the procurer, murdered and dumped at the back gate of the Circus Imperium.

Chapter 11
Bast Day

"Zagar failed to please his masters, after all," Muduzaya said. "First Halbard would not take a fall for him, and then you refused the victory he tried to hand you for nothing."

"From what I have heard," Conan answered, "one of the oddsmakers who was busy staking bets against you is named Sesoster. He would be one to talk to."

"He must have paid out a fortune. So he would not have felt lovingly toward Zagar."

The two conversed in the narrowing shade of the arena wall, waiting for the day's spectacle to commence. Just now, before the milling and largely uninterested stadium multitudes, Qwamba the black tiger was paraded through the center of the arena in a gold-painted cart, drawn by garlanded boys and followed by whirling, leaping, thinly veiled females. It was a religious display in keeping with the pious observance of the temple festival, Bast Day.

"That weaselly talent-procurer is a nuisance dead as well as alive," Muduzaya complained. "Now everyone who knew him is afraid to talk. It sorely interferes with my revenge."

"Your revenge has been going none too swiftly," observed Conan. "You seem to have other things on your mind."

"Well, now," the Swordmaster argued, "first I had to recover from poisoning, did I not? And then there is Babeth. Her healing baths and massages have helped me greatly, but she is most demanding of my time and strength. I can see now why you passed her along to me. Even so," he grudgingly added, "I thank you."

As the cat procession retreated, Commodorus stood forth on his balcony to announce the day's first contest. There had been no advance notice given, and the Tyrant's gold-trimmed staircase was nowhere in evidence, so Conan assumed that the ruler would not be setting foot in the arena today. He himself was not on the roster of single combatants, even though his sword-cut was practically healed. So he expected only to partake in the mass fight. As a trumpet-blast echoed through the great oval, he turned his attention toward the Gate of Heroes and the rostrum above it.

"Greetings, citizens of Luxur," Commodorus proclaimed from his vantage point. "I welcome you all to the Circus Imperium, and I join with you in celebrating this most sacred of feast-days, under the ancient tradition of our holy temple. Praise be to Father Set, and to his earthly pawns and arbiters," the Tyrant declared with every appearance of sincerity.

"I also commend your attention to the improvements we have made to our amphitheater," the Tyrant went on. "As you can see, both the east and west seating sections are now shaded and enlarged by the balconies we have added. By the next arena show, we expect to have the additional public areas open as well." He gestured left and right toward the soaring, graceful additions. "Here now to initiate our spectacle is Set's spokesman on earth, our exalted Temple Primate Nekrodias."

Briskly, Commodorus gave his place to the bald, skull-faced priest who so often presided with him over the games. Nekrodias, small and sinewy, spoke out in a practiced, oratorical rasp that hardly needed repetition by the criers stationed around the arena.

"Friends and minions of Set! Most fittingly, today's spectacle begins with an event that, gods willing, must affirm our simple, honest faith. The game will exact the full, harsh penalty of divine justice, and do so in a manner you will find edifying and interesting."

The arena, as Conan had seen, was laid out differently for this meet. Square pits, a dozen in number, had been opened at intervals across the sandy space; the cat-paraders and charioteers had been careful to thread safely between them, staying clear of the vertical drop-offs.

But now, as Nekrodias exhorted the crowd, a fast-driven chariot rolled forth from the Champions' Gate, carrying a slave and a smoldering fire-bucket behind its driver. As it veered perilously near the edge of a pit, the rider lit a torch and flung it in, igniting fuel in the bottom to produce leaping flame and oily smoke.

With that first blaze, a murmur went up from the crowd. Excitement passed from bench to bench; it grew into an eager, expectant ferment as the chariot-rider ignited one after another of the flame-pits.

"Faithful of Set," Nekrodias rasped forth, "you see before you the sacred power of searing, purifying flame! What can burn a soul cleaner, I ask you, than the punishing scourge of earthly torment? What is a surer test of faith?

"To be tried and purified here today, we bring forth the wretchedest and most depised malefactors of our empire: devil-worshipers, O citizens! False-souled heretics of the eastern waste! Instead of kneeling in the temples and shrines of our Holy Master, they choose instead to worship the raw rocks and cliffs of their heathen desert, and fall in prayer to the whirlwinds that mark the passing of evil sprites and *djinni*. They have forsworn our empire's simple, self-evident belief and turned their backs on sacred truth. Of all the gods we cherish, they revere none, but cling to their primal, atavistic evil."

Though the priest's words were lurid with religious fervor, his speech was relentlessly cold and even. He was an expert at lashing the crowd . . . as evidenced by the palpable waves of hatred that beat down into the arena like sun into an upturned mirror.

Then the heretics were driven forth from the Convicts' Gate—common-looking Stygians, a shade darker perhaps from desert sun, dressed in ragged, shapeless clothes that made them look laughable. There were women and men, young and old alike, half a hundred of them at least—no young children, as far as Conan could see over the fringes of shimmering flame and the tongues of smoke that rose from the arena pits.

"The terms of the ordeal are this: The heretics will be armed with wooden clubs, as will the gladiators, who are our temple's guards and protectors. Any heretics who make it past the flame-pits and the club-wielders will be allowed to exit by the Gate of Heroes. All who repent will be spared."

While Nekrodias grated on, Memtep came down the line of gladiators dragging a sack of round wooden staves and handing them out. As he gave one to Conan he repeated what he had told the others. "No steel. If they fall on their knees and make the sign of the serpent, spare them."

Signaled by a blast from the trumpets, the gladiators moved forward. Conan, seeing that the flames and screening smoke hovered thickest at the center of the arena, headed there. He had no great enthusiasm for this task, but a plan was taking shape in his mind.

Ahead were the so-called devil-worshipers, driven away from the gate by city guards armed with spears. There was no telling what the real beliefs of these unfortunates might be—only that

they had somehow offended the High Temple and
its political allies. Some of the younger heretics
ran forward swinging their clubs, ready to fight for
their faith, while most of the women and elders
dropped their weapons or let them trail loosely behind in the sand.

The gladiators rushed forward, always eager to
finish the fight and make a good impression; this
once Conan lagged behind the others, angling his
steps toward the area least visible to the raving
spectators, where smoke befouled the air and pud-
dled overhead in an obscuring screen.

All around him the battle was joined. Conan
heard desperate shouts, the thwack of cudgels and
the occasional softer thud of wood smiting flesh
and bone. To his left and right, he saw heretics batted or kicked into the searing fire-pits—never the
gladiators, even though they were outnumbered.
Some of the more combative devil-worshipers
were beaten down to their hands and knees, then
dragged or flung into the pits by vengeful adversaries who then had to shrink back from the heat
and flame that belched forth.

Ahead, in the smoke, Conan saw a man
approaching—a white-bearded elder in a tattered
robe, his cudgel cradled loose in his folded arms.
At the sight of the gladiator before him, the man
strode determinedly onward. He never looked back
at the plight of his companions, apparently oblivious to the screams and furious shouts that rang out
all around.

In the heat-shimmer and yellow smoke-shadow,
his gaze met Conan's.

"Strike me a blow, grandfather," Conan called out to him in low Stygian dialect. "Go ahead, knock me in the skull! I will fall down, and you can walk on past to safety."

The man, if he heard him, remained expressionless as he continued forward. He did not take his cudgel firmly in hand or raise it to strike; instead he came on as if to brush negligently past the Cimmerian.

Conan, unsure whether the foreigner could understand him, switched to the near-universal trade jargon of the southern deserts. "Go on," he challenged, "hit me as hard as you like! I'll stay down, I promise, and you can lead your people out of here." He moved over slightly to block the man's path, hefting his cudgel. "I'll pretend to put up a fight—no one will ever know the difference."

Coming up directly opposite Conan, the man stopped. His eyes, set in a weather-beaten olive face, fixed for a moment upon the Cimmerian's. He may even have smiled in the depths of his straggling beard. Then abruptly he turned away to one side. Conan said nothing.

More resolute than ever, the patriarch tossed aside his club. Before Conan could gather his wits and move to stop him, he strode straight to the edge of the nearest fire-pit and, with a deft half-step, jumped in.

Conan stood watching, astonished. Around him the so-called battle was already ending. No captives had made it as far as the Gate of Heroes, and no more heretics wielded clubs. The remainder of them had fallen to their knees in forced repentance.

Some, presumably, still hoped to be reunited with their absent children.

Feeling dazed, Conan wandered in a broad circle through the sand. The heat was intense, the air thick with the stench of tar-oil and smoldering flesh. Slaves were already hurrying to extinguish the fires, by shoveling sand into the pits. Meanwhile, the newly redeemed converts were being herded out through the Beast Gate.

"That was no pretty business," Muduzaya remarked as they trudged back toward the resting-stools. "I did not slay any of the poor devils myself," he added lightly, flinging his cudgel down on a pile near the arena wall. "I clubbed one over the ear and knocked him to his knees, but he passed as a convert. He started up a fashion among the others."

"Where do they come from?" Conan dully asked. "Did they even know what was happening to them?"

Muduzaya shrugged. "They were Altaquans, I think, from the southeastern part of the empire. Such heathen tribes have been butchered here often enough before."

Conan grunted, preoccupied. If the graybeard was from Altaqua in the near desert, he should have understood the speech Conan had used. Unless he was stone-deaf . . . why else would he have turned thus from Conan and thrown away his life?

Brooding, the Cimmerian settled onto his stool, scarcely noticing as the attendants sluiced away the soot and sand with pitchers of scented water. He sat pensive, all but blind to the subsequent events on the day's program. There were chariots, perhaps . . . costumed performers, and the sportive slaughter of some large animal. He lost himself in thought . . . recalling the brief fight, the look on the old man's face, his leap into the flames. All of it baffled him more than if he himself had been struck on the head with the patriarch's wooden club.

The code he had learned in his years and travels was one that clung fiercely to life. While a man had a hilt in his hand, so Conan believed, and a clear view to his enemies, there was always hope. Why would a brave man, to all appearances a vigorous clan-leader, resolutely turn his back on life? Conan had offered him a path to freedom, and beyond doubt he had seen it. Did his death, then, amount to bravery or cowardice? . . . a supreme act of faith or a surrender to hollow despair? Was his deed an expression of profound altruism—to stand up for his beliefs and mayhap cut short the slaughter of his kinfolk? Or was it blind self-seeking, because he believed his gods would reward him richly in the realms after death?

Conan's sullen abstraction lasted long, well into the afternoon's single combats. Saul Stronghand's name was bandied through the arena and screamed out by the crowd. He fought someone—Sistus, perhaps—and slew him.

Then, of a sudden, Roganthus was striding down the row of fighters with a fixed smile, clapping the Cimmerian firmly on the shoulder as he went. Conan heard Muduzaya shout last-minute instructions after him: "Use your weapon, Roganthus! Do not let him catch you in a grapple."

Flexing his arms jauntily overhead before the crowd's cheers, the strongman strode out into the sand ... to face Xothar, the Constrictor.

As Roganthus reached the center of the arena and squared off against his opponent, the circus champion looked supremely confident. He waved his sword high with a boisterous flourish, then cast it away into the sand.

The two wrestlers stooped forward, stalking one another. Roganthus feinted, trying to clap on a neck-hold, and was immediately caught by a powerful grip across his chest. Brutally he was forced down to his knees; then he sank to his haunches.

And never rose again.

The crowd's frenzy dinned remotely on Conan's numb ears. He felt light-headed—tremorous, as if the sandy expanse before him were a taut drumhead that quivered up and down under relentless strokes.

To mad cheering, Xothar departed the arena. Conan sat nerveless. Then he saw something that made him spring upright, clutching his sword.

The Red Priests were dragging Roganthus's body off toward the Gate of the Dead.

Conan darted across the sand with sword raised. He heard Muduzaya and the others call his name, but their cries rapidly fell behind. He bolted straight after the mummy-makers, leaping across the corner of one still-warm fire-pit, then another. The stadium crowd took notice, and shouts arose.

Ahead of him, the priests dragged their slack burden through the low-arched doorway, vanishing into interior darkness. Conan ran close on their heels, coming up against the wooden door just as it closed in his face. Heaving mightily, he shoved his way through.

The door banged shut behind him, and he was instantly blind. After the intense glare of the arena, whatever light there was within the tomblike chamber was as nothing to his watering eyes. He heard shouts and the scuffing of feet nearby and felt the impact of robed bodies. He raised his sword and, even as his blade and knuckles slammed into the low ceiling, felt the hilt wrested out of his grip. He laid hold of a scrawny assailant, lifted him off the floor—and felt an urn break over his skull, flooding his face with tepid water or, possibly, blood.

"Hold him! Pull him down! Hit him again!" The frightened cries echoed wildly around him. "He is crazed with slaughter from the arena!"

"Devils, damn mummy-stuffers!" Conan roared into blind, struggling darkness. "Give me back Roganthus! He is a proud Bossonian! They like to be buried in open fields, with flowers and grass— not gutted and wrapped and plastered up in a wall!"

In a spasm of rage, Conan threw off several of his attackers. He lunged forward—only to ram his head into an unseen pillar. The blow filled his eyes at last with light: bright pinpricks, swirling and many-colored.

"Enough now! Hold him, but let him lie down

flat." Amid the flaring pinwheels, Conan saw a true flame moving near his face and felt hard fingers probe his throbbing skull. "He is unharmed and still conscious . . . remarkable. You there, tell me, what is your name?"

By a dizzying effort, Conan managed to recall it and give form to the syllables.

"Good, now lie still. I am Manethos, Chief Priest here in the Circus mortuary. Calm yourself . . . we will not hurt your friend or do anything you do not wish us to."

As the lights within his skull faded, Conan could discern ghostly outlines of things around him. The room was lit by tapers hung in wall brackets, spaced at frequent intervals. The hollow-eyed, short-bearded priest who knelt over him with the others also held a candlestick in one hand. In the dimness, the red of their cowled robes looked black as dried blood.

"You cannot hurt Roganthus, not anymore," Conan told Manethos. "But what about me? You have tried to drag me in here before, and I was a good deal farther from death then than I am now! Do you intend to gut and stuff me as well?"

"Nonsense," Manethos soothed him, "we would not kill you, nor harm you in any way. My acolytes and I have no charter to deal with the living . . . not at this stage of our inquiries, anyway." There seemed to be a faint note of bitterness in his voice. "We serve only the dead."

"Am I to be turned loose, then?" Conan asked gruffly. "For, 'tis said among the gladiators that none who passes through yonder gateway ever comes back, be he alive or dead."

"That is utter nonsense," Manethos brusquely assured him. "There is no band of ruffians more foolishly superstitious than your gladiators! Come, now, and see if you can stand yourself upright."

With the help of his captors, Conan found his feet; almost immediately he reeled. As he pitched forward against Manethos, his eyes met with a horrific sight. There on a raised stone slab—supine, and laid open to the air with hooks, brass clamps, and wooden splints—was the slashed-open body of Sistus, the young gladiator lately of Dath's company.

"Fiend! Vile necromancer!" Shoving Manethos away, Conan felt himself instantly gripped on all sides—which was fortunate, in that it kept him from toppling over. "What are you doing to that poor lad," he croaked, "if not slicing and plucking him to pieces bit by bit!"

"The slicing was done by your associate, the one they call Stronghand, I would say," Manethos replied. "Blunt-Sword would be a better name for him, judging by his handiwork. He is the one who killed this boy; we are only examining the wounds and drawing what conclusions we can about the body and its parts, the miracle of the gods that you and your ham-handed friends love to defile and destroy."

"It is indecent, what you are doing here," Conan indignantly countered. "A man's innards are his own personal property. Peeking and probing at them like that violates his privacy."

Manethos laughed. "Better that it be done by vultures, flies, and rodents, I suppose?"

"Yes, in the natural order of things," Conan affirmed. "Any unseemly interest in the dead is foul and unwholesome, amounting to the crime of necromancy. The knowledge you obscenely quest after is beyond human ken, reserved for the gods."

"Nonsense," Manethos said, "it is all very straightforward. Tell me, have you ever really looked at the bodies you cleave apart?"

Moving aside, the priest commended the flayed-open corpse to Conan's view. "See here, this central spherule is the heart, which beats in your chest while you live. It works as a pump, just like the screw-pumps in the farm fields hereabouts, forcing blood humors to all parts of the body. And this bag here is the stomach, where food is burned up with acid to fuel the inner thermodynamic. It all works together, and every mortal is the same. Animals, too, are formed very similarly."

"Oh, so?" Conan, observing that young Sistus's body appeared to have been drained of blood—which had evidently been gathered in pitchers and basins near the foot of the slab—turned his face away in disgust. "What, then, is the end of all this hidden knowledge you lust after? Is it to command the dead, mayhap? Or gain fiendish power over the living, through some dark rite of your priesthood?"

Manethos shrugged, glum-faced. "First, to bind and heal the wounds your kind take such delight in inflicting. Second, perhaps, to learn enough from this mortal clay to help treat other sorts of ills, the baneful humors and indispositions that have plagued humanity since ancient times." He shook his cowled head. "Alas, our temple elders have enjoined us from applying these bold new arts, or otherwise experimenting with the cure and comfort of the living. For the time being, at least, our studies are confined to this dim workshop in the bowels of the arena. It is, fortunately, a perfect source of freshly hewn corpses—so long as we wrap them up neatly and consecrate them when we are finished. We are, as you say, mere mummy-makers."

"To my mind it is all unsavory and downright unhealthy," Conan stubbornly maintained, meanwhile probing at the sore dome of his forehead. "If such infernal dabblings be not wizardry, I warn you that they border closely on it."

"And then, of course," Manethos resumed, "there is a third possible fruit of our researches— one that may interest you more." He moved forward past Conan with his candlestick, letting the intruder and the encircling priests crowd after him. "It involves thinking up new and more effective ways of killing and injuring the human creature, using knowledge of the sort we have gleaned in our explorations."

Conan moved after Manethos, interested. The Red Priest had gone to kneel beside the body of Roganthus, which was laid out prone on a straw mat along one of the crypt's mortared stone walls. "This individual," he said, "has just died a singularly painless death at the hands of one Xothar, the temple killer from our eastern domain. I have seen only one or two examples of his work before, and the pattern is unvarying. You will notice that there are no wounds, no bruises, no purpling of the lips, nor any swelling or protrusion of the tongue and eyeballs. It is utterly characteristic."

Conan peered down in the flickering light at his good friend Roganthus. Even in spite of the intact and peaceful appearance of the corpse, he could not repress a shudder. "How does he manage it?" he asked.

"Quite simply. He is not a throttler, but a stifler." Manethos's long finger hovered in the area of the dead man's throat. "Through careful training, he does not wring the neck, crush the windpipe, and snap the throat-bone—nor even block off the mouth and nose openings, thereby trapping whatever air is left in the lungs. He takes his method from giant temple serpents, the pythons and boas."

Gesturing expressively with his pale hands, Manethos moved down the body to the dead man's chest. "By inhumanly concentrated strength, he expels the air from his victim's lungs—perhaps with the help of a harmless tap to the belly-plexus, here." With two fingers he prodded the dead man's thick middle. "Then, by maintaining intense pressure, he simply keeps his prey from drawing breath. There is no fund of air to be used up, no leakage, no intense panic and struggle, as with a strangling. Life simply ceases—a consecrated and holy form of killing under temple law, acceptable as an honored sacrifice to Almighty Set." Manethos folded his hands neatly. "That particular special skill of his is why they call him the Constrictor."

Conan shivered. "What you have described, Manethos, is just as evil and unsavory as all your doings here. Death is far better the manly way, with old-fashioned blows and bloodletting." He arose from his crouch beside Roganthus's corpse. "Still, if you are going to honor his poor remains . . ."

The Red Priest arose with him. "I promise you, temple law forbids us to do anything but a simple mummy-wrap, with spices and scents—"

"As a prized morsel for All-Father Set." Conan shrugged regretfully. "Very well. I do not think he would object, except to the manner and untimeliness of his death. As long as you swear to treat him decently . . ." He gazed around the room. "Now, you said I would be permitted to leave? I have had enough of these gloomy caverns—by Crom, what is that?"

For some time, murmurous shouts had been audible through the stone vaultings of the stadium above. Now, suddenly, a thunderous quaking shook the chamber walls and the very flagstones underfoot, while stone dust rained down from the joints in the ceiling.

"They are leaping and stamping on the benches," Manethos explained, looking resigned. "It is particularly troublesome when they shout and jump in unison."

One of the acolytes had dragged open the heavy door to peer out at the arena. "Your Holiness," he reported to Mantheos, "our services are once again required."

"Go, then. Fetch it." The Red Priest made his

way over to a second stone slab, this one vacant. In
the blazing rays from the open door he began shifting aside basins and handfuls of tools to make
space atop the table for a new occupant. "If you
go," he said over his shoulder to Conan, "let yourself out by the inner doorway to the tunnel. It will
spare both you and my helpers the mob's attention."

Conan, all but blinded once again by the glare
from the arena, nevertheless stood in the open door
watching two red-robed troglodytes drag yet another strong young body toward their subterranean
den. The name the crowd chanted, as their stamp-
ings and quakings gradually subsided, was clearly
discernible as "Baphomet." The Cimmerian was
curious now to learn whom the tough young street
fighter had vanquished in the third round of the
single combats.

The body, clanking and scraping across the
threshold in its canvas litter, looked heavy and
loose in its blood-spattered armor. As he watched,
the ungainly helmet was unbuckled and pulled off.
The stubbled face that revealed itself, lolling slack
and pale in the sunlight, was that of Conan's boon
drinking and fighting companion, Ignobold. A bit-
ter curse escaped the Cimmerian's lips.

"Your Holiness, this one yet lives."

One of the acolytes, having peeled back the
riven breastplate from the gaping wound across
Ignobold's shoulder, pointed to the neckward end
of the seeping crevice, between jagged edges of
cut flesh. There, tiny and inconspicuous in the gory
wreckage, a vein pulsed.

"By Mitra," Conan raved, looking for his sword, "if you put him to death I'll carve the lot of you!"

"Enough! Move aside there, get him up onto the table!" Manethos briskly directed his priests to surround the body. Meanwhile Conan, by an almost single-handed effort, stooped low and lifted the heavy fighter to the slab. When Ignobold's limp body clanked down onto the hard stone, an audible moan escaped his lips. The Chief Priest shoved Conan aside to get a closer view.

"You two, fetch needles and twine, and fresh mummy-wrap to wipe out the wound! You there, hold his head! Zevo, a basin of clean water at once. And you, gladiator, press inward on the lower part of his wound, just here! Place your hands thus, and thus—no, this way—and push! Harder—that's right. Hold him steady now, and keep up the pressure."

Conan, though unused to being ordered so harshly, did his best to comply. With blood seeping forth between his fingers, he had to struggle to keep his hands from slipping off Ignobold's clammy, waxen skin.

"But what does it avail us to try and push the blood back into his body?" the Cimmerian asked uncertainly. "Most of it is already run out into the sand."

"Just help him keep hold of what little he has left," Manethos replied, tight-lipped. Having received his washbasin and gauze, he was working his way along the wound, scrubbing, rinsing, and inspecting it by pulling apart its ragged edges and peering inside. "Deep, it is, but we may be able to do something. The bone is cut, see there, but it will knit. Hold steady while I pour—now loosen your grip and let me see inside. That's enough. Now press here."

The flow of blood had diminished to a mere seep, whether due to their hand-cramping efforts or just to a dwindling supply. Now Conan watched Manethos toss aside his bloody gauze, select a needle, and thread it, working deftly by the wavering candlelight.

"What strange ritual is this?" Conan demanded, suddenly suspicious. "Are you going to sew him a mummy-shirt to meet his gods in?"

Without comment, working closely between Conan's fingers, the Red Priest began to stitch Ignobold's flesh. The needle pricked in, threading though the varicolored layers in the riven wound; Manethos then pulled the thread painfully taut in a neat, puckered row. In mingled dread and amazement, Conan watched the Red Priest knot off one row of stitches like a seamstress and commence another, pulling the ragged lips of the wound unevenly together. He was aware that his own hands were beginning to weaken and tremble; then a cloud passed over his eyes and he fainted dead away.

CHAPTER 12

"I Have Done with Killing"

For a junior gladiator, Roganthus had a well-attended funeral. Aside from the usual oddsmakers, sports enthusiasts, and wailing crones in widow's weeds, all the members of Luddhew's circus turned out for the event—except Dath, who sent a wreath of laurel and lilies in apology for his absence. There were also a good many admirers of the fallen Ignobold—most of whom expressed astonishment to learn that he was recovering from his wounds in the Temple Infirmary. Whether they were pleased or disappointed by his nonappearance was not immediately clear. But they stayed on for the burial, although it was a mere double ceremony for Roganthus and his little-known teammate Sistus.

Conan, too, was in attendance. The gauze windings across his scabbed shoulder had been replaced by a single thick bandage about the crown of his skull. Apart from that, he seemed fit as ever, if subdued. His rush through the Dead Gate on the Red Priests' heels had been widely noted and whispered over; but he would say nothing of what had transpired there. He was naturally the object of a good deal of staring and speculation, both by fans and by oddsmakers, as they shrewdly tried to gauge his fitness for future matches.

During the plastering-up of the mummies, in spite of fierce scowls from the deceased strongman's associates, it was hard for the crowd to maintain a respectful silence. There were so many new developments to talk about—the rapid ascendancy of the wrestler Xothar, Ignobold's unprecedented escape from the very Gate of Death, and, most momentous of all, the pending reaffirmation of Commodorus as Tyrant of Luxur. For, although his seven-year term had technically expired on Bast Day, the Temple Primate Nekrodias had extended his reign to the coming Grand Spectacle a few days hence. There his reappointment as the city's ruler would presumably take place.

The prevalent view was that the old priest was simply bowing to the inevitable. When Commodorus was reordained, they said, it would be as Supreme Perpetual Tyrant, a lifelong post. The common mob and the various factions who supported the ruler would have it no other way.

Meanwhile, in the murmurous silence that followed the priest's last droned funeral invocation, the tightly clustered circus troupe gave voice to their feelings about their departed friend.

"Roganthus never should have joined the gladiators," Sathilda lamented. "He was no real killer— did you see how he threw away his sword before going to face that temple brute?"

Iocasta, one of the few present who was shedding real, verifiable tears, spoke up bitterly. "I warned him not to fight . . . his star-castings yesterday were the worst in months! But he would never listen, and he could not bear to disappoint his audience."

"He was a brave showman," Conan affirmed. "As to his wrestling prowess—well, I cannot say surely, for the only match we had was invalidated by a fault."

"While he was laid up all those months," Bardolph declared, "the loss of his public following hurt him more than his injury. It was that, and not the pain, which drove him to an excess of drink."

"True enough," Iocasta added tearfully, "he loved the acclaim. He was so pleased here in Luxur to be hailed by strangers in the city streets, and feted and fed by the city's nobility. You could say the Circus Imperium was the fulfillment of his life's dream."

"Aye," Conan agreed, "though in the end it killed him—and after none too long a term of glory. Now that he is gone, we must decide about our own future here in Luxur. Can we afford such popularity, when it places us all under the sword? There are bound to be more losses if we stay here,

losses we can ill-afford." He placed an arm around
Sathilda. "I, for one, do not like the choices it
forces a man to make."

"Conan, I can see that you are deeply moved by
the death of our dear friend." Luddhew himself,
speaking in a fatherly way, came over to clasp
Conan's shoulder and press against him in a formal
embrace. "I pray you, do not let it distract your
thinking overmuch. Most of us are not, after all, in
such great danger as Roganthus placed himself.
And the success of our concessions and exhibits
here at the stadium is most gratifying. I would not
worry excessively about losing more of our troupe.
We are, after all, skilled performers."

"You may not see yourselves in danger." Looking pensive, Conan turned from his employer to regard the rest of the troupe. "But I have been privy
to everything that transpires in the arena and even
in the streets. Whether I can go on as before . . ."

"Come, now, Conan, you are an indispensable
part of the show!" Luddhew moved forward once
again to comfort his star, though the Cimmerian
edged back from the circus-master's fatherly embrace. "If you feel that you are not getting ample
enough compensation, I'm sure we can work
something out. But then," he finished, "perhaps it
is best if we discuss such matters another time,
when we are all less pained and distraught."

From the ring of observers, the young knife-
thrower Phatuphar spoke up. "If you need another
gladiator to serve in your stead, Conan, or to fill in
for poor Roganthus's loss, I am ready to try. I
know my skill with blades would serve me well in

the arena. Jana and I"—he indicated the young
wife who clung affectionately to his waist—"will
soon be enlarging our family. We feel we can use
the extra wealth and reputation that such a move
would bring."

"How thoughtful of you, Phatuphar!" Luddhew
went off to confer with the young performer, taking leave of Conan, who remained sullen and
aloof. The rest of the group began to disperse, re-
morseful and uncomfortable at the sad occasion.
But Sathilda turned to her mate with an air of real
concern.

"Conan, I know this is a dismal situation, bury-
ing our dear friend. But you have not been the
same, I can tell, since you went running from the
stadium into the Red Priests' crypt. I ask you, what
enchantment did they work upon you? Did they
place you under some baneful spell?"

Conan, regarding her glumly, did not reply. And
Sathilda did not press the matter.

After they had parted, a messenger who claimed
to be from Udolphus found Conan. He led him
around the back of the Circus and up one of the ascending rampways, to a worksite at the north end
of the stadium, where a new balcony was already
being raised. Workers swarmed through scaffolding, pouring gray, pebbly flowstone into wooden
forms that had been braced up atop tall columns.

Surveying the work from above was Commodorus. He smiled and waved a welcoming hand
as Conan, leaving the messenger behind, came
striding up the ledges to join him.

"See how happily inspired this latest design is."

The Tyrant waved with a regal flourish toward the toiling slaves. "It gives the audience a loftier view and shades those who sit in the old seats below. On the whole it increases the paid seating capacity of this sector by one-half. Best of all, we are now using an improved conglomeration that my engineers adapted from the ancient Stygian formula for tomb-seals. It enables us to mold, pour, and finish a new superstructure in a matter of days, without waiting out long delays in stonecutting, fitting, and transport. I am personally pressing the work forward to be ready in time for the next Circus." He flashed a dazzling smile at Conan. "That way, all the more citizens will be able to witness my reordination.

"The timing must be flawless," he went on, "for I want to be able to make my final turn in the arena and impress the crowd one last time before ascending to my new, higher office. We have a truly astonishing spectacle planned for this coming show—something quite unprecedented, I promise you. Our workmen will be kept toiling day and night to bring it off on schedule." He pointed down to the flat oval, where more work crews were busy raking and carting sand and prying up floor panels to alter the arena's layout. "Needless to say, I am counting on you to guard my back as we agreed. So I rely on you to recover from this head wound, whatever the mishap was that you incurred yesterday, and be ready at my service."

Solemnly, Conan heard him out. "This scrape"—he touched the bandage where it crossed his forehead—"is nothing. Tender, to be sure, but no more. And my chest is all but healed." He patted the taut, knitting flesh below his armpit. "Even so, Tyrant, I cannot say that I am as sure of my place in the arena as I was. I may not be able to do your fighting for you—"

Commodorus grinned broadly. "The Set Priests have had their way with you, I can tell." He clapped a hand on Conan's shoulder. "I foresaw as much when you went charging into their den yesterday. They are a glib crew, well-practiced at manipulating the minds of simple honest folk, with scarcely any need for weapons or gold. Unfortunately, they have turned their backs on the manly virtues and skills that get things done in the real world of affairs. So they are ill-prepared to stand against men like me." He laughed in good-natured condolence. "Just rest a few days, get yourself back into shape, and soon their pusilanimous teachings will fade."

Conan levelly regarded the Tyrant. "Mayhap so, Commodorus. But what the priests showed me was sore troubling. I give you notice, I will not be ready to kill at your bidding."

The tyrant laughed again. "Nonsense, Conan. I hired you for defense, not murder. Remember, I intend to reap all the glory myself and keep you in the background. I only need a bodyguard, and a discreet, inconspicuous one at that.

"You know, things will change greatly in Luxur after this next Circus. I will then be in a position to move decisively with regard to the temple—or, if they should first try to unseat me, I can launch an open rebellion. My support from the people is strong enough. Nekrodias has let me grow too strong—the death-grip of these priests on the citizens of Luxur is near an end." He waved a casual hand. "But to carry through such great projects, I will have to stay alive. And that depends partly on you, Cimmerian." He peered jovially into Conan's face. "Remember, we have already struck our deal."

Conan nodded. "Since I have accepted your gold, I will carry out the task we agreed on."

"Very good." Commodorus grinned in assent. "Then I will be finished with the arena—you can be, too, if you wish it. But that does not mean you must leave my employ. There will be plenty of opportunities for strong, clever types under my new reign. Your prowess and popularity in the Circus will stand you in good stead, once you emerge from this current funk of yours, as I am sure you will."

After taking his leave of Commodorus, Conan spent the remainder of the day in household tasks—such as running the cat Qwamba in the exercise field—and in silent contemplation. That evening he took Sathilda in a chariot to Namphet's pub. But the place was quiet, having been abandoned by Dath's crew, and in any case, the wine did not inflame him as it usually did. After a morose hour or two, they returned home to an early bed.

The next morning his first visit was to Ignobold in the Temple Infirmary. The gladiator, though still anemic from the loss of his blood, was awake and capable of drinking soup and watered wine, so

Conan was told. On approaching his pallet, the Cimmerian was surprised to see that his eyes as well as his chest were bandaged. Kneeling down beside him, Conan asked him why.

" 'Tis because of the sand-grains that rascal Baphomet cast into them," Ignobold rasped, stirring weakly on his back. "That is the only way he ever managed to sword me, by a cowardly ruse."

"You are unable to see, then? Here, sip some of this," Conan added, spooning the broth he had been given to Ignobold's lips. "Do the priests say you will recover your sight?"

"Why, certainly," the prone man said after slurping down the first spoonful. "The gods have brought me this far, have they not? Would they withdraw their patronage now, before I am able to gain my revenge?"

"You will recover fully, then. That is good. Here, drink."

"Yes, Conan, and mark my words: I will be back in the arena by midsummer, where I will make myself a greater and more feared champion than ever."

"Here, take some more," Conan gently urged him. "Tell me, do you not think it a great miracle that you were spared after such a grievous wound?"

"Yes. It is very painful, but the gods work in mysterious ways. What keeps me alive now is the sacred hope of putting a sword through that gutter-whelp Baphomet and repairing my reputation, much as you and these priests repaired this sundered body. I have heard that you helped, Conan, and I thank you for it. Conan, can I ask one more favor?"

"Of course, Ignobold. Here now, take this."

"Do not slay him, Conan. Leave Baphomet for me. It is asking much, I know, not to kill him—but do you think you can do it?"

"Here, finish this. Yes, I'll give you my promise. You are growing tired, and I must be off." He patted the invalid's head. "Rest now, and do not fear. I'll not slay Baphomet."

After taking his leave of the frail, feverish patient and trying to dismiss the man's ravings, Conan did not feel any more at peace in his own mind. His encounter with the holy heretic in the arena, and later his bruising, dreamlike sojourn with the Red Priests in the crypt, had made a deep impression on him. It now appeared to him that the daily affairs of ordinary mortals were enwrapped in a tight, inextricable knot of murderous folly.

He was preoccupied thuswise all that day and the next, less than energetic in his sport and exercise, and scarcely regarded as boon company by his fellow gladiators and circus troupers. It was with dull resignation that he received a personal summons from the High Primate of the Temple of Set, the Priest Nekrodias.

The eunuch who carried the note led him directly to the Grand Temple where it brooded at the base of the same hill that upheld the Circus Imperium. They passed first through the Circus grounds, then into a series of viny courts and gardens where unseen shapes slithered away through the greenery underfoot. There followed more lavish vistas of priestly pavilions and dwellings set amid the verdure of the hillside. But, to approach the vast temple pile itself, the eunuch led Conan out to the paved city boulevard, up the broad steps, and in through the splendid façade.

The massive front pillars were carved from veined serpentine and etched with delicate scales to resemble the trunks of mighty reptiles. The polished stone gallery itself echoed vast and empty; for this was no day of worship, and at other times the public shunned the place. Dimly at the back, lit by the yellow snaking flames of oiled braziers, there loomed the vast golden spiral of the snake-idol, coiled as if to dart its fanged head down upon any who dared trespass. The red faceted gems that formed its great eyes were, undoubtedly, too heavy for a single man to lift.

But all this made only a fleeting impression on Conan, trailing along resignedly in his glum state. He followed his guide past the twin altars and the pediment of the vast idol, through a spangled curtain hung at one side of the back wall, and into a smaller but darker-vaulted chamber that looked to be the sanctum sanctorum, the private retreat of the temple's master.

"Come, foreigner, and stand before me. My eyes are not so keen as those of Father Set out there in the forecourt."

At the summons and eunuch's mute urging, Conan followed the beck of a pale, skeletal-looking finger around a high-backed ebony chair. He went before the broad table where Nekrodias, by the light of two green tapers, scraped his serpent-fang pen on a parchment scroll. The primate, his shoulders hunched forward under his stole of yellow snakeskin, finished writing in crabbed Stygian glyphs and looked up to meet Conan's gaze.

The archpriest, seen this closely, gave an impression of imponderable age. He could have been centuries old—in truth, there was no real reason why not, Conan reflected, given the church elders' arcane learning and close personal servitude to immortal gods. The primate's bald, cowled skull, his seamed and wizened face, his fleshless frame and gray, lusterless glance made it seem to Conan as if those bony fingers might only recently have peeled away their owner's yellowed mummy-wraps.

"Well—Conan the Slayer, so you are called. A new arrival, but a closely watched and well-regarded one, in spite of the wounds that have impaired your standing and performance of late." The priest flicked an ink-stained finger up at the bandage that still sagged loose around Conan's scalp. "Your prowess and fighting spirit have gained you notice in high places, and you have been entertained by notables other than myself."

"So far, I have not found this visit entertaining." Sparring with the priest brought Conan a flicker of his old fighting spirit. "Why have you summoned me here?"

With a creased smile but no laugh, Nekrodias laid aside his pen. "You have been overheard dealing with our ubiquitous Tyrant Commodorus, as well as his alter-ego Udolphus. You have been asked to perform a certain service for him. The temple, too, wishes you to undertake a service, and I am prepared to reward you a hundredfold over what our very generous Tyrant may have offered."

Conan shrugged. "I came to Luxur as an honest vagabond, knowing nothing of the feuds and intrigues between your city's various factions. I have tried, on behalf of my employer Luddhew and my fellow performers, to be open in my dealings— more open and fair than the folk of Luxur have been with us, I might add. Now, having seen so much blood spilled in pointless strife, I do not wish to become mired any more deeply in your rivalries than I already am."

Nekrodias raised his straggling eyebrows in surprise; real or feigned, it gave him an owlish look that was far from flattering. "Is my hearing, then, defective? Is this really Conan speaking, the one they call the Slayer, with an insatiable lust for combat and an eager blade that never rests a full night in its sheath? Is this the far-rumored thief and pillager, who has sifted the ashes of a hundred castles and a dozen cities, and never yet clutched enough gold or woman-flesh to satiate him? Is this the vaunted soldier of fortune standing before me, who does not have enough will to slay Commodorus at my bidding, and very likely make himself the new Tyrant of Luxur?"

Blankly regarding the archpriest, Conan sighed. "I do not know what you have heard of my past, Nekrodias, or what you may have divined through the clouded glass of sorcery. But to kill any man at another's bidding was never my way. I am no assassin."

"Come, Cimmerian, do not indulge your morose whims with me! I happen to know that Manethos, my chief embalmer, has been working his wiles on you. He is a clever fellow, a sly persuader—alas, his view of things is too far from the practical and positive ever to afford him high rank in our temple hierarchy. He may have blunted your edge a bit, true. The death of a friend is sad, and killing those pathetic, misguided idealists we call heretics may not have been a suitable chore for one with your lofty scruples.

"Even so, do not let this momentary fit of despondency ruin your chances. Now is the time for action and commitment! Commodorus is going to fall, regardless. My proposal does not necessarily involve murdering him, but simply letting an accident occur in the arena—where, as I understand it, you are to be his bodyguard. You may as well be close at hand to pick up his Imperial wreath and vestments. An adventuring hero like you may, after all, be just the figurehead we need."

Not regretting the lack of a place to sit, Conan stood solitary before the broad table. "That would be the rankest sort of betrayal. I do not strike a deal with one employer just to sell his carcass to another! Anyway, you claim that Commodorus is bound to fall—you try to overawe me with this mighty antique temple, your vast idols, and your maimed, mute servants—but I have seen your Tyrant's real power in this city, his sway over the people. I have heard your subjects rant and cheer at his appearances in the arena, and snore at yours. I have seen the aqueducts and broad city gates he has built. If Commodorus is so certainly doomed, why not simply refuse to reappoint him—you, who have the power under law?" He flung an arm impulsively aside, experiencing once again a faint flicker of passion. "Further, even if he were sure to die, and if it were true that you would name me as your city's ruler, I would still favor Commodorus! He, at least, has some mote of vision for this city, some thought of improving the lives of its inhabitants, and moving into a time of progress, rather than backward into the dark age of Set!"

"Aha," Nekrodias crowed in triumph, "there at last we have it! You, too, have fallen prey to his impious preachings, like many another credulous fool who believes in the high purpose he proclaims for his rule. He panders to the people's craving for material goods, and expands the Circus to satiate their ever-growing lust for blood! For his upcoming spectacle, did you know, he plans to flood the whole arena from bleacher to bleacher—fill it up with water from his precious aqueducts, launch a fleet of oarships, and fight a mock naval battle with real weapons and victims. He would send hundreds to their doom, while he struts and preens as admiral of the victorious fleet!"

Feeling resigned once again, Conan barely shrugged. "You, too, Nekrodias, have partaken of the arena's excesses, as have I. It has become the lifeblood of Luxur, the throbbing, pumping heart, as Commodorus himself told me. But he plans to leave it all behind."

Finally Nekrodias laughed outright—a grudging, unpleasant sound. "Ah yes, a commendable ideal, to quit the arena—if only our noble Tyrant could afford to! Alas, would it surprise you to know that, of all the touts and bet-fixers, Commodorus himself is the one who draws the biggest profits from arena gambling and keeps all the oddsmakers in his pay? That it was he who decided to feed your rustic circus friends to the wild beasts, and who has routinely ordered your fellow gladiators drugged and killed to inflate his betting-odds? Has he yet mentioned how much graft he skims off his splendid public works ... only to turn around and pay it out in bribes to undermine Stygia's church and noble families? Or how he uses hoodlums to collect his bets and enforces his own schedule of black tariffs on trade and smuggled goods? Does that fit in with your view of our godlike Commodorus?"

Conan, feeling suddenly as if the weight of all Luxur were being levered onto his shoulders, turned and strode for the door while he still could. "Nekrodias," he tossed back over his shoulder, "I do not care if your city's Tyrant is a living monster, a worse devil than Set himself! I will not join in your nefarious schemes, nor aid him further in his. I tell you, I am done with killing! It has lost its savor for me."

As memorable as Conan's encounter with the Primate Nekrodias was, it was not the one that made the deepest impression on him that day. For, returning home along the broad street which led past the temple portico, he encountered a goodshawker plying the crowds in a market plaza. The voice was familiar at first . . . and then the face, though it was attached to a body whose size made its owner hard to locate amid the milling passersby. At length he saw the diminutive peddler—Jemain, his youthful city guide of old.

"Baubles and trinkets! Pretties for your pretty . . . milady, might you be interested in a fine pendant of purest Argossean jet? A black tear to adorn a snow-white breast? Or you, sire? . . . oof, sorry, a thousand pardons—"

"Hold, Jemain, you need not flee me." Conan kept the urchin from flitting out of sight by seizing a tail of the coat that was also his warehouse—and no shabby coat, either, but a newish one, cut from sturdy cloth interwoven with bright silk threads. As he reeled the lad in, the merchandise jingled gaily where it was pinned inside his roomy coat-flaps. "Come, lad, hold still and tell me how you have been doing. Not too badly, I see."

"No, not badly." While keeping his face downward, the youth glanced warily up at Conan as if to gauge his disposition. "Events have kept me occupied these past days."

"Indeed. You seem to have set yourself up in business."

"Oh yes, to be sure." Growing bolder, Jemain held open his coat. "I carry a line of the finest trinkets and gewgaws. High-quality gemstones imported from the seacoast and set by master craftsmen into the purest alloy—"

"Yes, yes," Conan stalled him off, "I see they are of good quality. You have a sharp eye for counterfeits," he declared solemnly, "as when you recognized our friend Udolphus."

From the flicker of his eyes, Conan could tell that the youth was thinking of bolting again. "Do not worry, Jemain," he reassured the boy, placing a hand on his shoulder. "I can understand why you must have feared to say anything."

Uneasy, the boy blinked up at him. "Most surely, Conan. I would have warned you, if anyone. But to expose someone as powerful as our Tyrant would be far too dangerous . . ." He shook his head in embarrassment.

"His purse must have provided you with a stake for your inventory," Conan observed. "That is good. I think you will go far in business."

Jemain nodded, chastened. "And you have survived the arena—till now, with wounds." Blinking up at his bandaged hero, he almost stammered. "But, Conan, I would caution you—truly, be careful. With all these deaths—"

"I know," Conan said, sparing him further words that he might agonize on later. "The arena is become a more dangerous place, both inside and out. I myself am in far too deeply already. I cannot say what will happen." He patted the boy's shoulder, then released it. "You were wise to get out."

Jemain shrugged. "I was too small a player. In a game with such high stakes, there is no safety for the small bettor."

"We are all small players," Conan assured him.

As a gift for Sathilda, he bought the jet-black pendant from Argos—at a bargain price, so Jemain assured him. Then, bidding the lad farewell, he returned to the Circus grounds.

The next evening Conan never would have stirred himself from Namphet's pub, had not Muduzaya approached him at his solitary keg in the corner. Sathilda had declined to accompany Conan to the deserted tavern, so he sat brooding in silence, taking scarcely more than a desultory whiff of his *arrak*, when the black warrior wrung his shoulder in a heavy hand.

"Conan, I may have found Sesoster for us! He is likely to know something about Halbard's murder as well as my poisoning, so I thought you should come along. I am to meet him at once, at the north end of the Circus stadium. I think he chose the place because it has so many entries and exits."

"Muduzaya," Conan gravely asked, "are you sure you even want to pursue this? It is in the past, after all—Halbard is irretrievably dead, and you have regained your strength. Anyway," he added with a morose glance at his friend, "I misdoubt that you will really want to hear what he has to tell you."

"Nonsense, Conan," the Swordmaster chided, "revenge is not something to be set aside too long! That skulkard Sesoster has been in hiding for days; I finally lured him out by offering a bribe through his manservant, whom I caught in the bazaar. Of course," he added, clapping a hand onto his hilt, "whether he truly deserves an ounce of gold or a cubit of steel is something I will have to decide when I see him—"

"Well enough, Muduzaya," Conan said, rising up resolutely from his keg. "You may need me along to keep you out of trouble. And I too will be interested to hear what account the oddsmaker may give."

So saying, he followed his friend outside to a chariot, and they rumbled off to the city gate. Traveling at brisk speed, they nevertheless made certain to leave the vehicle at the downhill carriage yard. From there they proceeded afoot through the Circus grounds, so as not to attract undue attention.

Even so, the stadium was a-bustle when they arrived. Slave crews trooped in and out of the entry-tunnels, laboring by torchlight to ready the place for the forthcoming extravaganza. City gangs were busy trenching and scaffolding, preparing to divert the aqueducts and flood the pit of the arena. Construction was under way at both ends of the stadium as well: on the north side, a ragtag crew was busy raking and finishing the damp flowstone, where it had been poured into wooden forms to extend the broad viewing-balcony decreed by Commodorus.

As they mounted the stairsteps behind the hulking scaffold, Conan and Muduzaya could see that these toilers were no slaves, but ragged street toughs. They worked under the light of a torch held by none other than Dath. They had not poured the cement themselves, but were reraking it to cover a dead body they had laid into the forms—Sesoster the bookmaker, as Conan managed to see just before the face was covered over.

"You found him before we did," Muduzaya

complained, striding down the bench-rows to Dath. "That was most inconsiderate. We had questions for him."

"Ask away, he will not mind," Dath shrugged to the Swordmaster. "If you want to go to the horse's mouth, Zagar the procurer lies just over there." He pointed to a buttress that was more firmly set. "But I doubt whether, between them, they have much knowledge that I lack."

Muduzaya wrinkled his brow in the torchlight with gradual understanding. "You, then, are involved in the match-fixing and the other dirty dealings here at the Circus? But you are a mere upstart!"

The young ax-fighter stood holding his torch aloft, letting his free hand hang idle by the twin hilts at his belt. "I earned myself a place in the greater organization, true enough, by marshaling these wharf-rats." He nodded at the toughs who waited close at hand. "I think it's safe to say I've shown some skill at it. Of late our fortunes have been good, and our share of the take is proportionally increased. Our territory now extends to this very ground." He indicated the stadium around them.

Moving up behind Muduzaya, Conan spoke dully. "No doubt it was his men who killed Halbard as well. Or else one of the other gangs did it as a favor to him. Apart from their skirmishing and rivalries, they all collect arena bets and serve as leg-breakers and assassins around the town."

"Very true indeed," Dath said, smiling grimly. "All of us are part of the same butcher's-mill—you gladiators in the arena," he explained, "and my lads out in the street, where the work is better-paying and longer-term. All for the civic good, as defined by our leader Commodorus.

"You, in particular, should know that." Dath shot a pointed look at Conan. "Is he not your employer as well?"

Chapter 13

Extravaganza

When the day of the naval spectacle arrived, the city lay in a frenzy of expectation. All of Luxur had been drawn into the project in one way or another, as had countless merchants, officials, and procurers from far districts of the Stygian Empire and neighboring lands.

Aside from those employed in refitting the arena and redirecting the aqueducts, scores of river boatmen from the Canal Wharf were drafted. Their vessels, too, were hauled on caissons through the city to be set afloat on the blue waters of the flooded Circus Imperium. There were shipwrights and armorers from both banks of the Styx and even the far-off seacoast, imported here to build the one vessel too large to be trundled through city streets or hauled in through the arena gates. This massive construction was Commodorus's flagship, an authentic-looking war galley equipped with barrage towers, double oar-banks, and a heavy bronze ram.

To man the oars, slaves were obtained by the boatload from ports up and down the river. Ordinary servants and field hands would not do, for the rowers had to possess the skill to drive the vessels credibly and to ram and fight other ships at close quarters. Where possible, real naval officers and marine troops had been drafted, at least to fill out the crew and command of the flagship and its small accompanying fleet. It was considered essential that the Tyrant's fighting force put forward a good appearance, with full military regalia including banners, bugles, and kettledrums.

In the matter of the opposing fleet, an equal degree of attention and expense was lavished, but in a somewhat different way. Up and down the shores of the Styx and the Western Sea, brigs and stockades were scoured for the most infamous pirates, smugglers, and mutineers currently in captivity. They, too, were imported to Luxur to serve as fodder for the gladiators and the Tyrant's fleet. They would sail aboard small, fast ships with crews filled in from the dregs of the local jails. Since these sea thieves included some of the shrewdest navigators and fiercest fighters ever to bestride the waves, there was no great concern that the sea-battle would be one-sided.

Even so, to further spice the pot of sea chowder, the beast-gatherers had been set to work. From the shallow inland estuaries of the River Styx, rare freshwater sharks had been trapped and transported upstream by the bargeful. These good-sized, fast-moving scavengers, zealous man-eaters when the opportunity arose, were to be set loose in the arena's waters to dramatize the perils of open-sea battling. The crocodiles and river snakes that had become familiar stars of the Circus Imperium were to be employed as well.

To see this grand spectacle, crowds swarmed about the Circus and clung to the stadium gates from dusk of the previous day. They spent the night and morn before the exhibition in a sort of dizzy saturnalia, drinking, dancing, and singing bawdy songs, but never moving far from their cherished places in the entry line. Luddhew's performers, too, put on special early shows. Moving among the revelers with their wild beasts, bounding acrobats, and gambling and fortune-telling and health-tonic pitches, they were able to reap substantial profits even before the scheduled opening.

Needless to say, the city guards were called out in force. Additional help in controlling the mob was obtained from common street hoodlums. Under the direction of Dath and lesser gang-leaders, wearing headbands and formed up as pseudo-military units, they commanded swift obedience from the populace. In all, counting the spectators, performers, athletes, street vendors, enforcers, servants, administrators, and prisoners, it was likely that a large majority of Luxur's population was present in the clamoring crowd atop Temple Hill in the early hours of Reordination Day.

Conditions were rendered somewhat inconvenient when, toward morning, most of the gutters and ditches leading from the amphitheater became awash with water. The aqueducts, having once been diverted to flood the arena and keep it filled, could not easily be shut off. Therefore a continuous stream, overflowing the structure's caulked, reinforced gates and seeping out through leaks in the masonry, swirled away underfoot. It kept people from sleeping in the streets and was rumored to have caused minor flooding in the tenement districts, but was not seen as a serious problem.

At midmorning the stadium was opened, and control of the crowd immediately became more difficult. The iron gates were chained half-shut to keep the mobs from pushing through, and a corridor had to be cleared by the city guard to make way for the sedan chairs and chariots of prosperous latecomers. As the regular seat-holders trooped in, the anxiety to win a place waxed all the greater, because no one was really sure how much additional seating capacity had been added since the last show.

In short order even the newly expanded seats were filled to overflowing, and the gates were barred and double-locked. There still remained thousands crowding just outside the amphitheater, eager to be near the spectacle, if only to hear the cries of the thrilled observers. Luckily, as ever at these mass functions, there were individuals who posted themselves in the tunnels and archways to announce what happened inside. Passing along the news second- or third-hand, they repeated and embroidered the events for eager listeners.

Inside the stadium, words could scarcely have

conveyed the astonishment and splendor that awaited the audience. There, stretching from rail to rail of the broad arena, was a glittering inland sea complete with rocks, reefs, and beaches. There was even an islet or two adorned with palm trees, with crocodiles sunning themselves on the banks, and fin-backed sharks flitting smoothly between. True, the waters spread flat and still as any sheltered inland lagoon, rippled only by the lazy swimmers and the wavelets of the rapidly filling amphitheater. But soon they would be churned to fury by the oars of the two mighty fleets, which sat, teeming with crew and bright with sails and pennants, at opposite ends of the oval.

Conan, making his way in through an entry-tunnel with the other gladiators, had to blink in amazement at the spectacle the bright morning presented: the sparkling blue water, the massed fleets, the bustle of brilliantly costumed sailors descending the gangplanks—and above them, the mad panoply of spectators spreading through the amphitheater, crowding from the tunnels and flowing out along the ledges. The stadium itself had an utterly different appearance now that broad balconies sloped forward to shade large areas of seating on all four sides. With eager spectators swarming ahead to occupy the choicest vantage points, the impression was one of frenetic, intensely concentrated human energy.

Conan pushed his way through the crowd of costumed, armed, and armored fighters and sailors. Those costumes, however flashy, could cost a life; a chestplate or a pair of greaves would swiftly

weight a man down to the bottom of the lagoon—
which, indeed, might be a mercy in a sea full of
sharks and crocs. It so happened that Conan himself wore next to nothing—just a kirtle around his
waist and sandals that could easily have been
kicked off had he wished to take part in the naval
battle. He had generally worn much the same costume when he sailed as Amra the Pirate in years
past; only this time he lacked even a sword.

Ahead of him he spied the one he sought:
Commodorus, making his way down from the tunnel in a wedge of his guards. The Tyrant had been
hard to find in the last few days—hiding out, perhaps, or devising new schemes to tighten his hold
on Luxur. Conan had hoped to confront him and
fling his job back in his face, but the fellow had
been unreachable.

"Commodorus!"

Coming up from behind, Conan tried to push
through to him. The guards closed ranks; but, on
seeing that their leader recognized the intruder and
that he was unarmed, they let him pass.

"Conan, timely as always! And your head is
mended, I see."

The Tyrant was vigorous and alert-looking in a
trim naval toga, with his strong-toothed smile
polished to perfection, and his curly golden hair
encircled by a laurel wreath.

"Is this not a stunning festival we have put together? I look forward to fighting across the surging decks with you at my side."

"Commodorus, in sooth, I did not even intend to
be here. I wanted to give you back your gold and

begone"—he reached to the purse tucked in his waistband—"but since you relied on me to protect you, there is one fact you ought to know. The Priest Nekrodias sought to hire me to kill you ... here today, during the arena games."

"Nekrodias? Wanting to kill me?" The Tyrant laughed heartily. "Why, Conan, that is scarcely a surprise! And during the games, the time I am to be most vulnerable ... dear fellow, that is why I have you here! That is certainly no reason to change our plans."

"I am sick of the arena, and of killing," Conan said. "I want to quit the Circus and leave Luxur."

"Nonsense, man! You performers are all temperamental types, I know. But wait here, just one more moment while I conduct my business, and we will talk further. I'm sure I can make you see reason."

Splitting off with his guards from Conan, Commodorus strode out to the rim of his personal viewing-terrace, beyond the shade of the soaring overhang. After waiting for cheers and salutes from the still-moving crowd to subside, he began to speak.

"Citizens of the Imperial Seaport of Luxur, I bid you welcome ..."

After a fresh burst of laughter and cheering, he spoke on. Conan, meanwhile, turned and moved away, intending to leave the stadium without further talk. However, it proved impossible to force his way against the press of the crowd. He had to stand in an eddy out of the main stream. And wait, and think.

He thought of Manethos . . . he had felt drawn to the priest in recent days. But he had not sought him out, because he did not want to get him slain. He gazed down at the watery arena. There would be no Red Priests servicing this match. The Gate of the Dead was barricaded and caulked. Any fallen heroes in the sea-fight would be attended by sharks and crocodiles rather than embalmers—just as acceptable an offering to Father Set, no doubt. Where was Manethos now? he wondered—not very likely idling in this vast, unruly mob.

His eyes roved to the fleets massed at the near and far ends of the arena. The Tyrant's flagship resembled a gaudy joke—a top-heavy, shallow-bottomed, trellised and beribboned barge, whose towering sails had no conceivable use in the windless arena, other than to hamper the oarsmen's efforts. Such a craft would never stand a moment before the gusts and surges of the Vilayet Sea, much less the Western one. Yet, with its rams, its artillery, and its covering force of a half dozen smaller boats, it could prove victorious in this flat pond.

The pirate fleet, already manned and waiting at the far end, was a more realistic-looking assemblage, but far less likely to prevail. The slaves and felons at the oars, so Conan had heard, were chained to their benches. That would deprive the commanders of the bulk of their offensive force and make it well nigh impossible to capture enemy prizes.

The ships themselves, small swift cruisers, were ideal pirate craft. On the open waves, or in shallow river estuaries, they would have been impossible to catch. But here in the bayless oval, sealed in like cattle in a slaughter-pen, they would be hunted down in short order, their crews driven under the ram or else put to the sword.

The Imperial warships, by comparison, were crewed with gladiators and able sea fighters. The trained rowers in the oar-banks, though unchained, were also unarmed and would not take a willing hand in the fighting. So the match would not be wholly one-sided and not unduly brief. It was well-calculated to reflect glory on Commodorus, as commander of the flagship.

Conan reflected idly while penned in by the crowd, listening to the Tyrant's speechmaking give way to that of Nekrodias. A shame it was that the convict fleet was so far away. It was rumored to contain many noted pirates; there were probably some he would have recognized from his old days on the Black Coast, steering the ship *Tigress* with his pirate mistress Belit.

The decks of the Imperial ships, certainly, contained many gladiators and others he knew. Scanning the rows of oarsmen facing aft on the giant flagship, Conan caught sight of a face he recognized—or thought he did, just possibly. The man resembled someone he had seen only recently ... except for that unlikely mop of thick black hair.

Then Conan's jaw clenched taut. It was Xothar. There could be no doubt. Why, then, was the shaven-headed wrestler wearing a wig? It was hardly one that added to the colorfulness of his sparse costume.

As a disguise, then. To pass as a harmless, weaponless oarsman just long enough to get near the flagship's chief, Commodorus.

Of all the killers in the arena, Conan had no doubt that the temple-fighter was deadliest. If he could stifle a man to death in mere moments, the Constrictor could snap a neck in less time. Commodorus ought to be warned.

Yet there went the Tyrant now, having forgotten Conan or blithely assumed his participation—moving through the press of the crowd, from his podium down to the flagship's gangplank. He was escorted by uniformed guards; but they, in their helmets and armor, would not likely be going aboard ship.

In forcing his way through the throng Conan's height gave him an advantage, as did his gladiator's build. The spectators in his way, feeling themselves thrust aside from behind, scarcely had time to curse him—or recognize him as a champion and beg for his handclasp—before he pushed past.

Striding down the ledge-rows, he arrived at the gangplank. Commodorus was already stepping aboard the flagship's high poop. The eunuch Memtep, recognizing Conan, bowed with a courtly flourish and ushered him through the ring of guards.

No sooner had Conan stepped across the flagship's rail than the plank was jerked away from under his heels. He was in the fight now, in his place as the Tyrant's secret bodyguard, whether he liked it or not. Commodorus, unfortunately, was already passing down into the oarship's waist—

heading forward with a handful of officers to stand
in the bow, as no true sea-captain would. As he
went, smiling and waving for the benefit of his
ship's crew and the broader arena, he passed the
bench where Xothar sat, crouching there in the in-
board seat.

The bewigged wrestler did not look up. There
would have been no point in it; he would not make
his move until later, in the confusion of battle. But
as Conan proceeded past Xothar, intending to station himself behind Commodorus, he fixed the
wrestler with a direct, unflinching stare—and saw
it returned, the Constrictor's oil-sheened face half
creasing in a smile. Now there would be no misun-
derstanding.

Meanwhile, the order to dip oars was given, and
a kettledrum began its steady thumping. Wooden
shafts creaked in their tholes as, with the first
stroke, the ship's deck surged forward underfoot.
Simultaneously, from the far end of the arena,
there echoed a clanking of heavy chain being
drawn through eyebolts. That, undoubtedly, was
the sound of the pirate fleet being unleashed to
fight.

On the brink of combat, it occurred to Conan to
wonder if Sathilda was watching him. He had not
spoken much with her in recent days, or tried to
explain his true state of mind. She was still
wrapped up in the glamour and success of the circus and the sadness of Roganthus's death—closer,
in many ways, to her brethren in Luddhew's troupe
than she was to him. The two shared their bed and
routine daily tasks such as the care and feeding of

the tiger; but she busied herself ever more with athletic workouts and parties given at the arena by rich patrons, while he was content to brood in solitude.

Still she cared for him, as he well knew. And there, high above in the shaded seats that belonged to her noble friend Alcestias, he thought he could distinguish her seated form. Yes, indeed it was she; for there beside her was a deeper patch of shadow, a black reclining bulk which could only be the night-cat Qwamba.

If she had noticed him before, she could scarcely now distinguish him on the ship's crowded foredeck. The beak above the ram was full of gilded officers, with Commodorus strutting and preening at the fore. Just behind on either side the barrage towers loomed, with a dozen slingers and archers perched in each one. They were skeletal frameworks armored only with stiff, painted hides, but they were tall; it would take massed projectile-fire to clear them. To Conan they represented a handy bottleneck, making it hard for anyone to pass from amidships to the bow without going between. He stationed himself in the narrow passage at the middle, a few paces behind Commodorus, ready to intercept Xothar when the time came.

Turning his attention back to the approaching enemy fleet, he saw that, indeed, they had mustered forth in full strength. One ship in particular, the largest and stoutest ram-galliot, was well ahead of the others and rowing at double speed. It held the centermost position opposite the flagship, and looked to be fencing for a ram.

In response to the enemy's evident boldness, Commodorus turned and barked a command to his second. The bosun blew several short, sharp blasts on his whistle, and of a sudden the hortator's drumbeats accelerated. With the faster stroking of the oars the ship leapt forward, white foam beginning to bubble over the bows.

Conan glanced back to make sure that Xothar was still huddled in place, pulling his oar with the rest. He was surprised to see, however, that the other ships of the Imperial force trailed quite a way behind; some, indeed, seemed to be just getting under way. Evidently Commodorus had not adequately drilled his fellow captains as to the sailing order. The flagship with its triple oar-banks and picked slaves, even rowing against the burden of slack sails, was probably capable of making far better speed than its fellows. Very likely its commander, knowing his ship to be heavily crewed and well-armed, had fewer qualms about sailing into the middle of a pirate host. So the admiral had drawn well ahead of his fleet, perhaps unwisely.

Feeling a qualm of uncertainty, Conan gazed forward again at the opposing ship. It came on undaunted—and now that it was nearer, he noticed a curious fact. It was crammed with condemned slaves or captured river-dregs, able rowers who toiled earnestly at their single-banked oars. But on the narrow central deck there were almost no fighters—just a pair of striding, ill-clad ruffians who flailed long whips and kept the oars churning faithfully to the beat of a wooden clapper. There were no boarders, no defenders—they had presumably been placed aboard other ships in the pirate fleet. But why? Was the lone ship a spoiler—meant only to ram and hole the flagship, or rake away some of its forward oars? That would cripple her, true—but a single hole could soon be patched, and the big ship's crew would instantly grapple and overrun the smaller one, giving the Imperials a numerical advantage that would ultimately doom the pirates.

Then, of a sudden, a simpler and more menacing possibility took shape in Conan's mind. He grunted in rapid comprehension, and drew in a breath to shout a warning to Commodorus—

But already it was too late. At that moment another order was barked out, more blasts sounded from the bosun's whistle, and the tempo of the drum accelerated yet again to full ram speed. The creaking, cursing efforts of the oar-crews raised a tumult, while in the stadium above, the massed watchers began muttering and shouting in anticipation.

Surging forward at breathless speed, the flagship closed with the pirate galley. Now was the time for a seasoned captain to guide his ship skillfully, issuing sharp orders to the helmsmen and the hortator astern, or possibly even using hand-signals and bellowing commands to his rowers. Admiral Commodorus was riding in the bows, so this responsibility was left to a petty officer. But as it happened, the ship they were stalking did not even have steersmen manning the tiller-oars, so the result was the same. The flagship drove straight in toward the racing pirate's bow, and a likely doom.

Here lay defeat in victory, so Conan could foretell. The pirate scow, heavy and well-built, would foul the flagship's ram and halt her dead in the water. The weary oar-crews, trained and capable as they might be, would still have no easy time backing the big ship clear of its skewered rival. Meanwhile the other pirate galleys, following fast on the decoy's wake, would race ahead to outflank and surround the ungainly bireme. Thick with armed men, they would board her from all sides. This was their best chance of taking her by storm, six small ships against a single great one. The pirates, hardened sea bandits desperate for their lives, would fall on the arena fighters and officers, disregarding the unarmed rowers. Arrow-flights from the barrage towers would be blocked to sternward by the fluttering, ill-considered sails.

The fight ahead would be fierce; swift, too, and decisive. The remainder of the Imperial fleet, struggling to catch up, would arrive too late, and might even fear to close in and battle the pirates in their new, captured flagship.

From the tight, fast-racing wedge of enemies Conan looked back to the ill-arrayed stragglers of his own fleet. There would be no need, he saw, to defend Commodorus against Xothar's lethal embrace; the Tyrant would be killed or humiliated far more effectively by his chosen arena adversaries. He turned to warn him regardless. . . .

Then the two oarships struck. With a grinding and splintering of timbers, a shuddering lurch and a sudden upwelling of screams, the big ship's ram drove through the hull of the lone pirate craft. The

bronze ram-sheave tore in just behind the galley's
own beak and did not punch a neat hole; instead,
striking at a flat angle, it ground its way several
man-lengths down the stricken ship's keel, levering
apart timbers and opening a huge rent in the
for'ard hull.

Immediately water poured into the pirate. She
settled swiftly onto the flagship's ram, bearing
the forepart of the larger ship down in the water.
The impact of the mighty ship grinding and scraping to a halt hurled officers and fighters to their
knees and rowers from their benches. Simultaneously, ill-aimed arrows from marksmen in the barrage towers swept the pirate deck, slaughtering a
few rowers but missing the pair of overseers.
Conan saw the looks on their swarthy, unshaven
faces as they picked themselves up and ran astern
to hide; their expressions revealed no fear, but
rather sly triumph.

The stadium crowd looked on, rapt and silent at
the moment of collision. They saw the big ship's
ram smash into the galley; they saw it tear through
row upon row of the pirate's oar-banks, crushing
helpless men along with the timbers they sat on.
When water fountained up before the flagship's
bow, it frothed red; and where the victim's hull
gaped open, pinkish swirling plumes blossomed
forth into the pale tides of the Circus Imperium.

At this sight, a trembling roar commenced in the
great amphitheater. Promptly it swelled into a shattering, thunderous stamping and shrieking of applause, a massive primal frenzy in recognition of
fresh-spilled blood.

The sound was unnerving, even to a hardened arena veteran like Conan as he hauled himself up from the tangle of men and weapons in the bow of the flagship. What was most frightening about the noise was that, from its nightmarish crescendo, it did not diminish. Instead the sustained, shuddering roar was amplified by deeper and more widespread tremors and outcries. Once Conan had braced himself against one of the barrage towers and looked up from the ship's sloping deck, he understood why.

Under the leaping, stamping fury of the crowd, the new construction that had been added to the giant amphitheater could not hold. On the west side of the stadium, lying along the street-front, the largest of the great stone balcones was leaning and buckling with the sharp grating rumble of a mountain-face giving way. To the shouting, flailing horror of its occupants—even as they sprang up from their ledges and fought one another to get clear—it collapsed beneath them with a shuddering roar.

The thunder of falling stone fused with shouts and screams from all parts of the stadium—most particularly those underneath the massive, plummeting architecture. The shattering din gathered and funneled together in a single voice, a havoc that drummed madly on the waters of the artificial sea, then rebounded skyward.

Amid the ear-wrenching turmoil, the wreckage of the crushed balcony smashed the understructure of the stadium and slumped forward in a single massive avalanche. It plunged into the man-made lake, sending a giant wave sweeping toward the ships locked in combat in the middle of the arena.

CHAPTER 14
Survival Games

Outside the Circus Imperium, the masses unable to gain admission to the spectacle brought an air of hushed festivity to the surrounding streets. They clustered together in informal crowds with their attention focused loosely on the stadium, chatting and speculating on events under way inside the lofty walls. Gnawing fruit and pastry obtained from street vendors, they followed every rise and fall of crowd-murmurs from within the immense pile. With proprietary concern about the welfare of their bets, they listened to shouted reports from criers located atop the circus rim and in the mobbed entry-tunnels. "Now Commodorus boards his flagship," they were told. "The Imperial fleet is aweigh. Now the chief pirate ship attacks our Tyrant's vessel."

Not long after that last announcement, they heard the eerie murmur of applause rise to a thunderous roar, albeit strangely muted from within the stadium shell. Thrown upward to the sky and bounced back down, the tumult was nevertheless great enough to make the very cobblestones quiver underfoot.

"The flagship has spiked the pirate's bow," the cry came forth, almost drowned out by the applause. "A victory, a noble triumph!"

So great was the excitement that the crowd before the stadium burst likewise into wild cheering, madly elated over events they could not see. Their eyes were all on the Circus, their ears greedy for more reports and clues; but they were astonished to see the massive structure itself quake and tremble against the sky, as if its stone and mortar had been transmuted to quivering, excitable flesh. They heard a breaking, shuddering noise with repercussions deep in the earth. Meanwhile, the eerie sighing of the arena crowd rose in pitch from enthusiasm to a wail of fear.

To the groundlings' amazement they saw the great pile begin to dismantle itself, the plastered archways of the high façade detaching and dropping into the crowded court. Dust-plumes issued from the sloping tunnels, obscuring swift cascades of stony debris that drove out over the close-packed crowd. Ever-increasing shocks within the amphitheater caused a broad section of the street-front to swell outward, then fall in on itself in a chaos of rubble and plaster dust.

Standing dumbstruck in their places outside the

stadium gate, the onlookers then saw a more dreadful sight. For, within the fallen rubble there was a stirring and a shifting, as of some unthinkably huge beast awakening. From crevices in the still-smoking wreckage, dark tendrils emerged . . . and spread, and surged and sprayed over stone and mortal obstacles, as questing water found its way forth out of the ruin. The massive collapse inside the amphitheater had undoubtedly ruptured the wall of the flooded stadium; now the vast interior lake, vexed to mad restlessness, sought an exit.

The threat to the watchers was intense and immediate. Even as they screamed and turned to run, slipping and tumbling on the already wet cobbles, the torrent poured forth in full wrath behind them. Stone wreckage and fleeing bodies in the fenced courtyard were thrust forward and aside—driven up against the iron gates, then borne over and down along with them as the surging flood refused to be penned in. Unchecked in its rush, the wall of water drove outward into the streets, overtaking fresh multitudes and rolling them under, or else hurling them terrifyingly forward with its furious rush.

Those who managed to resist the first wave—clinging in trees and high barred windows, or kept afloat in the shallower eddies—were met with delirious and dreadful sights. For, along with the gray turbid water and the trundling stones that swept forth out of the arena, there were other less wholesome debris. Mummies of dead gladiators, fallen from the crumbled niches in the Circus wall, proved dry and buoyant in the flood—more so than the pliant, boneless dead already mangled in court-yard and stadium. And too, aside from mummies and the freshly drowned, there were less identifi-able and well-preserved remains, those of petty cheats and criminals informally interred in the sta-dium's walls.

From the rift in the arena, the torrent spread down the streets on the Temple Hill's flank. Drowning thousands in their flight, it washed countless others back to their flooded tenements at the foot of the hill. Along the way it filled the cel-lars and walled gardens of rich estates, populating them with sea-predators and deadly reptiles, and gouged hillside lanes into death-sewers banked with wrack and corpses.

While at its source atop the hill, as many knew, the fount of death flowed undiminished. The city's aqueducts, redirected for the sake of the great spectacle, gushed relentlessly forth, striving to refill the Circus Imperium even as the raging cata-clysm sought to empty it.

The great wave driven by the collapsing ma-sonry pile swept straight across the flooded arena. Gathering puny ships before it like windblown chaff, it instantly capsized most of the heavily armed Imperial fleet and swamped the lighter pi-rates. The flagship, largest of the lot, was torn free of its scuttled foe and hurled violently to starboard. After a giddy rush atop the fanged wave, the hulk slammed with a crushing impact against the far wall of the arena. Falling askew like a discarded toy, it hung there in a tangle of broken spars and slumped rigging.

The carnage among the rowers was fearful. The portside oars were flailed and levered in their oarports like titans' clubs by the pressure of the water outside; moments later, the starboard oars rammed and smashed inward upon collision with the stone wall. The splintering oar-helves snapped men's spines and drove straight through their bodies like spears. Most of the fighting-crew were swept instantly overboard by the crushing torrent; others, knocked senseless by the shattering impact, slipped quietly into the flooded bilges to drown where they lay.

Conan, soaked and battered but shielded from the worst of the havoc by the sagging wreckage of the barrage towers, appeared to be the only one left alive in the fore of the ship. Untangling himself from the debris, he saw that, amid utter chaos, there could be little hope of a coordinated rescue. It was every man for himself. Gazing at the ruin, Conan fleetingly wondered what the priest Manethos would have done.

As he dragged himself sternward to the mainmast, it was across inert bodies. Seizing hold of a tangled net of rigging, he hauled himself up hand over hand toward the rim of the arena.

Above, the cataclysm was far from ended. Both stadium balconies adjacent to the toppled one, weakened by the shocks to the arena's structure and the sudden, impulsive movement of the crowds swarming on top, had begun to sag and lean. As Conan watched dully, the northernmost structure slowly, agonizingly, gave way.

Crumbling with horrid deliberation, it slumped like a leisurely avalanche onto throngs of scrabbling, fleeing, tumbling spectators. Most of the debris, luckily or not, fell straight downward; its grinding flow halted at the railed edge of the arena, though some wreckage cascaded slowly into the water in a spray of muddy, bloody splashes.

Thus the collapse did not generate a second giant wave. But it was plain that, as a result of the damage to the amphitheater, the flooded oval sea had begun to drain out. The level of the restless, surging water did not noticeably fall, but clumps of cloudy silt and floating debris ... and struggling bodies, with hungry water-beasts worrying at them ... began to drift. Even whole ships, some with live crews chained in their benches, made their way steadily toward the murmuring, yawning crevice that gaped in the crushed wall of the stadium, to be sucked into the maelstrom. Closer at hand, no more than an arm's length from where Conan struggled to climb the barricade, panic ruled the crowd. Arena patrons shoved, tumbled, fought, and trampled one another to get out from under the sagging overhang and find an exit. Terrified watchers were spectators no longer, suddenly finding themselves contestants in a survival match more desperate than any arena game. Knives were bloodied, eyes gouged out, and skulls dashed fiercely against unyielding stone in numberless futile struggles over nonexistent space. Where the balcony above the Heroes' Gate shuddered and

sagged but did not immediately fall, Circus patrons
and civil officials by the score were shoved over
the brink in the blind stampede—down into the
flooded arena itself, there to shriek and flounder in
teeming waters which for them spelled hideous,
unimaginable fear.

But surely the worst trampling and crushing of
all occurred inside the last remaining uncollapsed
entry-tunnels. There the mad throng converged,
leapt, and clawed their way relentlessly inward,
faster than any crowd could possibly have exited. In
grim consequence, the lower reaches of the tunnels
were soon blocked entirely by crushed, hard-packed
bodies.

Meanwhile Conan, dragging himself up to the
arena rail, straddled it against the pressure of swarming, faceless humanity. He considered it mere luck
that none of the frantic crowd were trying to force
themselves down the mast into the ruined boat. The
crush of fugitives beyond the stone barrier was too
violent, too dense; so he stood atop the wall and
chose his way, steadying himself against the flagship's splintered mast.

Scanning the broad, shaded slope of ledge-seats
above him, at length he found what he sought: a
lithe female shape, flanked by a large and shapeless patch of darkness, the two striding and leaping
together through the mad, scattering throng.
Sathilda's athletic fitness gave her an advantage,
he saw, as did the presence of her black tigress
Qwamba. For the giant beast's satiny bulk was,
without doubt, one of the few sights that could turn
aside crazed arena-goers in full cry.

The two circus performers, running together, cleared the balcony's treacherous overhang as Conan watched. They appeared to be heading upward toward the rim of the stadium, rather than descending to find an exit. That, he decided, was a wise course.

"Conan, my friend," a voice came from below him. "Lend a hand here if you will!"

"Commodorus! I thought you were washed overside!"

Looking down behind him, Conan was amazed to see the Corinthian adventurer close on his heels, creeping up the same web of rigging he had himself climbed. The Tyrant looked unhurt—though drenched, with his short tunic loose and disarrayed. He needed Conan to make room for him on the rail, and extended a supplicating hand for aid.

"I was thrown into the water, in sooth, with the first great surge of the ship. The sea-gods must have favored me greatly, because another wave threw me back aboard."

Conan grunted in understanding. He found himself doubting whether, if any sea-god truly favored Commodorus, the mock sea itself would have thrown him back into the world of men.

That same moment, looking downward past the Tyrant, his attention was caught by a stirring amid the drowned and broken bodies in the waist of the wrecked ship. A familiar thick, shaved head looked upward at the two, and a familiar hulking form began to pull itself free of the wreckage. Wigless now, but still in the game.

"Come up, then, Commodorus. This wreck

might shift at any moment." Conan could tell that, with the artificial lake flooding out through the broken wall, the water level around the floating hulks in the arena was subsiding faster—and with it, the waterlogged wreck of the flagship. Bending and reaching down, he hauled his employer up onto the rail. There, with a restraining arm, he kept him from toppling forward into the shoving, staggering citizenry who flowed blindly past.

"This way now, follow me."

Stepping up to the mast's broken crosstrees, then literally launching himself over the heads of the throng, Conan leapt across to a row of carved, high-backed stone chairs that served as a kind of island in the desperate, streaming tide. Turning back, he caught hold of Commodorus as he likewise sprang across. The Corinthian, being in sound physical shape, made the jump easily. Behind him, to Conan's relief, the broken mast splintered with a further groaning and cracking, and slipped away out of sight.

"Now, Tyrant," Conan said, "you may command your subjects. Do what you can to bring an end to this panic."

"What?" In frank uncertainty, Commodorus looked from Conan to the faces of the swarming crowd, and from them up at the sagging, leaning amphitheater all around them. "What do you want me to do, prop those grandstands back up again? Keep this one from collapsing? It looks as if it will fall on us in a moment or two!"

"You boasted to me how much the people love and respect you," Conan growled at him. "Now is your chance to reassure them and call forth their loyalty. Come, fellow," he added a moment later in impatience, "is there no one you can command, no guards or officers you can call to your service?"

Looking ill-at-ease, the Tyrant peered down at the throng, whose racing frenzy had begun to burn down to plodding desperation. He leaned down from his perch and tentatively clasped the shoulder of a prosperous citizen—who stared briefly up at him, slack-jawed, then pushed on wordlessly past. "Nay, it is no use," Commodorus spiritlessly declared, shaking his head and turning back to Conan. "You are the only one who will listen to me. Now tell me, what is it you propose to do?"

Conan snorted in disgust. The shaded ledge-seats above them, to which he now pointed, were fairly clear of stragglers. By climbing upward at an angle beneath the deadly overhang, and avoiding the jammed, riotous tunnels, they could make progress. "This way," he told Commodorus, starting out from ledge to ledge.

"Where, then, are you taking us?" the Tyrant demanded, following along less than enthusiastically. "This whole place could crumble at any minute, considering the shoddy work of the Stygian crews who made it."

"More than likely the place is rotten through with all the bodies you've hidden in it," Conan rebuked him. "In any case, our best chance of escape is to flee across the rooftops." He had no idea whether this was really possible, but he wanted to reach Sathilda, who by now was somewhere near the stadium's upper rim.

"I see," Commodorus said. "That is as good a gamble as any, I guess. But, by Mitra," he complained a moment later, "this trek is cursed hard on a fellow's legs!"

Climbing from ledge to ledge, he lagged farther behind, and Conan likewise had to lower the angle of his ascent, for the giant upward steps rapidly drained the strength out of a climber's thigh-muscles and made the knees waver. By way of a rest, Conan switched over to a rightward ascent for a time and then back to the left—for he did not want to get too near the mobbed tunnel entry, whose upward-angling mouth was a howling, hellish funnel of curses and shrieks.

As they climbed into the deeper shade of the leaning, buckling balcony, the perilous condition of the whole amphitheater became more obvious—for they had to step over fallen debris, dodge past runnels of loose stone that came sifting down from overhead . . . and, at this higher level, they felt the very ledges under their feet tremble and shift from unseen nether disturbances.

"It is the water leaking into the Circus foundations," Commodorus panted as Conan let him catch up. "The arena itself should have held up, the engineering was good—but those shocks must have opened up fissures in the masonry. The outflow of water is very likely softening the earth and undermining the supports as we speak."

Conan grunted and forged on, feeling more and more the oppressive weight of the deadfall over their heads. At last the edge of the shadow loomed near, and they were out from underneath in the blazing sunlight, two-thirds of the way to the stadium's upper edge. Knots of fugitives were sparser here—since it was easier for fleeing, stumbling mobs to migrate downhill. Conan could see Sathilda and her big cat moving along the arena's rim; she turned back, saw him approaching, and started to descend in agile leaps. But Conan waved to her to remain where she was.

"So, my brave bodyguard," the Tyrant observed, "our escape path just happens to coincide with a lovers' tryst! But no matter," he added with a sly laugh, "I cannot think of a better protector to have than yon tiger . . . your brawny Cimmerian self included."

Climbing doggedly with nearly depleted strength, the two found themselves nearing the curving north end of the stadium. Here, well above the wreckage of the fallen balcony, in high, bright desolation, was a sparse population of the dead, of those crippled by falls and tramplings, and a few clots of frightened or mindless fugitives: refugees who hung back near the upper fringes to be as far from the terror as possible. For below them spread the huge, unstable piles of fallen stonework, the red-runneling drains and blood-dripping wreckage. There lay drifts of trampled bodies and the churning, still-vicious crowds that fought in the low places.

Below, too, was the horror of the flooded arena with its sargasso of drowned ships and men, its thrashing sea-monsters, its foul polluted lake that poured out through the unseen cleft under their feet. This unutterable terror was reflected in the faces Conan met as he climbed—stunned spectators, staring blankly down into the vortex of death the Circus Imperium had become.

Then the two of them, gladiator and tyrant, mounted to the topmost ledge where the anxious woman and the lazy tiger awaited them. In an instant, Sathilda was in Conan's arms.

But he, fatigued and breathless, was wholly distracted from her by the view that opened out to him beyond the stadium's rim. For, in the streets below, madness reigned.

The lanes before the Circus Imperium were gouged out by floodwaters and drifted high with silt, wreckage, and bodies—transformed to muddy, roiling rivers whose courses cut past ruins of undermined, half-collapsed buildings. The courts and gardens of the wealthy were flooded and befouled—haunted, too, by half-naked survivors who crept through them seeking a route to safety past drowsing crocodiles and shark-haunted shallows. This, in all truth, Conan might have foreseen.

But true havoc appeared to be loose in the town beyond . . . where shouts and screams of strife echoed, wood and glass shattered, and pillars of fiery smoke rose to the heavens. The cause was instantly evident: civil order had failed, the mobs fleeing the Circus had run amok, and the whole city was engulfed in pillage and riot. Luxur's nobles and officers, most of them trapped or crushed inside the arena, could scarcely hope to control the poor rabble who had been unable to afford a ticket to the death-spectacle.

Now, as Conan gazed down, he saw looters rampaging across the terrace of one of the stately villas nearby, dragging sacks of booty. Their leader he thought he recognized: one of the rangy, wild-bearded captives rounded up for the arena show. The river and sea-pirates, he guessed, would not take long to break their chains once they were washed free of the arena. Any gladiators who won clear of the devastation would likely prove to be equally spirited thieves. The few city guards remaining outside the Circus, in any case, would have slight chance against the ravaging hordes that now owned the streets.

"It is gone . . . all gone." The dull voice at Conan's shoulder belonged to Commodorus. "The arena, as I told you, was the heart of my rule here. And now that heart is pierced." He gestured down at the collapsed section of the amphitheater, through which the unseen torrent flowed, and into which desperate Circus-goers now flung themselves to find release from the doomed stadium.

Conan disengaged himself from Sathilda's embrace. "You might still restore things, if you regain command," he said. "No doubt many of your rivals are dead."

"They may be the lucky ones," Commodorus said glumly. "Even if I were to survive, I could never live down the humiliation of—all this." He waved his hand at the cataclysm around them.

"Mayhap," Conan agreed. "In any event, the first step is to get out of this place." He moved along the upper wall of the stadium until he came opposite the highest villa roof . . . that was, coincidentally, Commodorus's.

The lane between was narrow, and the buildings

tended to lean out over it. Even so, it was a considerable distance outward and down to the tessellated tiles of the villa's roof garden where they had dined. The viny arbor made a tempting target indeed; one or two others may already have tried the leap—and failed it, as was suggested by the presence of bodies crumpled facedown on the cobbled pavements below. Or perhaps they had merely been left there by the flood, or the surge of the fleeing mobs. Further, if any others had made it, they would already have fled inside the mansion. Conan scanned the drop critically.

His consideration was hurried along by the new tremors in the ledges underfoot. Screams and tremendous crashing burst forth on his left, reverberating through the very fabric of the amphitheater. The undermined, devastated portion of the stadium was widening beneath new clouds of dust. The collapse carried hundreds to their deaths and brought the danger much nearer.

"If we are going to attempt the leap, it had better be soon." He moved along the wall to where a flagpole, projecting out just below the stadium's rim, flew its colorful banner above the street. "What say you, Sathilda?"

Leading her restless tiger, the acrobat moved up beside him. "If the three of us could get a decent running start, we might drive ourselves out far enough. But I do not think—"

Just then, from behind them, there rose a forlorn chorus of screams, followed by thunderous tremors. The eastern stretch of balcony, the one from which they had so recently escaped, had finally given way. Those beneath it, most of them already dead or demented with fear, were pulped and buried instantly by the avalanche—which also caved in the stadium wall, reducing the full section of ledges beneath it to rubble.

Conan and his three companions, man, woman, and beast, now stood at the crest of a steep, unstable, and rapidly narrowing island.

"Qwamba, hold! Down, girl!"

The night-cat, with senses keener than any of the humans, was made uneasy by the oncoming cataclysm. She strained nervously at her leash, setting her big forepaws up on the stadium wall and peering over. Sathilda, seizing hold of her collar and using her harshest tones of command, had difficulty restraining her.

"Don't hang on too tight," Conan warned the woman frankly, "just in case she decides to go. Such a fall could mean your death."

Whether or not the beast understood his thoughts, her mistress chose to ignore his words. No sooner had he spoken than, with a fluid motion, the big she-cat sprang up the low wall. Sathilda, throwing a leg over the lithe satin-dappled back, clung to the jeweled collar with both hands even as the huge creature ran out onto the slender pole.

Tigerish strength and acrobatic toughness achieved the impossible. Rebounding from the end of the bowing flagpole, the giant creature hurtled through the air with the woman clinging to her back.

That the two females had trained, played, and

slept together was evident in the coordinated grace of their flight. The tiger's great paws came down soundlessly on the roof terrace; Sathilda rolled free across the tiles and sprang nimbly to her feet, unharmed.

"Here, then," Conan called out to her. "Take this—in case we don't make it across!" Reaching to his waist, he unlooped the drawstring of his purse and slung it across the gap to her. Sathilda tried to catch it, but it was too heavy; the gold-weighted pouch thudded onto the tiles at her feet.

"Conan, do not jump!" she called back while retrieving the purse. "Find another way, the distance is too far for you! Qwamba and I will go and gather up the circus troupe . . . if any of them are left alive. You can join us later."

"Aye, then . . . farewell," Conan said with a raised hand.

"Very touching indeed," Commodorus observed at Conan's side. "Though you know she might have had all the gold she could carry from my villa."

"If thieves have not already stripped it, or are not doing so now." Conan looked after the departing woman. "Still, I wager she is safe enough with that tiger of hers." He turned to Commodorus. "Now, to find another way out—mayhap across the rubble piles. If the arena drains, we might wade free—" Turning to survey the vast ruin that was the Circus Imperium, he stopped abruptly. His eyes fell on a figure that had come close up behind them, striding from ledge to ledge with supple, effortless strength.

"Xothar, the temple gladiator," Commodorus remarked in mild surprise. "So you, too, have survived today's grandest arena game . . . and now you come to join us, doubtless to receive your victory laurel." He reached in jest to his own bedraggled brow, but the wreath was long gone.

"Commodorus, beware." Conan spoke low as he stepped protectively in front of the Tyrant.

"What, then . . . oh, aha, I see!" Looking from Conan to the burly wrestler, who stood regaining his breath in an easy half-crouch on the next lower step, the Tyrant smiled in understanding. "As a temple fighter, you are Nekrodias's man. And Conan here, who was told by the High Priests to kill me, but feels honor-bound to protect me, now thinks that you are next in line for that most singular honor." He laughed heartily. "Well, Xothar, what say you? Is it really so?"

It seemed clear from the wrestler's oily, self-assured smile that he understood the gist at least of Commodorus's question. Conan had never yet heard the easterner utter a word in Stygian or any other tongue, and it did not look as if he was about to begin now.

"Commodorus," Conan said warningly, "you go on down to the wreckage and tell us if there is a way out." He waved back to the broken edge a dozen paces away, whence mighty rumblings and tremors still issued at intervals. "I will stay here with Xothar and make sure that he does you no harm." Keeping his eyes fixed on the wrestler, he spoke slowly and plainly to him. "Xothar, stay back. I do not want to kill anyone, including you—"

"You do not have to." Commodorus, brushing past Conan, stepped forward to face the temple fighter. "Come, fellow, if you want an arena match! I am more than ready to best you."

"Commodorus, wait." Conan laid a restraining hand on the Tyrant's shoulder. "He is the swiftest and deadliest I have yet seen. I might be able to take him, but I would rather not try—"

"And I?" Commodorus demanded arrogantly, with a sharp glance back at his bodyguard. "Am I not a wrestler, a soldier, and a skilled arena fighter? Do you think any temple-trained zealot or acolyte can outdo me? Do you doubt my ability to snap such a thick neck? Back off, before I am tempted to teach you myself!" With an angry twist of his muscular torso, he shrugged Conan's hand off his shoulder.

"Commodorus, you are a leader—or were one, and may be again!" Conan stepped forward. "I am a fighter, the one you paid to protect you—"

"Yes, and now, Cimmerian, I am paying you to stand by and do nothing. Let me handle it myself, I tell you!" Extending a palm, he shoved Conan roughly back. "This is my chance to regain my prestige, by defeating the temple's champion. Do you not see, all of this"—he waved a hand at the devastation around them—"it was a plot against me by the Set Temple, to undermine my rule! But I foiled them and bested their champion!" He winked broadly at Conan. "Once I am restored to power, I will build the arena all over again, bigger and better than before!"

Turning, he stepped down opposite Xothar. The temple fighter, by his gleeful grin, appeared to understand the situation fully. He waited for the Tyrant to make the first move.

However much he may have lacked in leadership, Commodorus retained his physical courage. Wrenching off his crusty, drying toga, he stood in his soggy breech-wrap in a wrestler's crouch, with his supple weight raised up onto the balls of his sandaled feet. Darting forward, he clapped a hand on the side of Xothar's oiled neck and sought, by sidling close, to throw his opponent over his hip.

The shorter, broader man, seeming in no great hurry, crouched low and kept his feet firmly rooted on the stone ledge. His response to the Tyrant's lunge was scarcely a shuffled half-step. By some quick, invisible exchange of leverage, he brought his opponent around before him and tipped him onto one foot. The threat of a fall to the next granite step made the maneuver that much easier; while Commodorus teetered, Xothar slid in close and upturned him.

The taller man toppled slowly to the pavement, with Xothar kneeling effortlessly close and controlling his fall. The temple fighter's thick, oiled, gleaming arms snaked pythonlike around his opponent's trunk, leaving the frantic Tyrant's clutching and beating futilely at his assailant's thick-clouted nether quarters. The squat wrestler's embrace was a close one indeed, and tight; the ruler's upturned face was pale, his eyes rolling wildly.

"Commodorus!"

Conan, looking down at the unequal match, waited for a sign—for some hint that he should intervene, after all, if that was indeed his employer's will. But the Tyrant, instead of beckoning to him, continued vainly to tug and pluck at his opponent's iron limbs.

The granite blocks shuddered and sagged underfoot, but Xothar remained unmoving. Commodorus's mouth gaped wide, forming syllables; but there were no words, no breath.

Then, after his brief labors, the Tyrant rested. His mouth fell slack, his eyes glazed over in a look of repose.

After a further moment, Xothar released his grip on the body. Where it lay loose, he rolled it over on its back, straightening out the legs and crossing the wrists over the breastbone: a tidy offering to Set.

"There, now," Conan told the temple wrestler, "your work is finished and mine is too. I'll go my way, you yours. I have no wish to kill anybody."

The wrestler's complacent grin signaled acceptance.

Turning, Conan made his way toward the stadium's slumping, ragged edge. He thought, mayhap, of riding a great stone block to the bottom.

Because of the deep rumblings and shiftings underfoot, Xothar's swift, catlike steps behind him went unheard. The first thing he sensed was the heavy, clinging grip of an arm around his neck.

"Dog! You have no voice, yet you lie like a pox-eaten harlot!" Breaking free of the wrestler's clutch, he delivered a swift, stinging blow to the man's shoulder. "I tell you, you do not need to trouble about me! I will have no more dealings with you, nor your masters, nor their much-feared enemies!"

The wrestler, barely shrugging aside the blow's effect, darted forth his hand with cobralike swiftness. Knotting it powerfully in Conan's hair, he sought to jerk the Cimmerian down to his lesser height.

"Arrh! Temple toad, did you understand me or not?" He smote out fiercely at Xothar's head; but the blow missed due to the temple fighter's quick sideward movement and merely glanced off his muscle-corded neck. Conan instantly recoiled his elbow into the crook of the wrestler's arm, causing Xothar's nerveless fingers to slip free of his taut mane.

"I know what has happened," Conan continued, squaring off loosely for a fight. "That fleshless skull Nekrodias thinks that, because he offered me the rulership of Luxur in Commodorus's place, I will be a contender. But I tell you, I am no threat! I will leave Luxur. I have planned to do so anyway!"

Eyeing Conan, shrugging out the crimp in his neck, the still-smirking wrestler ducked suddenly forward and sought to wrap both arms around Conan's middle. Conan drubbed him on the cheekbone, on the ear, in the temple and the mouth, and again at the base of the neck, meanwhile dodging backward to stay clear of his grip.

Xothar, grinning bloody-mouthed, came onward.

Conan smote him above the eye and felt sure his own fist had broken in the bargain. He thumped him in the taut belly, and it was like trying to punch through the side of an overfilled ale-keg. He landed swift blows on the jaw, chin, chest, rib cage, and flat rubbery nose, scarcely managing to blur the fellow's dung-eating smile. A knee delivered to the Stygian's groin, with little effect, made him doubt whether the man was wholly a man.

The wrestler surged forward. Conan, bracing his feet to drive a fist up into the sinewy throat, felt the stone ledge shiver and tilt beneath him. His sandal slipped off the side, his shin and knee glancing down against the hard stone edge. Even as the pain flashed in his eyes, he felt thick, ropy arms insinuating themselves around his middle.

"Accursed reptile," Conan spat. Then he saved his oaths, for he felt the python-grip steadily tighten. Xothar bound him close, waiting for the air to burst from his innards, the pressure more intense against his belly than his chest. The battered temple fighter could not lift and wring him about as he had the lighter Commodorus, but he bore him down flat with his bulk, head to waist, knee to throat. Fiercely Conan kicked and kneed at where he knew his opponent's face must be; but the wrestler ducked and lay blind, clinging to his victim closely as a mother to her child in a night-tempest.

Conan's air ran out. He gasped and ducked, drawing in the merest fraction of what had flown forth. His vision began to swim.

This, then, was the embrace Roganthus had felt. Him, and how many others? It had been part of

Xothar's plan, he guessed . . . to drive him back to the unstable edge of the stadium, where his footing must soon fail. Taking as much punishment as necessary along the way.

The dead air soured in his lungs. He gasped, choked, and this time drew in nothing, no breath at all. The snake-grip tightened further, squeezing bright daylight into darkness, pinching off the sun.

Beneath him, earth trembled and fell away. He felt his head strike something, then was plummeting free.

The grip loosened.

Then he was rolling, tumbling, flailing. He choked and convulsed—gratefully, on dry dust, sweet billowing dust! His limbs were free now; gloriously free to claw, scrabble, and abrade themselves on ragged stone. Sucked underneath a torrent of rattling, sliding rubble, he fought his way desperately to the surface, to roll and ricochet with loose shards.

His sliding, tumbling fall halted . . . except for the slow trickle of debris all around. He pried his extremities out of the rubble and was free to crawl unfettered. From somewhere near him came a sigh . . . a moaning, rasping exhalation.

Xothar lay faceup, pinned amid the wreckage. Atop his chest was a giant granite slab, firmly wedged and bedded against other massive debris. His face, dust-caked and seeping blood, hung inverted against a jagged stone pillow, with eyes and mouth agape.

Conan gazed down at him dispassionately, as Manethos might have examined a mummy-candidate. The jagged-edged slab was far too heavy to lift, without a doubt. If dislodged, it might slip further and shear off the victim's face.

Xothar stared up at Conan with mortal fear in his eyes. The wrestler tried to draw in breath, but failed.

A small river of dust trickled down, making a little white cloud over the supine man's face. When Conan brushed it away, there remained only a pale, motionless death-mask.

Turning, he began to pick his way down through the wreckage of the arena.

Chapter 15

"Long Live the Tyrant!"

Before he had wandered far, Conan happened across Muduzaya, who had clung to an oar of the Imperial fleet and been swept out of the arena. The Kushite's habitual preference for fighting nearly naked had saved him ... as had his dexterity at snapping crocodiles' jaws.

Although the city streets were lawless, and the citizens particularly mistrustful of any reminder of Commodorus and his ill-starred Circus, the pair were well adapted to survival. Food and drink were far from scarce in Luxur, at least during those first few days; and there were other sources of wealth, free for the taking, which ensured that they would not go wanting.

Conan heard that most of Luddhew's people had survived the cataclysm and set up camp in the temple grounds, as keepers of the sacred menagerie. Their former hilltop environs were rendered pestilential by the mass death and flooding, even after the aqueducts were shut off . . . so the old, easy life was over. But Conan did not doubt that the circus troupers would soon again find an audience for their varied talents.

"Muduzaya," he remarked one morning, lying in the feast-hall of the rich ownerless villa where they made their home, "it has been long since I saw Kush. Tell me, do the wild parrots still bend the trees with their weight? And do roebeasts yet flock like termite-swarms through the veldt?"

"Aye, Conan, they do," his friend affirmed. "Your speech makes me homesick, I must say."

"I have been thinking that I would like to do some fine hunting. Get away from cities and priests and tyrants, and live close to nature once again. Does your fancy turn southward?"

"Aye, surely enough," the former Swordmaster said. "But what of your girlfriend and her pet tiger? I have been expecting these past few nights to waken and find that creature drooling over me, and her over you."

"Nay, Muduzaya," Conan confided, shaking his head. "In sooth, I do not think I am cut out for circus life. And I am sure she is not cut out for any other. Things are better left as they stand."

With that resolution made, they did not linger long in the city. It was just as well; for there ensued in Luxur a fortnight of civil uprisings and reprisals against foreigners. After all, had the great cataclysm not been a result of adopting ungodly foreign ways? And had not the final slaughter of gladiators in the arena been an omen, a symbolic triumph and revenge of Stygia's ancient beast-gods?

At the end of it, when the fires were extinguished and the hated Corinthians finally driven out of the capital, a stern commander was named Tyrant of Luxur. He was a ruthless young enforcer named Dath—who, by uniting the street toughs to fill the dangerous vacancy of power, restored order to the city and won the trust of wise old Nekrodias, High Primate of Set's Temple.

Once he was installed in his seven-year term, Dath's first public decree was to level the unsightly ruin of the Circus Imperium. There was to be built in its place a tomb, one in which all the mortal remains of the victims would be piously interred.

Thus was the ancient city of Luxur preserved, and its people brought back to their age old traditions under the just rule of the gods.